SECOND HOUSE
from the CORNER

ALSO BY SADEQA JOHNSON

Love in a Carry-On Bag

SECOND HOUSE

from the CORNER

Sadeqa Johnson

Thomas Dunne Books

St. Martin's Press ≈ New York

THOMAS DUNNE BOOKS.
An imprint of St. Martin's Press.

SECOND HOUSE FROM THE CORNER. Copyright © 2016 by Sadeqa Johnson. All rights reserved. Printed in the United States of America. For information, address St. Martin's Press, 175 Fifth Avenue, New York, N.Y. 10010.

www.thomasdunnebooks.com
www.stmartins.com

The Library of Congress Cataloging-in-Publication Data is available upon request.

ISBN 978-1-250-07414-0 (hardcover)
ISBN 978-1-4668-8581-3 (e-book)

Our books may be purchased in bulk for promotional, educational, or business use. Please contact your local bookseller or the Macmillan Corporate and Premium Sales Department at (800) 221-7945, extension 5442, or by e-mail at MacmillanSpecialMarkets@macmillan.com.

First Edition: February 2016

10 9 8 7 6 5 4 3 2 1

In loving memory of
Geraldine Murray aka Mommom
Missing you.

To my parents,

Tyrone W. Murray and Nancy Murray,

for giving me what you have. Your love has always been enough.

All that I am is because of you.

PART 1

To love means to embrace and at the same time to withstand many endings, and many many beginnings—all in the same relationship.

—CLARISSA PINKOLA ESTÉS

ONE

The Witching Hour

That four-hour window between after-school pickup and bedtime? It's like walking a tightrope with groceries in both hands. The slightest hiccup will land any mother in a quagmire with her legs in the air. For me the whole afternoon was a fail. I locked myself out when I went to pick the kids up from school, but didn't notice the missing house keys until I pulled in to the driveway. The snacks had been demolished at the playground, so the hunger meltdown began on the drive to my husband's office for the spare key (a drive that usually takes seven minutes, but ended up being twenty round-trip because of traffic). Things got even shoddier once I discovered we were out of Kellogg's Corn Flakes. My children will not eat baked chicken unless I dip the pieces in buttermilk, roll them in corn flakes, and bake until crispy. The oven was preheated, the potatoes were boiling for the mash, and I was thirty-three minutes off schedule without the magic cereal that makes my chicken finger-licking good. No time to change the dinner plan. So I swap in seasoned bread crumbs and cross my toes that they won't notice.

"Mama, this doesn't taste right." My son, Rory, frowns.

"Just eat it. There are children right down the street who are starving."

"But it's disgusting," whines Twyla.

How does a four-year-old know what disgusting is?

"Just eat."

"I have to go pee pee and poo poo."

"Stop smiling at me. Mommy, she's smiling."

"Can we just have dessert?"

"Maaaaaaaa."

"Mommmmm."

"Momeeeeeeee."

Like a song on repeat. Like it's the last word in the English dictionary. They call "Mommy" until my lips pucker, eyebrows knit. And it takes all my strength not to respond with that inside voice that nobody hears, that you wish would stay quiet, that tells the truth you don't want anyone to know. That *damn voice* is hollering.

Shut the fuck up!

At what point do I get to shout *What the fuck do you want from me?* I wouldn't drop an F-bomb in front of the mommy crew at the park, and I hate to see parents on the street cursing out their kids. But here in my kitchen with everything working against me, I would like to liberate myself just once and let the profanity rip.

It's the nipping at my nerves that gets me. The feasting on my flesh like starved sea urchins. Them, fighting like thieves for their individual piece of me. Me feeling like I have nothing left to give. Any mother who says that she has never felt like her whole life was being sucked out through her nostrils is a damn liar. I feel it every day.

Especially when I don't get at least five hours of shut-eye, like last night. Twyla (whom I call Two) walked her four-year-old self into my room every hour complaining about being scared. *Scared of what?* The curtain, the bed, the wall—she had an excuse for each visit. Never mind that she had to walk past her father to get to me.

They never bother him. It's always Mommy. So I upped and downed all night while he slept like a hibernating black bear.

Breathe.

I hate when I feel like this. My chest rising and falling. Momentum of failure piled. Anxiety has swept through my belly and is curled against my organs like a balled fist. Just one happy pill would make it all better. But I've been on the happiness-comes-from-within kick for a few months, so no more pills. Instead I've started tapping.

Tapping out my emotions so I can get back to feeling right. It's that new technique where I say what my issue is and use my fingertips and hit my meridian points until I'm back to even. It usually takes about five minutes and several rounds before I feel centered and strong. My husband, Preston, calls it woo-woo, but he's not at home with three children all day. I am, and I have to use what I've got to carry me through. I turn my back to the kids at the kitchen table, take two fingers, and tap the side of my hand while whispering my setup statement.

"Even though I feel stressed out, anxious, and tired of being alone and responsible for my kids I love and accept myself."

"Mommy, what are you doing?"

"Calming down." I try whispering the statement again but Tywla is out of her seat.

"My stomach hurts."

Rory puts his fork down. "I'm full."

My fingers stop. I haven't made it through one minute, much less the five I need. I take a deep breath and usher everyone upstairs. Maybe Preston will surprise me and come home early.

The *damn voice* laughs. *When was the last time he did that? He never makes it home before their bedtime and I bet that's on purpose.*

Rory moans. "That's my boat."

"Dad gave it to me."

"No, he didn't."

Breathe. "Cut it out and get undressed."

I run their bath and sneak in a quick tap. Repeating my setup statement, I move from my hand to my forehead, to the side of my eye, under my eye, under my lip, under my chin, full hand on chest, bra strap and top of the head. Fill my lungs with air and exhale.

Twyla and Rory are back. I read my body. Better.

"Can I bring this in the tub, pretty please?" Twyla clutches the mesh bag with their toys.

"Sure."

They climb into the bathtub and play.

This should give me a few minutes alone with the baby.

"Guys, I'm going to change Liv into her pajamas. No water on the floor."

"Can we have more bubbles?"

"No."

"Awwww, man," Rory replies, imitating Swiper the Fox. "You only gave us a little bit."

I cut my eyes in the direction of my six-year-old and hold his gaze for a beat longer so that he knows I mean business.

The upstairs of our house is small, and it only takes three long strides to the girls' bedroom. Liv, the baby, squirms in my arms and I find solace burying my head in her neck. I could sit and smell this child all day. At ten months old, she still has that fresh-to-the-earth smell that forces me to slow my pace. It's hard to look at her without feeling deep sighs of relief. She is our miracle child.

When I was twenty weeks pregnant with Liv, a routine sonogram found something suspicious. I was sent to the Robert Woods Johnson Hospital in New Brunswick to see a pediatric cardiologist. There was a pinch in her heart that could hemorrhage. Her chances of being stillborn were high. When the doctor suggested that we terminate the pregnancy, I was bilious. By then I had already heard her heartbeat, felt her flutter and kick, loved her. Preston didn't even look my way when he simply told the batch of white coats that we would take our chances.

On our way home, the traffic on the Garden State Parkway held us hostage. I slobbered and blubbered against the passenger seat window, trudging through my past, knowing which karmic act brought this down on our family. My husband kept patting my hand, but when that didn't work, he pulled our ice-cream-truck-size SUV over to the side of the road and pressed the hazard lights.

"Foxy, look at me." He is the only person who calls me Foxy, and even with hearing my personal pet name, I couldn't bring my eyes to his. Tilting my damp chin, he forced eye contact. "This is not your fault."

But it is.

"You trust me?"

I shake my head, of course, because there really is no other response when your husband asks you that question.

"So the baby is healed. It's done, no more worries." Preston clapped his hands, as if he had just entered a contract with God. "Now stop blaming yourself, you didn't do anything."

As our vehicle crawled up the Parkway, he informed me that we'd name her Liv.

"Not short for anything. Just Liv."

I knew what I had done to deserve this even though my husband did not. I wanted it to be all right. Needed something to cling to, so I agreed to everything that Preston offered because the only hope I had for a favorable outcome was him. I had burned my bridge with God a long time ago.

"Ooooh! I'm telling!" Rory shouts.

Liv is snapped up in her sleeper and on my hip.

"What's the matter?" I round the wall to the bathroom tub, and what I see makes my stomach sail over a steep cliff and capsize at my feet.

"What the . . ." I can't even finish my sentence because my mouth is filled with saliva. Twyla has my forty-five-dollar hair-nourishing cream clumped in her curls and pasted all over her body. When I move in closer, conditioner is floating in the water and smeared onto the sides of the tub. I pick up the bottle. It's empty.

"I told her to stop," pipes Rory with globs in his hair and oozing down his back.

"Why didn't you call me?" My voice slams into Rory and he shrinks and shivers. "Two, how could you do this?"

Twyla just looks at me and then on cue she opens her mouth. Out comes that nerve-pinching wail that makes me want to drag my fingernails into her veins and make it stop.

I walk away. Damn the tapping. I need to get out of here. I recognize the rage coursing through my body, and it's all I can do. I deposit Liv into her crib and she starts crying immediately. I keep walking, knowing that everyone is safer with me heading in the opposite direction. I get as far as the kitchen, where I grab my cell phone off the countertop. I text Sam, my teenage sitter.

Can you come over now for a few hours?

As I lean against the countertop waiting for her text back, the evidence of my unsuccessful dinner is on the table, chairs, and floor.

I'm in no mood to tackle the cleanup. Not right now. I need to get out of this house before I morph into screaming, raging, mean Mommy. The one who presses against my eyeballs begging to be set free.

The racket upstairs has escalated in the three minutes I've been gone. Rory is yelling at Two, Liv is still crying, and I hear something crash to the floor. I tuck my phone in my shirt pocket and head toward the litany of tears. My daily mantra, "All is well. The Universe supports me," is on replay in my head.

I hand Liv a stuffed bear and a teething toy to pacify her. That will buy me a few minutes of quiet as I face what's happening in the bathroom. When Two sees me at the doorway she looks like she is ready for another round of the sobs, but I cut her at the neck.

"Don't even start."

I reach for her arm and stand her up in the tub.

"I'm the one who should be crying. Look at this mess," I say.

The water has gone down the drain, but balls of conditioner still wiggle around the bottom of the tub. I stand them both up for a quick shower, hoping that the conditioner doesn't clog the drain. Then I'll have to hear it from Preston for adding another chore to his honey-please-do-it-over-the-weekend list.

"Rory, go check on Liv," I say, rubbing a little lotion on his face and kissing his cheek. He tosses me his Mommy-don't-be-mad-at-us smile and then scampers out of the bathroom. I hear him open his drawer for his pajamas and then Liv's giggles when he climbs into her crib. Two children settled, one to go.

Twyla looks as guilty as a bank robber with a bag of money and a smoking gun. "Two, why would you do this?"

"I, I, I don't know," and she drags out *know* in that whiny way that only a four-year-old can muster.

As I dry her off, my phone dings. I slide it from my pocket. It's Sam.

Be there in ten minutes.

I sigh. Smile. Feel like throwing my hands up in the air and doing a liturgical dance.

"What, Mommy?"

"Nothing."

"Why are you smiling?"

"Because I love you." I swat her bottom and send her on her way.

It's still a bit early for bedtime, so I bring them downstairs to clean up the tornado that is my living and dining room.

"Who's coming over?" Two cocks her head at me.

"Sam."

"Where're you going?" Alarm rises in her voice.

"I have to run an errand." I untangle her grubby hands from my leg and point. "Go clean up."

"But I don't want you to go," Rory comes over, now wrapping his arms around my waist.

"Please, Pudding Pops, clean up before Sam thinks we live in a pigsty."

Our dining room is the official playroom, and I leave the kids with the task of tidying while I open the door for Sam.

"Thanks for coming." I give her a light hug.

She removes her headphones and smiles her no problem, mouth full of adolescent braces grin. She's been coming over for more than a year and knows our routine well—a book each, brushing of teeth, prayers, and then bed—so without worry I move through the kitchen snatching up my escape weapons: keys, wallet, lip gloss, and ear buds for my cell.

"Be good." I kiss each kid on the forehead and push them in the direction of Sam. Rory is happy on the floor, crashing two of his dump trucks into the coffee table, but Twyla follows me to the door. I can't shake this girl with a backwoods switch.

"Mommy, I want to come with you."

"Next time, honey." I try to pull the door closed but she won't budge. "Twyla, sweetie, please go find Sam." This is how I speak to my children, soft and sweet. The angrier I am the lower my voice gets. Right now I am damn near whispering.

"You didn't give me a kiss."

I kiss her lips.

"The other kiss, Mommy. The marry kiss."

I kiss her long, holding her lips to mine. She calls it a marry kiss, because it's how Preston and I do it.

"You didn't give me a hug."

My temperature is rising. Girl, please go on. I squeeze her shoulders while shoving her enough to close the door. I lock up and run, yes, run down my front steps to my SUV parked in the driveway. The humid air drapes my skin. I've been inside with the air conditioner on and forgot we were in the middle of a July heat wave.

Inside my SUV, sweat gathers under my arms, and my back burns against the leather seats. My car is in reverse when the familiar lump clogs the back of my throat. I'm not sure what to call the feeling or the vision, but I'm having it, again.

Me, riding away into the sinking sunset with only the clothes on my back. Driving for hours until the car runs out of gas. Then walking for miles until my feet give out. Then dropping down to my hands and knees and crawling until my skin is ripped from the bones and bloody. And then sitting, right where I am, tired, hot, thirsty, but with the taste of freedom.

I glance at the house before turning the corner and spy three little faces pushed against the front window, watching me.

You are a terrible mother for even thinking about leaving them, especially since you know what that's like.

I wave, blink away the picture of my other self, and curse the *damn voice* for always being up in my business and holding me awful and tight.

TWO

The Escape

The State of New Jersey has been smoldering for five straight days, with temperatures averaging in the high nineties and the heat index off the charts. As much as I love summer, I've had enough. The air conditioner is taking too long to cool me off. I floor the gas pedal hard on Liberty Avenue, cut through the supermarket parking lot, and merge onto Route 22. I don't know where I am going until the sight of the Wine and Spirits shop ahead on the left catches my eye and cools my skin like a pool of water. I haven't snuck a drink into a movie theater since I was in college, and that's when I decide that's exactly what I'm going to do.

The four-pack of merlot nips fit into my barrel-size purse beneath a pack of baby wipes and a forgotten tangerine. I'm bubbling with excitement until I catch a glimpse of myself in the reflection of the silver-blue paint of my car. In my haste to get away, I've walked out of the house wearing ratty yoga pants and a two-pocket pullover, my hair snatched up in an untidy bun. My one pledge to myself was to never be one of those housewives who run around town looking like they are too busy to put on decent clothing. I've mumbled under my breath about these women, but tonight I am one of them. I laugh out loud at my own irony and fasten my seat belt.

I have no idea what's showing when I enter the theater, but just the smell of being close to my acting cohorts unbuttons me out of my mommy suit and connects me to my higher self. The me who tripped, and then fell head over heels in love with acting while watching the very first episode of *A Different World*. That late '80s sitcom was my rock, my sword, and my shield through my teenage years. If Hillman College had really existed, I would have gone there for my undergraduate degree. Every Thursday, I would tape the latest episode, then watch the show until I mastered every character's part and memorized the entire show. I was obsessed with imitating Whitley Gilbert, the southern belle with all of her daddy's money at her disposal. I drove Gran crazy because I made her sit and be my audience. This is what convinced her to come up with the money to send me to the acting camp at The New Freedom Theater on Broad Street the summer before my senior year.

I remember how I ran around asking my acting teacher, Ms. Diane, how to get an agent. I was ready to throw my wings in the sky and fly toward Hollywood, but she just looked me over and said, "Learn your craft first. Study acting. Don't just imitate what you see, feel it."

It's not until I'm in line that I decide on a film about a woman, played by Nicole Kidman, who has an affair. It starts in eight minutes. Perfect timing. I shove my ticket into one of my breast pockets and head for the almighty concession stand. Nachos smothered in cheese and jujubes will make everything all better. With my goodies in hand and my mind two-stepping over what's stashed in my purse, I make a beeline to the theater. And then I hear my name called. It's

Monday night. No one I know should be cracking at the seams but me.

I spin on my sneakers and see Monroe McKenzie, president of the Dames and Culture Club. Just my freaking luck. I plaster some remnants of something I hope says pleasant to see you and move in her direction. Monroe looks dazzling in a spring pink suit and over-the-top pumps. Her cherry-blond hair is pulled into a side bun, and her cheeks are round and plum. Under normal circumstances it would be great seeing Monroe. As an artist, Dames and Culture is the club that I've been wishing myself into with obsessive osmosis for the past two years, but they haven't even given me so much as a finger wave. Membership is restricted to women who have distinguished them-selves in art, music, literature, philanthropy, or just enough wealth that none of the above matters. It's an invitation-only club and Monroe, with her perfectly painted red lips, can unlock the door with her key. I push my shoulders back and pretend that I am not stand-ing in the middle of the movie theater dressed like the cleaning lady.

"Felicia Lyons, is that you?" her tiny eyes disappear altogether when she smiles. I touch my frizzy hair with my free hand as if to confirm it is still in a frazzled snatched back. My lips smack against each other in search of moisture. I could have at least remembered to put on some damn lip gloss before I got out of the car.

"Are you here alone? What's going on with your hair?" she grabs a loose strand and flips it back, grinning.

I shift my goodies to the side. "Yes, alone. Just catching a breather."

"Well, I'm glad I ran into you. I have a favor to ask."

I look at her.

"Rumor has it that you are a celebrated actress."

I wouldn't exactly say "celebrated," but the compliment remedies her flicking of my hair. White girls should really know better.

"As you may or may not know, the Dames' annual fund-raiser is in three weeks and I'm the chair. We call it the Afternoon of the Arts. We have our headliner. Are you familiar with Audra McDonald?"

"Am I?" My mouth gapes open.

"I figured you would be. Well, she's the headliner." Monroe claps her hands. "It is such a coup to have her. I've been working with her manager for over two years to secure her."

"That's amazing. I saw her on Broadway a few years ago and she's just awesome."

"Tickets are practically sold out. Now we just need to fill in with our supporting cast. I've already contacted an opera singer, cellist, and a modern dance group. What's missing is a dramatic interpretation of some sort."

"Are you asking me to perform?" My doe eyes widen, revealing too much glee, but Monroe continues on as if she hasn't noticed as she runs down the business.

"Proceeds will go to the underserved girls at Cross River High. We are trying to extend their library by two thousand square feet and put in a media center. What's the commercial you had running? Bounty?"

"Bounce fabric softener," I say, letting it roll slowly off of my tongue. It's the one thing that people know about me because it ran during the Super Bowl. That was more than two years ago, and I haven't booked a job since. My agent doesn't even call regularly because I missed so many auditions after Liv was born. I'm still ten pounds over my headshot picture weight and can't remember the last time I had my mane colored and cut. But I'm about to work on some changes. Felicia Lyons is making a comeback.

"We need something funny, of course," Monroe continues on, like she's reading a checklist from her clipboard. "Needs to resonate with the two hundred and fifty women in the audience, something to which we can all relate."

"It would be my pleasure."

"Great. I'll put your name on our nomination ballot and be in touch with more details."

My face slips.

Monroe pats her lips. "Darling, the Dames vote on everything. But with your celebrated accomplishments, you shouldn't have a problem."

"Sounds good." I take a step back.

Monroe turns on her heels and gives me that toothpaste grin. "Ciao, darling, and be careful eating all of those nachos," she says with a wink.

Not at all what I was expecting when I stormed out of my house today, and my mood improves a bit. The theater is half empty and I let my mind wander over the excitement of performing for the Dames. Perhaps this could be my ticket in. An incredible show could earn me the coveted purple and yellow pin. The pin I'd never take off. The pin that would finally elevate me to . . .

Girl, please, the Dames are not letting you in their posh little club. Not with your history, the *damn voice* interrupts my happy thoughts, and as usual I hate her logic, reason, and timing.

I sink lower into my seat, dipping a salty nacho into the warm cheese and then shoving it into my mouth. My cell phone vibrates from inside of my purse and I see Preston's name flash across the screen. I send the call to voice mail.

The Dames will see right through this little facade you've created and see you as the fake that you are. You are a wannabe. Always have been and always will. She cackles.

My knees knock against each other. This is why I liked my happy pills, because just one would have kept her demonic voice away. Just one would have let me enjoy this small moment of victory. Just one would have let the past be forgotten and forgiven and I would have been glad to feel the fake glee. My hand gropes the jujubes.

Nicole Kidman is bent over the sink with her lover's hand in her hair and I will myself to be lost in her story. My sleeve sops the raindrops from my chin and I swallow small sips straight from the bottle.

THREE

The Good Husband

Preston is waiting up for me. It never fails. No matter what time I come home, my husband is always waiting. I polished off two of the four miniature bottles of merlot in the theater, and I'm all cried out. When I saunter into the living room I feel toasty and relaxed.

"Where have you been?" Preston looks up from his tablet. His brown eyes darken beneath his horn-rimmed glasses. The History Channel is on, as usual.

"Hello to you too, darling." I stand in the middle of the floor with my hands on my hips.

"You went out dressed like that?"

"I know. The kids were so out of control tonight I didn't even realize that I hadn't changed until I was damn near at the movies. Least you know I'm not cheating on you." I bend down for a peck.

"You went to the movies?"

"Mmm hmm," I move to pick up Rory's yellow dump truck and carry it into the dining room/playroom. "Why, what's wrong?"

"You didn't answer your phone. I had no idea where you were."

"The picture had started." I grab his hand and pull him up from the sofa. "It was a hard day."

Before he can pout further, my lips are on his. My yoga pants are old but tight and it's not long before Preston's hands glide over my ass like he's a horny teenager.

"Next time send me a text." He moans in my mouth and rubs his groin against mine. Preston is easily four inches taller than me, but somehow we fit. My husband is the sun, and I am the flower stretching toward his ray.

"I didn't even know what to pay Sam." He tugs me tight.

"You paid her, right?"

"That's not the point. I don't want to find out my wife's whereabouts from the babysitter."

I push back. "Oh, Preston, get over it. I'm entitled to some time alone."

Sam is usually good about having the kids clean up after themselves, but tonight toys are all over. Preston must have walked in before she had a chance. I open the toy box that we keep in the corner of the dining room and start shoving toys in. Honestly, I give my husband a long leash. I don't check his whereabouts. He comes and goes when he pleases, but my leash is short and tight. My unbuttoned mood tightens back up.

"Good night," I say, with Rory's shoes in hand.

"What's wrong with you?"

"Nothing."

"Come here." Preston is on his feet and cuts my path before I can make it out of the living room.

"So dramatic." He breathes on me. "Can't a brother be concerned about his wife?"

His lips graze mine and I thaw. Preston smells like sand and something smoky and I inhale until I'm full. Breathing me out, I take him in, all of him.

On the sofa, he's right next to me. Arm wrapped around my shoulders.

"How was your day?"

"I picked up two new accounts in Sparta." He lifts my shirt over my head.

"Oh," his breath cinches. I'm wearing the pink satiny bra that smashes my breasts together.

"One is a big fish that I'd been working on for weeks." His tongue teases over the length of my cleavage while he unhooks my snaps.

"So proud of you, honey." I move my arms and thrust my boobs forward so he can have full access. Preston traded in his nine-to-five and started The Lyons Group when Rory was born. He represents companies for health, life, and disability insurance. A traveling salesperson with a small office at the foot of our town, and he rarely makes it home before the children go to bed. Long leash.

"What are you thinking about?" He has come up my body and we are eye-to-eye.

"You."

Preston's lips feel like pillows of marshmallow. His hands move with grace and I lean back so he can touch all of me. Even after ten months of dating and seven years of marriage, it takes him only about thirty seconds to make my mind turn to fuzz, to erase all of the bumps in my day.

"You taste so sweet," he purrs against my stomach.

I bubble. Arch my back. Hug him with my knees. My womanly parts are swollen, panting for our connection. My fingers are in his hair. Preston crawls up my body.

"Foxy, you are so beautiful," he whispers against my bottom lip. I gasp as his fingers work my pleasure. My leggings are around my ankles and the thong I by chance wore is shoved to the side. My husband claims me, devours me, does me good.

"This is what I've been waiting for." He groans as we find our connection and swim. Long, deep strokes. The couch rocks on its tiny hoof heels.

"Should. We. Close. The door?" My brain floods with watery images of sleepwalking children. I lick his neck and squeeze his lower back. My thighs are soaking wet.

"They're gone. I just checked. Relax, baby."

But the thought is in the air and now I can't let it go. His tongue finds my ear, my cheek, and his breath feels like warm cider as it rushes down my throat. Preston grabs both of my hands, placing our palms against each other, and we dance. He drives my body into the sofa and talks that stuff that I like, but my mommy brain won't fade. I lean into his waist, give a push, and then slip away.

"Foxy," he whines, hands out like one of the children.

"One sec." I swing my hips hard as I move through the room, closing the living room shutters and turning off the television. My fleshy ass wiggles and I know I'm giving him a show. The light from the cable box gives just enough blue so that Preston can see me.

"What you want, baby?" I put my hands on my hips so he can see all of me. My curves, my stretches and pulls, the map of my life on this body. I stand like it's a curtain call.

Preston is sitting up. Legs ajar. His eyes glow with greed. "Come." I fall into his arms, sink, sigh, surround him.

Warmth courses between us. He clings to my hips and I undulate. The friction is automatic and in no time I grip the back of the sofa and spill.

His patience has waned and I am tossed on my belly. Teeth are on my back, fingers where I like them. I sense the quickening, feel the urgency in his rhythm, paw the sofa, and then surrender to the release of my husband's storm.

Spent, we lean with our legs crisscrossed. My head is listening to Preston's heartbeat. His fingers draw circles on my arms.

"Better?" I say.

"Yes." He adjusts himself on the floor, with his back resting against the sofa so that I am sitting between his legs.

"What made you go to the movies?"

I tell him about the fighting car ride, forgotten keys, commotion over dinner, and the hair-conditioned bathtub.

"I'll drive them to camp tomorrow for you."

"Really? Tomorrow's Wednesday." Preston only drives the kids on Tuesdays and Thursdays.

"My morning meeting got pushed back so I can do it."

I squeeze him tight and kiss his chest.

"You're too good to me."

FOUR

The Aftereffect

The next morning, the tempest has passed. The water has receded. I can't even remember what the storm was all about. I tighten the strap on my cotton robe and move into the girls' room to start their day. I kick some dolls and crumpled tutus out of my way to reach the beds.

Two has climbed into Liv's crib and is wrapped around the baby like a lover. Rory also abandoned his room in the middle of the night and is snug in Two's bed. Our nights are filled with mattress movement.

"Two," I rub the small of her back.

"Rory, good morning," I call. He wiggles away from me so I sing, "Good morning, good morning, little chinchilla."

I'm on the second verse when Two pops up.

"Monkey!" she shouts and Liv raises her messy head.

"Good morning, little monkey, good morning, kitty cat and colorful peacock. Good morning."

With that we are on the steps, Liv on my hip, Two's hand inside of mine, and Rory right beside me. At the bottom of the stairs, Rory scrambles into the kitchen. He dashes into the chair next to the window. Two is right behind him.

"That's my seat, Rory."

"I sat here first."

"It's my turn. Move." She pushes.

"Twyla, sit here," I point to one of the three other chairs at our table. For the life of me, I can't figure out what makes that particular chair so special.

"That's not fair." She crosses her arms over her chest. Her ponytails have come loose and she looks rested and beautiful.

I kiss her cheek and then whisper, "Tomorrow will be your turn. Promise." She's mollified for a moment and gets distracted by the Cheerios I've left for them on the table.

I serve my normal diner-style breakfast: waffles and bacon for Rory, a bagel for Two, and oatmeal for Liv.

Preston comes into the kitchen wearing long sweats and a fitted T-shirt. His eyes look sleepy and his mouth twists into a shy grin.

"Morning, Fox." He kisses my lips with his hands on my waist. "You felt good last night," he says, only loud enough for me to hear.

I blush.

"Here." He stuffs my thong in my hand and then closes it.

The basement door is open so I toss the panties down the steps. "What am I going to do with you?"

"Love me." His eyes twinkle.

"Don't forget you promised to drive the kids."

"Awww, I want you to drive us," the kids chime from the table, but I pretend not to hear them. I shoot Preston a you-got-this look, and then head upstairs to lay out their clothes.

Before I am finished, the smell of freshly brewed coffee wafts through the house. I love that Preston makes this his morning task.

"Kids, finish up," I call down from the top of the stairs. While I wait, I make their beds and put the dolls and stuffed animals away. Rory dresses himself, but I help Two button her blouse.

"Brush your teeth and no fighting." I give them a hard look and then head down to the kitchen.

"Smells good." I pour two cups and hand one to Preston. He is standing at the counter bent over the newspaper.

"Are you checking the lottery again?"

"I forgot to play yesterday. I hope my number didn't come out." He flips the page.

"You sound like an old lady."

"I'm serious."

"You know, all you'd get back is the money you've put in."

"This is my po' black man's stock market. You won't complain when I hit big." He rolls the paper and swats me on the butt.

I stick out my tongue. Preston has never hit for more than a few hundred bucks, but whatever makes him happy. We all need something to believe in.

I'm at the door waving good-bye when the telephone rings. I know its Gran before I answer it. She phones the same time every day, and starts in on her constant chutney of chatter before I croak a proper good morning.

"Oh, didn't expect you to be home. Ain't it your day to drive the kids?"

I wonder then why she has bothered to call, but I say, "Yeah. Preston took them. They left a minute ago."

"Well, I'm glad I caught you. Wingdings on sale at ShopRite this week for seven ninety-nine. Should get two or three bags and put 'em in the freezer. I ain't seen them lower than nine ninety-nine in months. They good to have."

My Gran's favorite topics are food and God. It just so happens that the supermarket chain that we both frequent is in New Jersey and Pennsylvania. From Philadelphia she tells me what to buy for my family.

"You're right," I oblige.

"How's Preston?"

"Fine." She drops quiet. I can sense her stiff, arthritic fingers struggle with turning the circular as her right eye squints hard. A chunky, black Magic Marker is pinched between her pointer and thumb. When Gran spies something for the church she'll check it, my aunt Crystal's food gets an X, but for me, there are loopy rings safely enclosing what she deems fit.

"Oh, Faye, five-pound bag of those red potatoes you like only two dollars. Cook that with some forty-nine-cent cabbage and you got a meal."

Liv slithers her way into the kitchen. She's small for ten months and instead of crawling, she slides, one arm commando-style across the room and grabs my ankle. I kiss her cheek and then put her in her high chair and tie on her bib. She gnaws on a Baby Mum-Mum rice biscuit and watches while I pull a bag of whiting from the freezer. I'll fry that tonight with some potatoes and string beans.

"Oh, I remember what I wanted. The nursing home called. Said your mother would be doing a lot better if she had some visitors. You know I can't get all the way out to no Valley Forge. Not less Mr. Scooter takes me, and his hip is bad so I don't wanna call on him too much."

"Let Crystal take you." I wipe at the syrup spot on the kitchen table.

"I ain't getting in the car with Crystal. Is you crazy? 'Sides, that's your mother laying up there. You need to go see her. How long has it been?"

I can't even remember.

"That's what I thought," she snaps, as if I've said it out loud.

My other line clicks.

"Gran, I have to take this call. Let me talk to Preston and I'll get back to you."

"Don't take too long." She hangs up the telephone. Gran never says good-bye.

"Hello."

Nothing.

"Hello?"

Breathing.

The line goes dead.

It's just as well. I only have an hour to get out of the house. Liv has her Mommy and Me music class at eleven, which is the high-light of my week. The pile of laundry waiting for me to fold at the foot of my bed gets ignored. The baby's ExerSaucer fits in the opening of the bathroom door. I've become accustomed to show-ering with a breeze.

The class is a fifteen-minute drive. Liv babbles while I listen to the local NPR station, absorbing my dose of current events and news. As I pull into the parking lot, I can see that it's chaotic. The four-room building where the music classes are held also hosts a kids' art studio and preschool movement and yoga. Children's classes in the suburbs are big business. Every mother wants to make sure little Honey-bunch has every advantage and is ahead of the curve, so we bump ourselves until battered, piling on classes in music, Man-darin, art, swim, and Gymboree before our little people can even walk and talk.

As I unlatch Liv's car seat, I ponder over how I, Felicia Lyons, with a BFA in Theater Arts, a Super Bowl commercial, and various plays notched into my sash, how that girl ended up a stay-at-home-mom-domestic-chauffeur-short-order-cook. Maybe it was decided for me when "The Incident" occurred, the one that took my mother away.

My Gran, bless her heart, did the best she could but there is noth-ing like *your* mother. The woman whose skin smells like home, whose touch is filled with familiarity, and whose heart has your face smack at the center. This is the woman I am for my children. Front, center, and available, with their needs motivating my every move. A full-time job would distract me from being the type of mother you see on television, the one with all the white-picket-fence trimming. Nothing like how I was raised, in a North Philly box with food stamps and that disgusting welfare cheese. Gran was downtown taking care of Mr. Orbach's children, while I was latchkey with Crystal, my aunt who was only five years my senior and far more interested in fooling around with big Derell in the basement than watching me. I showed a brave face every day, but the lump of loneliness for my mother lingered in the crevices of my soul, and even though I was very young, I vowed that my children would never meet the pain of motherlessness. So here I am. Even during those burned-out times when I don't want to be available, I'll tap myself into oblivion and take a time-out at the movies with baby-size bottles of wine to bring myself back to center and focus. But I'm here.

Once inside we remove our shoes and take our spot on the colorful rug. The wide and open classroom is painted sunshine yellow. In orange letters, scripted on the wall is this: "Music is a moral law. It gives soul to the Universe, wings to the mind, flight to the imagination, and charm and gaiety to life and to everything. Plato."

In this circle, all of the mothers look the same. Washed-out skin, worn-out eyes, wearing wrinkled clothes that they found in a pile on the floor. Bone tired. Starved for conversations that don't include cooing. I must admit to feeling a bit superior because I combed my hair and I'm wearing my cute capris, so I do a lot of smiling.

"Hi, morning," I nod to Melanie. She's a mom friend. Her kids go to the same preschool as Rory and Twyla, so I know her well. Melanie is pregnant with her fourth child.

"How are you feeling, honey?"

"It was hard this morning but I made it." Melanie grins and rubs her baby bump. Her skin is a mousy olive and I don't think I've ever seen her without a limp ponytail.

I lower myself next to her and pat her knee in agreement.

We all say we come to these types of classes for the kids, but we really come to find our tribe. A mom we can talk to while our real friends are off at work. Someone to share coffee with and chat about how little Junior wouldn't go to bed, a person besides our spouse who understands the lingo and knows what the witching hour means. It's for the socialization. The getting out of the house before it consumes us. The need to have an adult connection, even if it's over "Mary Had a Little Lamb."

Ally, the music teacher, walks in and places on the floor a plastic container with eggs that shake when the kids rattle them. Liv slithers to the center and grabs the blue one. Into her mouth it goes and I cringe.

"Don't worry, I just wiped them down a second ago," Ally reassures me. We know each other well. I've been taking this class since Rory was ten months old and I'm arguably the only mom in the room who has been through all six CDs more than once, and have committed every song, intonation, hum to memory.

Liv is the only child of color in the room. I am the only African American mother. The rest of the browns are nannies. I'm polite to the working women because we come from the same place and I don't want them to think I'm uppity. But I'm never overly talkative. It's a delicate balance but I've become used to that part, too.

Ally picks up her guitar and we all chime in on the Hello song.

"Now remember moms and caregivers, it's important to sing out and dance to the fullest because your children learn from watching you," Ally encourages.

We go through a few warm-up songs and then Ally walks over to the closet and comes back with a box.

"Scarves." She dumps all sorts with varying textures, colors, and patterns, and the kids crawl and run over to pick one. I hang back eyeing the purple, and to my delight I get it. We dance to a Greek wedding song and Liv gazes at how much fun I'm having and wants up. So we dance, we fly through the air, twirl around the room, float through the sky caught up in our lavender world and I am ecstatically breathless and happy. So is Liv. I am a good mother.

"You ready for our walk?" I ask Melanie outside, in the parking lot. She and I walk after music class for a little exercise. It gives the children some fresh air and us a chance to talk before we are confined in the house for nap time.

"Mind if we skip it today? I didn't sleep at all last night." She puts Jeremy, her thirteen-month-old, up on her hip. "Between my sciatica and Bob's snoring, I tossed and turned all night."

"You should make him sleep in the den," I joked.

"I wish."

"How many weeks left?" I rub her belly.

"Five, but who knows? I was two weeks early with him." She ruffles her son's hair. He has the same dirty brown hair as her, and when he realizes we are watching him he sticks his thumb in his mouth.

"Take a nap with Jeremy today. That's what I used to do with Twyla when I was pregnant with her," I say, squeezing Liv against my breasts.

"I do have some fall fling business to catch you up on. Are you picking up today?"

"Yes."

"Okay, we'll chat then."

The walk would have been good for Liv but I could use the extra time to fold the laundry. I play the class CD for Liv on the drive home to keep her awake. I need to feed her before she naps or she won't sleep long. I sing and make faces at her through the rearview mirror and it works. As soon as we walk in the house she wants her

food and I bounce her around on my hip while I warm her organic
sweet potatoes and chicken. The telephone rings.

"Shh, shh," I say, placing Liv in the high chair with two crackers.

"Hello."

"Felicia Lyons?"

"Yes."

"This is Ashley from SEM&M."

My pulse quickens. My agent. I make my voice cheery while glid-
ing Liv's chair with my foot to keep her from crying out.

"Yes. Hello, Ashley. How have you been?"

"Oh, fine. Summer has been slow so I've managed to do a few
fun things."

"Are you still taking surfing lessons?"

"Yeah, just got back from Hawaii last week. It was incredible."

"Wow, Hawaii is on my list."

"It's beautiful. I had a great time."

"Wonderful." I pause.

"I have a go-see for you tomorrow at eleven A.M. for Samsung
Galaxy. Is your e-mail still the same?"

"Yes, nothing has changed."

"Great, let me give you the address."

"Hang on while I grab a pen."

Liv has lost interest in the now-soggy crackers and I see in her
face that she is about to let me have it. I mute the phone, snatch her
out of the seat, and sway her in my arms while I open the kitchen
drawer and search for a pen. I can't ever find a pen in this damn house.
Desperate, I take the information down with a green crayon.

"So I'll e-mail the copy right over. Good luck."

"Thanks so much for calling, Ashley. Please give everyone my
best."

When I hang up the phone, I scream. Liv starts crying.

"I'm sorry." I soothe. But I'm light on my toes. First Monroe with
the Dames' fund-raiser and now an audition. Things are looking up.

Liv looks at me with those eyes that say *Mommy, pay attention*, so I sit and feed her. Once she's taken care of and down for her nap, I send Preston a text.

Audition tomorrow at 11:00. Can you work from home with Liv?
Asking Preston is a long shot. So much to do. I have to get ready for my audition tomorrow and start writing my monologue for the Dames. Preston's text comes through.

Sorry, Foxy, but I can't. Back-to-back meetings tomorrow.
For some reason I'm not overly concerned. I'll ask one of the mom friends on the playground today at pickup. We interchange children and fill in where necessary for each other. I have at least two possibilities; I'm sure one will say yes. I twirl and head down to my little office in the basement to print the e-mail. I have an hour and a half to look over the audition copy before it's time to pick up the kids.

The commercial is about a woman who's late for work. When she pulls out her cell phone to call her boss, it falls into a puddle. She picks it up and wipes it down with her fancy scarf, and when she puts it to her ear, it works. She gets through to her boss and explains with a sigh of relief.

I can do this. I go over the copy, marking my spots, and as I move through my living room, my inner actress pours through. Damn, I've missed her.

FIVE

The Little Red School

I wander down the driveway of the Little Red School a few minutes before dismissal. Liv is still asleep, so I carry her in the detachable car seat. The year-round nursery through kindergarten school is in the town of South Mountain, which was chosen in *New York* magazine as one of the best places for commuters in northern New Jersey to live, play, and raise kids. The article said, and I quote, that it was "the type of town where the mice bring you breakfast and birds chirp lullabies to the children at night." It's where I would give my right pinky toe to live, but Preston won't cosign on the taxes, so I live out my fantasy through the children's nursery and activities.

The school is in what used to be a farmhouse and has and old-time-before-life-became-complicated feel. The education is Montessori in style, which I thought was a must for our future Barack and Michelle Obamas. I round the corner and see Melanie from music class, and Erica Prince, standing at the gate, watching their children play. I pick up the pace. Before I can say hello, Rory comes running like a dutiful puppy and laps me with kisses and hugs. He just turned six and will be going to a new school in the fall.

"I missed you all day," he says, and then runs in the opposite direction. The school yard is huge with a pint-size jungle gym, playhouse, seesaw, sandbox (which I hate and I'm sure every other black mother who has a daughter with a thick head of hair hates), and bridge.

"Hey there." Melanie greets me with a smile.

"Where's Jeremy? Did you get some rest?"

"Yes, I slept for two hours and then Bob surprised me by coming in early so I left Jeremy with him."

"You look cute." Erica looks me over.

"Thanks."

Erica has a baby boy the same age as Liv but her son is twice Liv's size. She has him in a front carrier and rocks on her heels. She's a pretty woman with a short, reddish natural, and light freckles on her cheeks and nose. New York City cute with a suburban flair. She quit her job in publishing after her oldest son, Coltrane, was born, and started a public relations business. Her husband is a musician and travels often, but when he's home they throw the best parties. I'm delighted every time our names appear on their guest list.

"How come you never put Liv in the front carrier?" Erica looks down at the baby carrier that I'm struggling with.

"She was asleep when we left the house and I didn't want to wake her."

"It's so hard on the baby. Being juggled around on the other kids' schedule." Melanie shifts on her feet.

"We were just talking about the fall fling," Erica informs me. "The day will run from one to five P.M., with activities and crafts for the whole family. Warren is going to do a music moment singalong with the kids at around three P.M."

"Are you sure he's going to be able to make it?" Melanie is the president of the parent organization and takes her job as seriously as if she were the mayor of South Mountain. Warren was supposed to play at the spring fling, and Melanie sold a slew of tickets based on his celebrity. But Warren got stuck in Los Angeles and couldn't get back in time. Melanie hasn't gotten over it. It was like her date stood her up for senior prom. "Last time we had to refund tickets and—"

"He'll be there," Erica cuts Melanie off.

"What do you need me to do?" I ask, more to break the tension than anything.

"Will you be at the meeting next week?" Melanie asks.

"Yes."

"Perfect. We will break up all the responsibilities then." Coltrane runs over to Erica, crying.

"I guess that's my cue." She takes her son by the hand.

"Rory, tell Twyla to come on," I call.

Melanie goes searching for her twins.

Damn! I almost forgot. "Erica, I need a favor?"

She slings Coltrane's backpack over her shoulder. "What's up?"

"I have an audition tomorrow in the city."

"Ooh, nice."

"I know, it's been a while since they've called. Can you watch Liv for a few hours?"

"Of course. Tomorrow's a light day and my mother will be there with me if a call comes in."

"How's that going?" I ask.

"Girl, don't get me started," she huffs. "That woman is a piece of work."

"How much longer is she staying?"

"Who knows? It was supposed to be temporary but she's getting mighty comfortable. All I can say is pray for me."

I laugh.

"Miss Liv is definitely welcome. McCoy would love to have her." She kisses the top of his head. Text me when you are on your way."

I thank Erica and we all head our separate ways. Getting our minds prepared and our emotions right for those hours after school that can feel like a full nine-to-five.

. . .

The children don't give me a hard time leaving the school playground, so I'm feeling optimistic that tonight's dinner, bath, and bedtime will be a breeze. My SUV isn't fit for three car seats, but it's my little piece of luxury and I make it work by cramming the car and booster seats together, tight like cigarettes in a fresh pack.

"Can I have a snack?" Rory asks as soon as he's buckled in.

"Excuse me?" I eye him through the rearview mirror.

"May I have a snack?" He corrects himself and I reach into my bag and toss back two granola bars. On the avenue, I ask the children about their day, but neither remembers anything.

A few blocks later: "Stop." Two shouts.

I look through the rearview mirror and fix Rory with a look that says please leave her alone. But it's too late. Two has started wailing. The baby whines and now I'm pissed.

"What's the matter?"

"She dropped her granola bar on the floor."

I pull over in front of the Ukrainian church to sort things out. But thrusting the bar in her direction doesn't stop her howling. This is Two's time of day to be wound up, and she loses control in seconds. She doesn't just cry; she screams like someone is drawing blood with a butcher knife. Nothing I say works to calm her. I consider pushing her out on the curb and leaving her to find her way home but realize that's a bit dramatic, so I pull back in to traffic, turn up the radio, and tune her out.

I've barely pulled in to the driveway of our house, and Rory has already broken free of the seat belt and is hopping over Two to be the first one out of the car. This makes her shriek harder.

"Rory, can you please wait." I unbuckle Two's seat, and pull the baby from her car seat onto my hip. I have both backpacks and Two's hand in mine, but she's still going.

"Stop," I hiss. "Does everyone on the block have to know that we're home?" Of course they do, and she keeps it up. Rory takes the keys from me and runs up the stairs to unlock the door. We just manage to get in the house when Two throws herself on the floor and continues the tantrum.

Liv's fuss has flamed to a full throttle cry and I know she wants my milk. I'm weaning so she's down to two feedings a day and she only had one before her nap. I send Rory to get his math workbook, lift Liv to my breast while cuddling Two on the other side. Two's tears slow to a sniffle as she pops her pointer finger in her mouth. The evening has just begun and I'm dog-tired. Why is this always so hard? The kids have been with me less than an hour and I already feel like the mother in that commercial; Calgon take me away. It would be easier to manage if Preston were home a few nights a week to help me.

Well, someone has to work while you are playing house with the kids. Bills don't get paid on their own.

I bare my teeth ready to do battle with the *damn voice* but then I remember myself. Remember that I have a toolbox for moments like this. I shift Two onto a pillow, tuck Liv under my arm, and then tap two of my fingers against my hand.

The whiting never got fried. Instead they are munching on my go-to ten-minute meal: chicken nuggets from the toaster oven and vegetable fried rice (frozen peas and leftover rice sautéed on the stove). My salad is an afterthought, and by the time I sit down they are nearly finished and rice is everywhere.

"Would you like some more?" I asked them both while spooning Liv harvest squash and turkey from the Earth's Best jar.

"More chicken nuggets." Rory chews.

I'm tossing him two nuggets when the telephone rings. Preston's house rule is that no one answers the telephone during dinner. But he's not here and I'm wondering if it's my agent with last-minute notes about tomorrow's go-see. I snatch it up and put my finger to my lips to silence the children.

"Good evening." I sound cheery.

I hear breathing.

"Hello?"

A man's chuckle.

"Hello?"

"My, my, my, I can't believe it." His voice is low and baritone. "After all this time, I've finally found you."

My lips part and if my skin wasn't a decadent brown, I would have turned pasty white.

"Who is this?" I demand, all business-like. Knowing, but not wanting to know. *It can't be.*

"Felicia Hayes," he produces my maiden name. "Come on now, it's me, Young Sister."

The phone slips down to my shoulder. He always called me Young Sister, and the sound of the nickname that I hadn't heard in ages has me feeling light-headed. My hip presses against the countertop for support.

"Ms. Hayes?"

"It's Mrs. Lyons."

"Mommy, who is that? Is it Daddy?" Two looks at me with suspicious eyes and I flick my wrist to hush her.

"I don't have much time. I've been down for a couple of years, but I'm on work release now."

Down? As in jail down? My tongue lays heavily in my mouth and my eyes don't blink.

"They got me in the hot Georgia sun picking up trash and cutting grass along roadsides. Burning up out there in this ridiculous orange jumpsuit. Damn right embarrassing. But I'm being released and will be home in a few weeks. Will you come to Philly to see me?"

My breathing is shallow.

"You have no idea how many nights I've stayed up thinking about you. Wondering . . ."

"Mommeeee," Two is up from the table, tugging on my shirt and hollering.

"Hang on, please." I put the phone down. "Have you lost your mind? I AM ON THE PHONE. Are you finished with your dinner?"

"Yes, ma'am," she says, all of a sudden remembering her manners.

"Rory, go put the television on and you two sit and watch one show."

"Really?" he looks up surprised. There is a cardinal rule of no television during the week. Both look at me like I've lost it.

"Go now before I change my mind."

They scramble out of the room and I let Liv down to slither after them.

"If I hear any arguing, I'm turning it off."

I run my fingers over my hair before putting the phone back to my ear.

"Martin." His name feels foreign in my mouth. "How did you find me? My number isn't published."

"Don't say it like you're not happy to hear from me. How long has it been? Fifteen, sixteen years? You must be as pretty as ever."

I warm from the compliment, thinking it's been more like sixteen years and five months. But I don't say it out loud. It's not like I've been counting. Or have I? I let the question go as quickly as it came.

"How many kids do you have?"

"Three."

"Look at my Faye, all grown up. It's so good to hear your beautiful voice." He pauses. "I remember how you use to walk around the church with your head held high. Couldn't keep my eyes off of you."

My mind struggles with whether reminiscing with him is right, but the battle is lost, and I'm headfirst with Martin down memory lane to that long-ago place I've forgotten.

His hands on my waist, making me move to his beat.

"Slipping out with you in Daddy Gracious's Caddy was the highlight of my week. You used to like those moments, didn't you?"

Yes, I was a young, hungry girl, sneaking off with this man, who kissed my wounds away and made them all better. This man who is talking in my ears like a lifetime hasn't passed and still having the same effect.

"It's been so long since I've laid my eyes on you." His voice feels creamy, soft, and hypnotizing. Martin could say anything to me with that voice and I'd quiver.

Get down on your knees and beg, Young Sister.

"When you stopped coming to church I missed you."

"Yeah, well . . . things happened." I snap out of it and my feet are back in reality. Back to why I stopped going to church altogether and Martin had everything to do with it.

"I know all about it, Young Sister," he soothes. We both pause, letting his words hang in the air.

"What do you want?"

"I have to go now. Time's running. Can I call you again? Is this time good?"

Preston is never home before nine, and when I open my mouth, I'm not thinking. "Yes, this time is good."

"Perfect," he replies, and I feel his smile through the telephone. "Sweet dreams, Faye." His voice fades into the lobe of my ear. I stand there clutching the phone so long that it takes me a few seconds to realize the line went dead.

"To bed," I call to the kids and never mind their protest. My hands are as shaky as a cup of Jell-O. I thought Martin was buried with my past.

"Mom, *Wonder Pets* is almost over," Rory calls. I grab Liv from the floor and hold her to my heart in an attempt to slow down the thumping.

"Meet me upstairs as soon as the credits start rolling."

I take the steps two at a time, wash Liv's face and hands, and rock her against my breast, trying to stay a step ahead of the constant thought *I can't believe Martin called me.* When Rory and Two make it upstairs, I tell them to brush their teeth and get in bed.

"What about our story?" Two's eyes get big.

"I let you watch a show. I'll read extra tomorrow."

"But Mommy."

"Don't 'but Mommy' me." I wipe the toothpaste from the side of her mouth and then pull the covers over her.

Rory's bedroom is across the hall and I tuck him in, kiss both cheeks, and head downstairs.

"And if I have to come back up here, it's going to be some serious trouble," I say halfway down. My body hasn't settled, and I'm grateful to find an unopened bottle of merlot in the cabinet. I pour myself a healthy glass, promising to pump and dump the milk before bed. I carry the glass to my gazebo in the backyard, drop the mosquito net, and light the citronella candle. I still cannot believe Martin found me. After all of these years. Who can I call? Who can I tell? The only person who knows everything that happened is my Aunt Crystal, but I'm not dialing her because I don't know what state she might be in. Crystal runs hot and cold, and if I catch her on the wrong day, she's liable to pick up the phone and tell Preston all of my business. This is not the type of thing I'd share with any of my mommy friends. Shayla knows, but . . .

I take a long gulp. Shayla knows, but . . .

Would Shayla have connected Martin to me? I scroll through my phone and find her on Facebook. Shayla and I grew up together on Sydenham Street in Philadelphia. She was my best friend, had my back through thick and thin, but it's been years since we've talked.

Once I went to college our lives went in different directions and we lost touch. Three years ago she found me on Facebook and tried to meet up but I canceled every time. Blamed my lack of availability on my children and Preston working, but that wasn't it. Shayla knew the before-Preston me, and I wasn't that North Philly girl anymore. I had rewritten my history, so to speak, and I didn't want any ghosts from my past haunting my chance at picket-fence happiness.

She eventually stopped asking to see me and we dropped down to a happy birthday on Facebook, and a like here and there, but nothing real or substantial. That's why I amaze even myself when I send her a direct message.

Are you around? Can we talk?

I hear Preston calling me.

"Foxy?" he looks through the back window.

"I'm out here."

I put my phone down. Preston comes out with his tie dangling and a beer. He looks worn out and I'm glad to be able to shift my thoughts to him.

"Did you eat?"

"Yeah. I got your text about the chicken nuggets so I picked something up on the way home."

"How was your day?"

"Ugh, I don't want to talk about it. Yours?"

"Me either." I put my legs in his lap.

"Good."

We sit with our thoughts, listening to the crickets and enjoying the fresh air. If Preston had a penny for my thoughts, it would be detrimental. I wonder briefly if it would be the same for his.

SIX

The City

I am dressed in all white in the alley of the Daddy Gracious One Church. I slink back behind the fire escape, where no one can see me unless they were determined to find me. There is a draft stirring between the buildings, but I don't feel it. My lips are parted and my skin is piping hot. Martin is pressed against me, working two thick fingers under my skirt, inside the mouth of my thighs. His breath is in my hair. Our hips crash, creating the friction I desire, and I forget to inhale. The tension starts to strengthen in my lower belly, build, build, build. I've sped past shy and can't control myself from smashing into his fingers with so much force that I erupt and spill. Soaked with my fragrance, I collapse against his chest. He holds me tight and breathes a whisper.

"You're ready, Young Sister. Next time."

As I struggle out of bed to hush the alarm, I'm aware of the stickiness between my legs. The dream is at the top of my memory and I shake my head to let it go, but that hurts. That's when I remember. One drink with Preston turned into three. Three! What the hell was

I thinking? Did I say anything incriminating? I think for a minute. I have an audition in a few hours. Christ. I pad into the bathroom and look at my hungover face in the mirror. My lips are cracked and stained red from the wine. My mascara has run and pooled under my eyes. I pop two Advil, sip water from the faucet, and will the wooziness to stop. I'm scrubbing my face when Rory enters the bathroom. Murky water is all over the sink.

"Mommy." He puts his arms around my waist.

"Hey, baby."

I can honestly say I don't have a favorite child. Each one touches me in a different place. But Rory's space is special. My only boy. My firstborn. I squeeze him back.

"How did you sleep?"

"Okay."

"Just okay?" I turn off the flow, pat my face with a paper towel, and then get down on my knees so that we are eye-to-eye. His features are Preston's, nut brown, curved eyes, and a strong nose. I can't locate anything of me. I kiss his cheek and then we walk hand in hand to wake up Two.

I manage to get them all ready on time, and Preston drives the kids to school while I run around the house making sure I have everything for Liv, the audition, and my trip into the city. I slip a cute purple romper over Liv's head and fasten the snaps. I bring her into the bathroom with me and take the extra time with my stage makeup: foundation, blush and shadows, mascara, lipstick, translucent powder. I go at least two layers heavier when I'm in front of the camera, and I'm grateful Liv is sitting still for a half hour to let me get it all done.

The anxiety sifts like flour in my belly as I rehearse my lines one more time in the mirror. I need this audition to turn into a callback so that the agency will put me back on their top call roster. The clock races faster than me. When I bend down to scoop up Liv, she's got styling cream all over her romper and fingers. What is it with my children and freakin' hair products? The outfit is ruined and now I rifle through her wardrobe looking for something else. I can't send her to Erica's house looking anything but cute. Coltrane and McCoy are always dressed well. Most of the laundry is piled in my room and I don't have time to iron so I pull down a yellow sundress with the matching "panty bottoms" and head downstairs.

Snacks (can't ever leave the house without snacks), diapers, wipes, change of clothes, toys, books. My left arm is weighed down so I've scooped Liv up with my right and head to the car. Our block captain, Ms. Minnie, is watering her lawn and I give her a quick wave and shout good morning while strapping Liv in her seat. She squirms and kicks her feet. She pulls on my shirt and I know she wants to nurse. We are fifteen minutes behind schedule and there is no time. I hand her a sippy cup filled with diluted apple juice and round the car to the driver's seat.

I can smell the tangerine floating from the belly of my favorite flowers and I let the window down for a gentle wind, but as I turn onto Liberty Avenue, the breeze has my hair blowing and I can't chance the frizz. Air-conditioning it is.

Erica lives a few blocks from the kids' nursery school, up the hill and close to the South Mountain reservation. I lug Liv and all of her things down the winding walkway while balancing in my skinny heels. I ring the doorbell. Liv starts up a little fuss and I bounce her on my hip, hoping with all my might that she doesn't throw up on me. The door opens, I look up, and there is Erica's husband, Warren.

"Hey there," he greets me, smelling like some kind of essential oil.

"When did you shave your head?"

"Oh," he reaches up and touches his head like he's just remembering his new look. "I'm shooting a small scene in a movie."

"Really?"

He ushers me into the open-concept living room.

"Nothing big. A walk-on really but the director asked me to shave so I thought what the hell."

"It looks nice."

He gives me a wicked grin. "My wife likes it."

"It's sexy as hell on him, isn't it?" Erica floats into the living room, wearing faded cutoff shorts and a baby tee. She's thinner than me and the outfit makes her look youthful. She squeezes Warren's hand and they gaze into each other's eyes. I feel shy, catching them in an intimate moment, and turn my attention to smoothing down Liv's hair.

I can smell something baking, buttery and nutty. Warren excuses himself to his den. Erica throws her arms around me and then reaches for Liv.

"What is all of this stuff?"

"Just in case."

"In case what? You know I have every toy she could think of with these monsters I have running around here." Erica leads me into the kitchen. She places my bag on the white marble center island. There is an office nook off to the corner with a big window looking out onto the deck. It's only my second or third time in Erica's kitchen and I feel like I'm in the middle of a magazine spread.

"What time is your audition?"

"Eleven."

"You better hurry."

"I know, thanks so much. If you need me for anything . . ."

"Felicia, go."

Erica's mother walks gingerly into the room. I hear her shuffling before I see her. "Oh, 'scuse me. Didn't know you had company."

"Have you met my mother?"

"No. I'm Felicia."

"Gweny." She leans heavily against the counter like she's short of breath. Her hair is cut short and she's wearing dark glasses. "Lord knows I'm tired. Just pulled a load of clothes from the dryer and folded them. Then picked up all the toys in the playroom. Coltrane is big enough to pick up after himself. You need to start training him, Slim. You want me to change the linen on the beds too?"

"Mom, won't you go relax?" Erica chides.

"Just trying to be helpful."

Erica waves her hand for me to follow her. "Come on, let me walk you out."

"You keeping her baby?" her mother calls after us.

"Yes!" Erica shouts back. At the front door she whispers, "Honestly, that woman is going to have me drinking scotch by lunch."

"Be grateful you have her," I say, thinking of my own mother.

Erica blows her breath and then smiles. "Break a leg today, and don't worry about Liv. We've got her."

I merge onto Route 78 and take the New Jersey Turnpike. I flip the radio to 1010 WINS to hear what the traffic is like. The Lincoln Tunnel is a twenty-five-minute wait, so I take that route, praying that the traffic around Forty-Second Street isn't too bad. All the cars slow as the traffic merges to get to the toll at the tunnel. I flip through my phone to calm the nervous energy. On Facebook I see that Shayla replied to my direct message.

If you can get away, let's do lunch. Midtown works best.

With all the hustling this morning, I almost forgot about Martin calling.

That's perfect. Twelve o'clock. You pick the place.

I drop my phone in the passenger's seat. Shayla. What am I doing reaching out to her? Last I heard she was living that underworld, fast-money life. When we were growing up, I never wanted any part of the street game, but Shayla's always been down for climbing up by any means necessary. Lunch at a public place should be fine. It's not like I'm inviting her to my house, where my family lives. Introducing her to Preston. I'd never do that. Seeing her might help me get to the bottom of how Martin found me, and just get that man off my chest. That's all I wanted.

The audition is at Fifty-Second and Eighth, and I maneuver into a parking lot a half block away. The cost is exasperating, but what can I do but cross my fingers that this commercial will pay back dividends?

Now, you know the odds are against you. Actresses come a dime a dozen.

But I ignore her. I pop down my driver's side mirror to refresh, recheck, and regather. My Louise Hay affirmation is taped to the visor on a yellow Post-it so I read it out loud while looking myself dead in the eye.

"All is well. The Universe supports me at every turn." Preston thinks talking to myself in the mirror is bonkers and maybe it is, but I do it anyway. When I step out of the car I am ready.

"Morning." The petite blonde smiles at me from behind the small desk.

"Felicia Lyons, here for Samsung Galaxy."

"Room eight."

She hands me the copy and I'm relieved that it's the same lines I've practiced. Sometimes they change them at the last minute.

There are two women waiting in front of me. I give a polite smile; one smiles back, and the other nods. We all have similar looks but I'm the brownest of the bunch and I hope that works to my advantage. My mocha doe eyes are my best feature. I do an awesome surprise, and watch out when I have to gush and cry. I haven't relaxed my hair since college, so my natural is long and thick and full of body. I go over my lines one more time, and when they call me in, I tell myself it's all mine.

Shayla messages me to meet her at Landmarc at the Time Warner Center in Columbus Circle. I've never been inside the building, and when I see the directory of stores I wish I had more time to buy myself something. As always I'm on the clock. I have about an hour to meet with Shayla before I need to dash back for the kids and figure out dinner.

At the entrance of the restaurant, I see Shayla sitting at a table by the window bent over her tablet. She is as beautiful as the day is sunny. I envied that when we were kids. Shayla woke up pretty. I always felt like I needed to do a little work to catch up. Her shiny hair was bone straight, hanging down her back. She had coal eyes, high Ethiopian-like cheekbones, and a natural pout to her mouth. When she turned to face me, I saw her hand-size breasts mushed together with a demi cut bra. No surprise there. That's been Shayla's trick for cleavage since we were eleven.

"Faye." She steps and hugs me. She smells expensive. I squeeze her back. She's taller than me by an inch and her waist is small.

"You look great, as always." I slip into the seat across from her and glance out at Central Park.

"You look good. How many years has it been?"

"A few," I say, knowing damn well that I haven't seen her for at least seven years, before I married Preston.

The waiter comes out of nowhere and is smiling down at me, asking for the order.

"What are you having?" Shayla looks over at me.

"Chopped salad."

"Salad? That's bird food. Give us two cheeseburgers and surprise us with your favorite draft beer." She winks at the waiter.

"I don't drink beer in the middle of the day. I have to pick up my children from school."

"One beer won't kill you. Chill out. Damn, you uptight."

I feel weird. "So what you been up to?"

"Business, that's all." She said business like it wasn't the type of thing I needed to know. So I changed the subject.

"You want to see my kids?" I unlock my phone and pull up pictures. The waiter drops off the beers.

"Damn, Faye, they are beautiful. Don't look nothing like you."

"Whatever."

She looks over each picture slowly, studying at least ten before handing me back my phone.

"You could have made me godmother to at least one kid. Damn. I am your oldest friend. You didn't even invite me to your wedding."

"Girl, please, you've never even liked kids. Swore on a stack of Bibles when we were thirteen years old that you would never have them."

"Still."

Preston texts me.

How did the audition go?

I text back, *Well. Heading home soon.*

I check the clock before stashing my phone in my purse. The burgers come and Shayla chews.

"Did you give Martin my phone number?" I say abruptly.

"What? Martin?"

I watch her face for the lie and keep my eyes even.

"Who the hell is Mar—oh, wait, Martin from—"

"Did you?"

"Girl, no. Is that what this is about? Why you finally had time to see me?" She shakes her long hair. "I haven't seen that fool since, damn, like back before things happened. Probably wouldn't even recognize him on the street."

I believe her. "I don't know how he found me."

The waiter approaches and drops off two waters.

"You're a frazzled mess." Shayla touches my arm. "What happened?"

I tell Shayla about him calling the house and catching me off guard. "You should have seen how my middle daughter was cling-ing to me. Like I was having an affair or something."

"It's probably because you were all flushed like you are now. Look at you. Breasts all full. Face, cheery and shit. You still got feelings for the old dude?"

"Nooo."

"Faye, you ain't got to fake it with me. It's obvious. You gonna fuck him?"

"Shayla!" I touch my fingers to my throat and look around to see if anyone has overheard our conversation. "That's not what I want. I'm married. Happily married."

"Mmm hmm." She stares me down. "Does your husband know about—"

I cut into her quick. "No. And he doesn't need to."

"Okay, Faye." She holds her hands up in surrender. "You did make me solemnly swear to take it to my grave."

I was about to remind her that nothing had changed, but her phone rings. She checks the caller ID but doesn't answer.

"So what does the man want?"

"He's about to be released from prison. Asked me to come see him in Philly when he gets home."

"You going?"

"I don't even go to Philly to see Gran."

"My mother used to say, best to let sleeping dogs lie." She sips her beer. "But it looks like that dog is wide awake. I'll cover for you."

"You'll cover for me? What are we, sixteen?" I laugh.

"You know it's something about that first man who pops your cherry. You just don't ever get that dude out of your system. It's like they live inside of you. Forever. Time doesn't change that."

Her words unnerve me. My appetite is gone.

"I need to go." I pull two twenties from my wallet.

Shayla pushes the money back toward me. "I wouldn't dream of letting you pay, Faye." The waiter passes the table and she thrusts her credit card at him. "That's insurance, so that I'll see you again."

I gather my things. Purposely stand without the usual promise to touch bases with available meet-up dates. A quick hug and then I am walking out the front door.

SEVEN

The Man, Mr. Martin Dupree

As I maneuver my car back through the Lincoln Tunnel, my mind swerves. I thought downloading with Shayla would help me move on, but it has untied my system. Memories gush to the surface. It's as if someone has wrenched me open like a fire hydrant on a hot day.

It's hard to remember Martin without thinking about the Daddy Gracious Church. Gran was a fool of a fanatic back then. She worshipped Daddy Gracious like he was the Second Coming of Christ, going to church services five or six times a week. It was all one big charade to me.

The church was in the neck of South Philadelphia, less than a mile south of Rittenhouse Square. Before Sunday service, Daddy Gracious would start at Twentieth Street and cruise down Fitzwater in his long, white Cadillac convertible with the tomato-red interior. The top was always down, so that his shoulder-length press and curl blew with the wind. Martin, his driver, drove slowly enough for Daddy Gracious's drill team to keep up on both sides of the car and behind him. Everyone in the neighborhood knew his theme music, and the children came running when they heard the tambourines, drums, and horns. Flags, pom-poms, and batons moved through the air as dancers' feet stomped, twirled, and kept the rhythm. Sunday morning was more entertaining than late night television.

Daddy Gracious kept a cooler filled with ice-cold canned sodas in the backseat. As he passed the people in the street he would crack open a soda, sip it first, and then give it to the outstretched hands. Followers believed his lips were anointed, and the folks would line up for blocks, hoping to be blessed with a kissed can. By the time the entourage pulled in front of the storefront church at the corner of Sixteenth and Fitzwater, the music from the drill team would be thunderous. The trumpets blared, the drums would beat harder, and the choir stood singing on the curb with the doors of the church open.

"Here comes Daddy. Here he comes." The singers' hips swayed. Teenage boys stood guard at the curb, and at Daddy Gracious's nod they would roll out this bright red carpet that only he could walk on.

But Daddy Gracious didn't walk. He tiptoed on high-heeled boots, much like the shoes Prince wore. Daddy glided across the red carpet, swinging his long lion's mane back and forth. His fingernails were long and curved like a predator's, and he wore a rich, white cape that swished and cracked the air when he moved.

"Give Him some praise. He's worthy. Now give Him some praise."

When he entered the church, the whole congregation would jump to their feet. Daddy Gracious hoofed it down the aisle and then fell into his center pulpit chair. Two ushers would fan him until he caught his breath and was on his feet again. The show would continue until the audience was riled up and breathless.

Martin Dupree was always with Daddy Gracious, driving him around, standing as his bodyguard, and playing bass guitar in the church's band. He was thirteen years my senior and he was Billie

Dee Williams in *Mahogany* fine, Brad Pitt in *Troy* fine, Denzel Washington in *Mo' Better Blues* fine. Every time I walked into church and saw him up in the pulpit rocking his instrument, my heart skipped a step. His gold-flecked white shirts stood out in the sea of bright white we were all required to wear. His hair swept away from his face in a fit of shiny black curls, hazel eyes, and thick lashes. Seemed like a sin to waste so much pretty on a man when so many women ran around the church looking like wet ducks.

Every Sunday, Gran made us sit in the same pew, fifth row from the front, left-hand side in the aisle, and as soon as I was seated I'd feel Martin staring at me from behind his dark shades. The small circular ones that seemed sewn on, because no matter how hard he plucked the strings of his bass guitar and rolled his instrument, the glasses never moved. When Martin and I would later bump around the back of Daddy Gracious's car, his frames stayed still then too.

Living with Gran had shamed me. Losing my parents had deadened me. But when those catlike eyes peered at me in a way that wasn't obvious to anyone but me, things inside of me came alive. My body was like the earth thawing after a long, harsh winter. Just a look from Martin made my throat curl toward him, and I inhaled until the thin material of my collared dress ballooned and my bra felt like it would burst. The first moment Martin called to me, I came in heat.

Gran was down on her knees praying hard and loud, no doubt for my salvation as well as her own sanity, when I snuck away from the carnival. By then Crystal had been excused from Sunday services on account of her job at Payless shoes in the Gallery mall. I was shocked when Gran allowed that, but Crystal was pregnant with little Derell, needed the money, and according to Gran couldn't be saved.

"That chile always had the devil in her. Don't you follow in her footsteps," Gran would say, thumping her Bible at me. Crystal was crazy but it wasn't the devil. She was an ornery teenager with raging hormones and I would soon relate.

I was in the church corridor, dipping my head for a drink of water from the fountain. My hair was pulled into a high ponytail, and my white ensemble fit me well. When I came up wiping the dribbles with the back of my hand, Martin was there. Smelling like a dream. Smiling wide. Standing too close. Eyes lapping over my curves. Gran had finally let me wear shoes with a little heel to church, so I was tall enough to look up at Martin with my Cleopatra eyes.

"How are you today, Young Sister?"

"Fine." I tried to back away but there was the concrete wall.

"You okay?"

I nodded. He kept his eyes on me until I gave him a shy grin and then looked down at my ankles.

"I wanted to give you something," he whispered and then pressed a strip of paper into my hand. His thumb flicked against my palm, like a match to the striking surface. The friction turned my hormones inside out, and I leaked with love or lust or both. At fourteen, I didn't know the difference.

I kept the paper tucked in the bottom of my shoe until I reached my bedroom and could savor it alone. It simply read, in blue ink, "I'd like to get to know you better, Young Sister." I blushed all week whenever I pulled the note from inside my pillowcase, where I kept it.

Next Sunday I sat in our pew trying to keep my nerves under control through all the hoopla that led up to the sermon. As soon as Daddy Gracious One said "Let us pray," Martin nodded to me and walked toward the side door. I took that to mean he wanted me to follow. Gran's eyes were closed, so it was easy to get away. He waited for me at the fountain.

"You look pretty today," he greeted me the first week. "Like your hair," the next. By the third Sunday we had worked up to, "That dress is wearing you well, Young Sister."

He always called me Young Sister. And I liked the way it sounded from his mouth. Like we were in the middle of a revolution and he recognized the part I played. On our fourth meeting we went from talking by the water fountain to leaving out the side door of the sanctuary.

"You want to see the inside?" Martin asked, with a wink at Daddy Gracious's car.

Everyone referred to his Cadillac as "that Fat Hog." It was the finest thing in all of South Philadelphia, at least on the black side of town, which ranged from the trolley tracks down to Oregon Avenue. So asking me, a fourteen-year-old orphan girl, if she wanted to get inside the car when I was used to catching the bus, was like asking a kid if she wanted to board an airplane to Disney World with her twenty closest friends.

I followed him down the alley to where the car was parked. It was a cool day, so the top was up. Martin opened the door for me, and when I got inside, we were completely isolated. The leather was smooth against my back and easy to snuggle against. Martin turned the radio on and we sat next to each other. He hummed the song on the radio, something by Force MDs. I felt grown.

"You sure are pretty. Tender." His smile gave me tremors and I didn't know what to do with my hands. I had dressed more thoughtfully since Martin began showing attention, wearing Crystal's low-cut blouse and a skirt with a split.

"You okay?" he touched my chin.

"Yeah."

He dropped his hand on my thigh and I never wanted those shivers to stop.

Martin became all I could think about during the week, and the next Sunday I was the first one ready for church. Gran eyed me.

"What the devil's gotten into you?"

"Nothing, just didn't want to be the cause of us being late today. I know how important church is to you." I didn't bat a lash.

Gran let the moment pass.

I imagined that Daddy Gracious loved to see the women holding themselves and falling all over the place in the name of the Lord. He kept them juicy with sweat, ripe and heavy, so that they could give it up at offering time. The ushers would pass the plates around while Daddy walked up and down the center aisle, punctuating each thought with a whip of his cape.

"Don't put nothing in the basket that jingles, now. Don't hurt Daddy's ears." *Whip.* "Give the Lord something that folds. And you'll be blessed now." *Whip, whip.* "Daddy's got sensitive ears, now. Make sure you give something soft." *Whip, whip, whip.* He'd give a swivel of the hips and then return to the pulpit. Nothing ever rattled in those plates. Even the broke folk put in dollars.

After the collection, the congregation would pray over the money. But I never prayed. I had my eyes on Martin, eager for his signal to sneak away.

We were two months into hanging out in "that Fat Hog." The clouds were drizzling, and I was glad that I had pulled my hair into a tight bun so it wouldn't frizz up. Martin opened the door and then was beside me with one hand on my thigh, working the radio station with the other. We didn't talk much, but the chemistry was connective. Martin stopped fiddling at a Keith Sweat song. Our time together was limited, and Martin seemed to advance on me more each week. I knew where we were heading, but I didn't stop him. Little beads of drizzle pitter-pattered against the window while his hand moved to the top of my pantyhose. When I didn't push his hand away, his head moved in close and I could smell Doublemint gum. I tilted my head and he kissed me. His fingers were cold on my belly, then caressing the rim of my panties, before his whole hand curved down my pelvis into my mess of hair. His fingers played my delicate spots like a melody on his guitar, soft and sweet, then long and hard. I was sweating under my clothes. With Martin I was gone. When he was around I didn't have space to think, to breathe, which made it impossible to do anything but what he wanted. I rocked my hips to melt into his rhythm. I moved my butt back in the seat and tilted forward so that his finger could go deeper, and then the sensation was building and needed to be released and I let it. I reached out for the dashboard to steady myself. This time the orgasm ricocheted through my entire body. My forehead was wet and I when I finished gasping I was washed in shame.

I worried that Martin would think differently of me, but when he moved his fingers from my panties he pulled me to his chest, kissed my forehead, and whispered.

"You're almost ready."

The next week Martin used two fingers, removed my left breast from my bra, and pulled on it with his teeth until I thought I would lose my sanity. When he went back to the pulpit to play, I sat in the bathroom until I felt normal. I couldn't get enough of that feeling that Martin gave me. During the week, I'd wait for Crystal to leave for work so I could run to the room we shared and touch myself, pretending that my hands were Martin's. Once I had discovered the release, I couldn't make myself stop. All I wanted was to feel myself shake and come undone. It wasn't the same without Martin but it was enough to hold me over until the sermon started.

By now Martin had taken me to first and second base. I wasn't sure about third, but I was okay with skipping it and heading straight for the home run. That Sunday Gran had her eye on me. She hadn't slipped into her coma-like state. Instead, she kept passing me her Bible, telling me to look up passages. When I said I had to go to the bathroom, she clucked her tongue.

"Hold it. Show Daddy Gracious some respect."

I saw Martin slip out, and it was all I could do not to disobey Gran. The next week I had my period, so I didn't go to church. I told Gran my cramps were so bad I couldn't get out of the bed. By the last Sunday of the month I was craving Martin like a marathon runner thirsty for fluids.

Gran was good into church that week and was down on her knees before Daddy started up. I was up and out the door before Martin and had to wait for him in the alley. As soon as I saw him, he kissed me full on the lips like I was a woman. Didn't even wait until we got in the car.

He turned the music on, let whatever station was on play, and then his hands was all over me. I could tell he was trying to control himself. I wanted the pleasure from him so bad my toes tingled. Martin slipped one finger, then two, eased them in and out, in and out, in and out, deeper, deeper, and just when I felt myself coming apart, he stopped.

"What?" I asked, big worried eyes, like I did something wrong.

He unzipped his pants and put my hand on his erection. I told him I had never seen or touched a man's part.

"I want to stick it in," he whispered. "I'll take it slow."

My mind went to spying on Crystal and Big Derell humping in the basement. The back of the preacher's car wasn't my idea of the ideal spot to lose my virginity, but I would do anything for Martin. Martin slid me underneath him, pushing my legs apart, and then lowered himself inside me, with the same slow technique he had been using with his fingers. When his skin broke into mine, it wasn't what I was expecting. It hurt so bad but felt so good. Mixed emotions poured through me. It was all I could do to keep my scream trapped between my teeth and tongue. The leather seats squeaked as the car rocked, his sweat pouring on top of me. He grunted and I felt fire, splitting fire, and I wanted to tell him to stop but he held me so tight I felt smothered with love. More love than I felt in the three years since my daddy took my mommy. And I clung to him for dear life, praying it would never end. But it did. Badly.

EIGHT

The Groceries

Since I'm coming from the city, I don't have time to stop at the grocery store before I pick up the children. Preston would have a fit if I do a quick-fix nugget dinner two nights in a row, so I'm forced to cart all three into Ashley's Gourmet after camp.

Rory has karate today, and the stop at the market is going to prevent me from taking him home before class. Thank goodness I remembered to throw his stuff in the trunk this morning. I hand him his *gi* and tell him to change in the car.

"But someone might see me," he says, crouching in the backseat and covering himself with both hands.

"Boy, we are in a covered parking lot. I guarantee that no one is breaking their neck trying to see you."

Two climbs over the center console and drops in my lap. I smooth her hair while she sucks her pointer finger and I make a mental grocery list. I'll throw together a chicken noodle soup with cornbread for dinner. To make it hearty, I'll add a can of pumpkin to the broth. I slip Liv into the BabyBjörn carrier and grab the hand of each kid.

We come in through the back door, and as I select my carrots and celery, I see Monroe McKenzie poring over the cucumbers. I haven't heard anything from her since the chance collision at the movies. Since I am coming from the city my makeup is done and my outfit is just right, so I approach her first. Time to get my Dame membership rolling.

"Hello, Monroe." I smile.

She spins on her heels. "Felicia, how are you, dear?" She looks down at the children. "Boy, you guys are getting big."

Two hides behind my leg and Rory just give his shy boy look, which teeters on the verge of a look that says leave me alone.

"How's the performance piece going? I really want you to wow the Dames," she says, cocking her head. Those perfectly painted red lips smile out at me and I mindlessly wonder how she keeps the red from bleeding.

"I started sketching it this morning but I had to run into the city for an audition. I'll get back to it tonight." It's a partial truth but it makes Monroe's eyes brighten.

"An audition! Really? What for?"

"Samsung Galaxy. It's a national, so keep your fingers crossed." I beam, glad to have something to brag on, showing her that I *am* Dames material.

"And toes," she says.

Rory slips off and I spy him out of the corner of my eye.

"I didn't get that e-mail from you with the details for the meeting."

"Really?" Monroe whips out her smartphone and starts scrolling through. "It's next Friday at six for all potential talent. I hope you can make it."

I do a mental check and declare that Friday works. It's my first time being invited to anything Dames, and I try to keep the excitement from bubbling outward.

"What's your e-mail address again?"

"Here, it's easier if I type it in." I take her phone. Liv squirms and I bounce on my toes to quiet her.

"Rory, come over here," I call without looking.

"Mommmmmmeeeeee," he says back.

When my eyes flick over, I see apples, lots of them tumbling in all directions from the apple stand to the floor. Rory has three in his hand. Two rushes to help him. Five, six, seven apples spill from the cart like water and roll in all directions.

I hand Monroe back her cell phone.

"Rory," I say with my voice even, straining to keep my black mama scorn from showing up in front of company.

"Start picking those up." It's fruitless because the apples continue to fall twelve, thirteen in all directions. I am at the stand trying to plug in the hole to keep more apples from falling. Monroe is watching Rory and Two crawling all over the floor, so I dismiss her.

"I'll look for your e-mail and see you next Friday. Call me if anything changes." I give a short finger wave, and as I do, a store clerk is at our side.

"I've got it from here, ma'am." His facial expression is polite, and I pat his forearm in thanks.

Breathe.

In the canned goods aisle, I'm up on Rory. "How did that happen?" I hiss between my teeth.

"I was trying to get an apple so you could put it in my lunch box for tomorrow." Rory pouts, and I can tell by the way his brows tilt down that he is two seconds away from crying.

I soften. "It's no big deal, honey. Accidents happen." I pull him to my hip. "Let's get the chicken for the soup tonight and get out of here."

We head to the other side of the store and pick up the rest of our list. When we get in line, Rory tugs my shirt.

"Mama, I don't have my karate belt."

I look down. He doesn't. It's been a long day. I just want to get out of this store, take off these tight clothes and high-heeled shoes.

"Sweetie, where is it?"

The tears brim.

Oh, my goodness. Please stop it with the tears. What you need to be is more responsible with your things. Mommy can't be in charge of everything.

"I had it when we came in."

"Maybe it fell by the apples?" The apples are on the other side of the store and I stand there while the cashier rings up my purchases, half on the conveyor belt, half in my cart. Liv starts a fuss.

"Rory, go back to the apples and see if you dropped the belt. I'll meet you there."

His small eyes widen.

"Are you afraid?"

"Can Twyla come with me?"

Twyla grabs his hand and leads the way. That's one of the things I like about Two. She ain't never scared.

The cashier gives me the total and I run my Amex card with my eyes in the direction that the children just ran in.

"Gosh, I ran out of paper. It'll be just a minute." She smiles. I don't smile back.

Hurry the fuck up.

My eyes swing around the store. She puts the paper in and taps a few buttons but nothing happens. She takes it back out.

"I'm sorry, I put it in backward."

The apples aren't far, they should be on their way back by now. Oh, for the love of Christ, come on, lady.

"You know, I'm okay with no receipt."

"I've got it now." She presses a button and the receipt skirts out. "Sorry for the wait."

I stuff the paper in my pocket and then swivel the cart back toward the apples. Liv's fuss is now a cry.

"All is well. The Universe supports me at every turn," I murmur.

As I pass the canned goods aisle, I see a yellow karate belt lying on the floor. My affirmation worked. He must have dropped it when we were getting the pumpkin. I pick it up and rush to the apples.

The kids aren't there.

My hand rubs my mouth as my armpits sweat.

"Rory, Twyla," I call. Shoppers bustle around the store. I move back toward the gourmet cheese. No kids. Where could they be? Okay, stop it, Felicia, the store isn't that big. This is what I tell myself as I picture a hairy white guy carrying my kids out the back door. I move towards the chicken, calling their names. This isn't Walmart, where the folks act a fool, so I'm still trying to be subtle.

"Rory, Twyla."

They are not by the chicken.

How long has it been, five, ten, twenty minutes? Liv is now full-out crying. I want to howl. She wants her milk now. Preston is going to kill me. Where are my children?

You are failing at this just like your mother.

Shut up! I want to scream at the *damn voice*. Liv's fingers cling to my shirt, the bounce no longer working. I never have a pacifier when I need it. I rub her back with my free hand and push the cart with the other, swinging my eyes from aisle to aisle.

The prepared food, I rush over to the stations.

"Rory."

"Mama," he turns the corner. Twyla is in tears.

"We thought you left us." She hurls herself at my leg. My feet are aching.

"Why would I leave you, huh?" I'm down on my knees kissing her tear-stained cheeks as my pulse makes an attempt to slow, but it's fruitless. I squeeze both kids in a hug. Then I look them both over, confirming that they have two ears, two eyes, and a nose. "Let's go."

"But my belt. Mommy, I can't go to karate without it or Sensei will give me fifty push-ups." His voice raises another teary octave.

"Honey, calm down. I have your belt." I thrust it in his direction and hurry the children to the car.

I now have ten minutes to get him to karate on a fifteen-minute drive, and Liv wants her milk. I am wearing my good push-up bra instead of my easy access nursing one, so I have to unfasten the clasp in the back to get the boob out and in her mouth. Liv relaxes into her milk.

"That's mine!" Rory shouts from the backseat. "Twyla, stop it. Mommmmeeeee. Twyla won't give me back my car."

"Twyla, please give it to him. Guys, I need silence."

"Mommmmeeee! She's laughing at me."

"Stop it, now!" I screech.

The car is silent except for the sound of Liv sucking and gurgling. I try to relax but I can feel the pressure of getting Rory to karate and the chore of dinner circling my spine. I inhale, then exhale slowly while Liv feeds. When she's had her fill, I strap her in her car seat, give her a plush toy to chew, and get behind the wheel. Then I push it. We pull up to karate eight minutes late, which now cuts into my preparing-dinner time. I pull in front of the karate center, unhook Rory, and stand by the car so that I can watch him and the girls at the same time.

"Don't come outside until you see my car."

"I know, Mama." He goes in. Karate makes him too cool for a good-bye kiss. I wait until he crosses through the second door and then wait some more to make sure he doesn't come back out and say that he's forgotten something.

Liv and Twyla have entered their own world with words I can't understand when I get back into the car. It only takes five minutes to get home and I park in our driveway. Drag the girls up the front stairs.

"Play with Liv," I tell Two.

Shoes off, clothes thrown on the sofa. I'm in my underwear. I want to go upstairs, hide from my children, from cooking dinner, lock myself in my closet, chug a stiff drink, and push the pressure away. But I only have thirty minutes to get the soup on the stove, so I force my body into the kitchen. As I pull the ingredients from the refrigerator, that overwhelmed feeling is there, taking shape as words in my head. The monologue for the Dames, I see the scene playing out before my eyes. Drowning mom. I drop the chicken on the counter, find Rory's notebook and a pencil, and start jotting down what comes.

Husband ain't home when I need him. Things are so bad that I hid in the back of my closet. I was back so far that I was behind the tan wool coat that my mother bought me when I was working in corporate America. My head against the slinky black dress that became too tight two pregnancies ago. I'm saving the clothes in case I wake up one day and have a life. If I wasn't so damn responsible, I'd have a bottle of hard liquor hidden here, in a crumbled paper bag to slurp down on days like this when I feel like I'm suffocating in my own skin. This job called motherhood feels like—

"I'm ready, Mommy."

I glance down at Two. She has ignored my command to play with Liv and has gone to the closet for her apron.

"I wanna help."

"Hang on, baby."

"Please."

"Give me a minute." I clutch the notebook and read over what I wrote. It's a good start. I can make this exhausted, overworked mom funny and relatable. Say with this character what mothers don't usually say to each other. That sometimes motherhood sucks. Sure we love our children, but the job is taxing and thankless. Most mothers like to pretend that raising children is the best job in the world, but the reality is, we didn't know what we were getting ourselves into and now we're stuck, grinning, bearing, and medicating ourselves through it. Yes, that's what I am going to portray in my monologue to the Dames. It's risky, shedding a light on what's real, but so what? I was taught that acting is imitating life. The Dames will not accuse me of playing it safe with this piece. I'm bringing my A game.

"Mommy, are you going to let me help or not?" Two has her hands on her hips, looking grown.

I'm wondering where she has learned to ask like that, but then she smiles that goofy grin that makes me cave and I kiss her fingertips.

"Okay, baby. Let's wash our hands."

I hold her wrists as she pours the chicken stock and shakes in the seasonings. She loses interest when Liv starts eating her doll's hair and I start sautéing the chicken. Five minutes before we need to pick Rory up, I turn the soup to a simmer, pop in the cornbread, and head back out with the girls. Luckily it's summer and I don't have to fool with coats. Rory is standing in the window. I wave and he comes out onto the street.

"How was it?"

"Good. I'm glad we found my belt. Trevor didn't bring his belt, and Sensei gave him one hundred push-ups."

The light turns green and I gun it for home.

When I get out of the shower the children are fast asleep and Preston is home. He hasn't called to me but I can feel his energy moving throughout the house. I pad downstairs, the television is on, and he's splayed on the sofa.

"Hey, handsome. Hungry?" I lean in for a kiss. He holds me until I fall into his lap.

"For you."

I rub his face and put my head against his heart.

"I made homemade chicken noodle soup and cornbread."

"Smells delicious."

"So why didn't you make yourself a plate?"

He looks at me sheepishly. "Because you do it with so much love."

"Bullshit," I tease on my way into the kitchen. My husband is spoiled. He'll sit and wait an hour for me to bring him his dinner rather than plate the food himself. His scratch-offs, keys, and wallet are on the kitchen counter, so I know he's been peeking in my pots.

The phone rings. I move to the receiver attached to the wall and check the caller ID. Shayla Douglas flashes across the screen. Huh? I'm not even sure how she got my phone number. What could she want? I bite my bottom lip and decide not to answer it.

"Are you going to get that?" Preston calls to me.

"It's Crystal," I lie. "Not in the mood for her drama, baby."

After four rings it stops. I'm not used to lying to my husband, but I'm not about to go into who Shayla is tonight, or ever, for that matter. I hope she doesn't think that lunch means that we are back to being instant friends. I carry the meal into the living room. Preston has taken off his dress shirt, socks, and shoes and is watching *Storage Wars* on A&E. I place the hot bowl in front of him with a napkin and spoon.

"What do you want to drink?"

He looks up at me. "What's wrong with you?"

"What do you mean?"

"I see the anxiety all over your face." He slips his spoon in the soup.

"Nothing." I walk into the dining room and start busying myself with putting away forgotten toys.

When you start with a lie, you have to keep lying to cover your tracks. It never ends.

"Foxy, what are you doing?" Preston pats the seat next to him. I put the stacking cups in the basket. "Come sit. Stop moving all the time."

"You know I hate a mess."

"Just relax. The food is delicious."

I lower myself next to him.

"How was the audition?"

"Oh, yeah." I fold my legs under me as I recall my moment in front of the camera, happy to switch to something pleasant.

"And I started writing my monologue for the Dames." I tell Preston the ideas that I've sketched.

"Sounds like you're on fire." He smiles and I love having his full attention. Often our time together is nothing more than a quick toss of information revolving around the kids. It feels good that just for a few moments, it's about me.

NINE

The Weeds Need Pulling

Two days have gone by. No more calls from Martin. I hope he doesn't ring me again. If he calls I'll tell him point-blank that he needs to stop contacting me. My husband is one of the good ones, and I can't chance what we have by keeping in touch with a ghost from my past.

It's finally Friday. My favorite night of the week. Friday nights mean no rules, no home-cooked meals, no begging kids to eat vegetables and to clean up. It's pizza and movie night and I am all too happy not to have to uphold the law. Tonight the kids won't get baths, stories, or songs. Toys can stay wherever they are abandoned, the children can pick out mismatched pajamas or sleep in their clothes. I don't give a shit, and that feels good. While we wait for the pizza to be delivered I pick up the remote to pull up a show on the DVR.

"I want *Dora*." Two bounces on one foot with her hands folded in the prayer position. I kiss the tip of her cute little nose and grant her wish.

"Not fair," Rory says with a pout. "That show is for babies."

"No, it's not," protests Two.

"Yes, it is." He pushes her.

"Hey, no hitting, Rory. Don't let me see that again or you won't get to pick the next show."

The telephone rings and I feel that nervous ripple in my chest. I take it in the kitchen.

"Hello."

"There's my girl."

"Martin." It comes out breathless. My breasts get that heavy feeling and he hasn't even said much.

You're supposed to tell him to stop calling.

"How are you, Young Sister? You are all I've been able to think about. Having a good week?" He purrs in my ear. His voice makes me lose my senses. I glance at the clock. Preston shouldn't be home for an hour so. I'll talk to him for a few minutes and then tell him to stop calling.

"Yeah, things have been okay."

My tongue starts moving like I'm a child at Christmas, sitting on Santa's lap. I tell him about my audition this week and the monologue I need to write for the Dames.

"Wow, an actress. I should have known. My Faye, all grown up." His voice drops to silkiness and it unravels my female core. "I always knew you'd take the world by storm with your gorgeous self. You probably just make them television people fall deep in love, don't you?"

My face presses closer to the phone to absorb every word. I'm fifteen again, wrapped up in his arms in the back of the Hog.

"I'm getting out soon and I want to see you."

"Martin." His name feels way too delicious on my tongue. "I'm, I'm married now."

"I know, Young Sister. It's just been so long. You know?"

"What do you want?"

"Isn't it obvious?"

"No, it isn't." I twirl the telephone cord.

"You like making a man beg, don't you."

Us fogging the windows of the Hog. My knees pressed against his chest. He liked when I wore the red panties.

Hotness flares my skin.

"You were something else. Our time together was precious."

A girlish giggle passes through my lips.

"You left the church so abruptly I never got to give you a proper good-bye."

"Yeah, well . . . things happened."

"I know all about it."

I fan.

"Where're the kids now? Mighty quiet today."

"They're watching television."

"The oldest one?"

"He's in the living room watching *Dora* with his sisters."

"How old again?"

"Rory is six."

"Not that one, Young Sister."

The heat in my blood runs ice cold. There is an echo thumping in my ear. "Wha, what do you mean?"

"Come on, Young Sister, don't play games with me. I know what we made together."

Saliva fills my mouth. No words travel from my brain to my lips for a full thirty seconds. "What are you talking about?"

"Oh, don't be like that, pretty girl. We really need to talk and get things straightened. Don't you think it's time for me to meet my child? Boy or a girl?"

Our front door drags when it opens. The children scream "Daddy." I slam down the telephone. I move away from it like it's got bird flu and open the refrigerator so that Preston can't see me shaking.

You should have told him that you were married and to stop calling you the moment you answered the phone. Always looking for attention. Now look at your new mess.

"Hey, Foxy Mama," Preston calls, opening his arms to me.

I emerge with two containers that need to be cleaned out and give him my cheek.

"Who was that on the phone?" He's on me, arms at my waist, pulling me close. But my body resists.

"It was Gran. My mom isn't doing well." The lie is slippery on my tongue like a tadpole.

"You think you should drive down to see her?"

"Yeah, maybe."

He looks at me. I look away.

"Is that all that's bothering you?"

"Headache. I'm going to run to CVS. We're out of Advil."

"I'll go for you."

"No. Thank you, Preston, but just keep an eye on the kids."

He steps back from me but I don't care. My sandals are on my feet and I call over my shoulder that I'm going to leave out the back door. Before I go, I slip into the basement and take the phone off the hook.

Inside the car my body is shaking and my fingers curve like they are cupping a cigarette. I haven't smoked in seven years, not since I met Preston. He doesn't even know I'm an ex-smoker. My neighbor across the street is doing something in his front lawn and I give him a tight wave before pulling onto the street. I pass the cleaners on Liberty Avenue and instead of stopping at CVS on the right, I make a left onto Long Avenue and park the car in front of the neighborhood bar, Tanky's.

Preston and I have come here on occasion for a quick drink. I'd sit at the bar and pop my fingers to the jukebox while he got up a game of pool. The place isn't date night material; it's more a hangout for neighborhood degenerates and full-time drunks. I've come out in yoga pants and a tank top again, and the men stare as I make my way to a corner seat like I'm a virgin maiden looking for a sailor to take me home.

"What can I get for you, doll?" The bartender cocks her over-permed curly head at me.

"Jack and ginger."

Across the bar a man puffs on a Marlboro Red. I watch him pull it in and breathe it out. I can almost taste the nicotine curl between my jaws.

"You want a cigarette, doll?" The bartender puts my drink in front of me. "We sell loosies for fifty cents."

"I thought smoking in bars in the State of New Jersey was illegal."

"Drinking at ten A.M. should be, too, but that don't stop no one 'round here."

I put my quarters on the counter and she brings me a Newport 100. There is no hesitation as I place the filter between my chapped lips and light the match. The amber roars against the tobacco and like a lover rediscovering its first crush, I pull. The intimacy goes straight to my head, loosening the crust around my memories. They come like a flood.

TEN

The Blasted Past

George H. W. Bush is just days away from being sworn in as the forty-first president, Bobby Brown's "My Prerogative" is number two on the *Billboard* charts, and Toni Morrison entered the year having won the Pulitzer Prize for *Beloved*. I know this because my tenth-grade English teacher loves Toni Morrison and read parts of the winning book to us in class.

I'm fifteen. It is a bitterly cold New Year's Day in Philadelphia. Four weeks have passed since I've seen Martin at church. It's like he just disappeared. I'm sick with worry over what we've made and I need him to help me sort things out. Besides that, I miss him. My body won't breathe without him and it feels like I've punctured a lung. According to the pamphlet Shayla brought me from Planned Parenthood, I am too far into the pregnancy to have an abortion. I have missed four periods and my pudgy belly sticks out.

Gran has been stalking me. In my face, walking in my bedroom without knocking, asking questions about my every move, picking up the phone line, and eavesdropping on my conversations with Shayla. Since Crystal and the baby moved around the corner to Big

Derell's, Gran ain't got nothing better to do than study me. It was Shayla's idea for me to go to Martin's house.

"I know you have his address." She popped her gum.

I did. Gran was a willing worker at the church, so on the last Saturday of each month I helped her clean. I was dusting the church office when Miss Doris, the secretary, handed me the new members' files and asked me to put them away. I filed Lorna Dickerson, and two files behind hers was Martin Dupree. Whenever I got to missing him I sucked on the sweetness of his address—1783 Ellsworth Street—like it was saltwater taffy.

New Year's Day provided the perfect escape plan. Shayla and I said we were going to the Mummers parade on Broad Street, but she was going to her boyfriend's house in West Philly and I was going to mine.

"I hope that nucka don't act a fool when he finds out. If he don't handle his responsibility I'll—"

"It'll be fine, Shay," I replied with false confidence. In reality, I was as nervous as a long-tailed cat in a room full of rocking chairs. The last thing I needed was to be stepped on or crushed. I dressed up for the trip to South Philly in a pair of kitten heels Crystal left in the closet, and the only jeans that still fit with a palazzo shirt, and my red Michael Jackson leather jacket with the zippers. The look wasn't warm enough to make it to the subway, and Gran let me know it on my way out the door.

"You gon' freeze and catch pneumonia all in your hind parts, goin' out there half dressed."

Shayla and I agreed to meet at the McDonald's on Broad Street and head back home together to make our stories believable.

When I looked up Martin's address on the bus map Gran kept in the kitchen drawer, it seemed to be about six or seven city blocks from the church. I decided to catch the bus there and walk the rest of the way. Bad choice. It was January and cold as the dickens. By the time I reached Martin's house, my thighs were stinging and the balls of my feet felt like I had trotted on needles. Daddy's Hog was parked a few doors down, so I knew I had the correct address. The row house was red brick with a mud-colored trim. The drapes were drawn and the banister tilted from years of service. From across the street I stood behind a parked Pontiac, staring, having lost my nerve. What was I thinking coming all this way? By the time the front door to his house opened, my fingers were like Popsicles. I heard Martin's laugh before I laid eyes on him. His laughter was loud and infectious. Even at the church in the midst of the Holy Ghost's hallelujahs I could identify that hardy, deep-belly cackle. It rocked through me and warmed my chilly spots.

Then I saw her. She was curvy in the hips with big breasts, like a woman who had given birth a few times over. A long wig hung from her pear head, and she wore platform heels so high I willed her to trip and die. Her cheap perfume slithered toward me on the opposite side of the street and assaulted me.

Martin emerged with his beautiful mouth shaped in a smile. He was dressed in navy, a color that looked good on him, and I felt myself lean forward, craving my name on his lips, in my ears, on my neck, talking that mess that made me do anything for him. Martin was the master of my universe and now he was wizard to someone else's.

They walked down the street as close as two people could, with Martin's arm wrapped around the women's waist. He tucked her into the car. I made eye contact with him as he walked to the driver's side. If he saw me he didn't let it show; his cocky stride didn't stumble a beat. Seconds later, the Hog pulled off without warning. Billows of smoke colored the air chalky. Frozen to the cement, I watched as the car headed down Ellsworth, and I would have testified before a judge and a jury that I saw him look back at me through the rearview mirror. But he didn't turn back.

. . .

I didn't even bother meeting Shayla at the McDonald's. Couldn't muster up the energy to tell her what happened. When I got home, I ran the bathwater with the intention of drowning myself. I figured it was the best way to go. I wasn't one for a lot of blood, so I couldn't slice my wrist and bleed out. We don't have a gun in the house, and although Shayla's brother could probably supply me with one, I didn't want everyone in my suicide business. I thought about tying a noose around my neck and hanging from the ceiling, but that felt a little too Ku Klux Klan for me. Holding my head under the bathwater and letting my life go was the most logical thing to do. Nothing mattered now that Martin was gone.

With most of my body under the water, I said the Lord's Prayer, the Hail Mary, and then blessed myself with the sign of the cross. I took a few deep sighs, and just as I was about to plunge my head under the water, I spied a cockroach crawling from a crack in the wall right beside the tub. I hated cockroaches and I considered whether I should just go for it or kill him first because I didn't want him making his way into my water, messing up my death scene. That's when I heard a rattle in the door. It sounded like a key. Unaware that the bathroom door even had a key, I was stunned silent when Gran burst into the room. The heavy belt that she whipped Crystal with was hanging around her neck. Her feet reached me before I could scramble for my towel and she saw. I know she saw because she started calling on her Lord and Savior to give her strength as she yanked my arm, forcing me to bang my knee trying to get out of the tub. Gran had never beaten me before, but on that day she brought the belt down on my body like she was the overseer and I the runaway.

That thick strap rained down on me so many times I lost count. Welts popped, skin tore, blood poured, everything ached, and I moaned and tried to protect my face. Maybe Gran would beat me to death and that would be the end of it. That would stop the pain that had no words. Gran's motions slowed to a stop. She was out of breath and dropped down on the top of the commode seat, sweat pouring down her face, tears from her eyes as she coughed out one sentence.

"How could you?"

ELEVEN

The Backwoods Baby

In June, Gran said it was time for me to go. It was my first time leaving the City of Brotherly Love. I'd been to Englishtown in New Jersey on a bus excursion with the church, but that didn't count as real traveling.

I was supposed to leave in May, but Gran was waiting on some money that never came. So I stayed holed up in the hot house the first week of June. The neighbors couldn't see me, but I saw the kids when they got home from school: playing in the water plug, jumping double Dutch, blasting Public Enemy and KRS-1 on the boom box, eating cherry water ices and salted pretzels, drinking grape soda. Anything to enjoy the time off and beat the heat.

Gran didn't have an air conditioner because she didn't want to run up her light bill. She put the fan in the window, but turned it backward so the hot air blew out of the room. Didn't work, so I was as miserable as a nun in a whorehouse where only sin was for sale.

Gran's friend Mr. Scooter came to pick me up on a Tuesday night when the sun went down and the block was quiet. When I waddled from the house, I placed my postage stamp suitcase in front of my belly, as Gran instructed. I wore her fancy church trench coat, the one she wore when her choir group, The Blessed Hearts, sang at their anniversary. It was blood red with a gold and magenta broach at the breast. Gran flattened her matching pillbox hat onto my head at the last minute. I knew she was trying to make me look respectable, so I didn't say nothing. While I push myself across the backseat of Mr. Scooter's car holding onto his headrest, Gran reaches in between her large breasts for her wallet and gives Mr. Scooter five dollars for gas. I hear her tell him what time my bus is leaving. She had already shoved the money for my ticket and three extra dollars into my pocket before I left the house. On our ride down, Mr. Scooter makes small talk while I work my finger into a tear in the vinyl seat, fumbling my fingers around the cottony filing.

We take Broad Street. Pass Temple University. Pass Hahnemann Hospital, where my grandfather died, and around City Hall, to Market Street. Then we cut over to where the bus station is, at Tenth and Filbert. Mr. Scooter pulls to the curb.

"You need help, Faye?"

"No, I'm fine, Mr. Scooter. Thanks for the ride."

The bus station is vibrant for that time of night. Four of the ticket counter lanes are open and I get in what I hope is the shortest. A homeless man draped in a pound of blankets walks past me, rattling a dirty coffee cup with coins in it. I quickly turn my head before the smell of him makes me puke. I hear Keith Sweat crooning "Make It Last Forever" on someone's radio. The song made me feel hot and cold at the same time. It was the fourth song on the slow jam tape that Martin played that one time I told Gran I was meeting Crystal at the Gallery mall to look for church shoes. Martin got me from the corner of Eighth and Market Street. We drove in the Hog down to the Lakes, and did it under the highway overpass. It was the first time I got completely naked in the car.

"Next."

I step up to the counter and purchased my ticket to Virginia.

"Boarding in five minutes," the clerk tells me with vacant eyes. The job has desensitized her.

The ladies' room is in the back left corner, and I head over to pee before boarding. It smells more horrific than the station and I hold my nose, breathing only out of my mouth until I finish my business. I feel like vomiting, so I hurry out of the bathroom before it catches me. I couldn't imagine heaving on my knees in this filthy place. I find a peppermint in the coat pocket and shove it into my mouth. The sleeping pill I stole from Gran is in there too, and I make sure it's secure.

"Greyhound bus to Lynchburg, Virginia, making stops in Wilmington, Baltimore, Washington, DC, Richmond. Transferring in Richmond, then stopping in Charlottesville. Lynchburg will be the last stop. All aboard. All aboard."

I crack the orange pill in half and it affords me a long rest on the first leg to the transfer. In Richmond, we have about ten minutes to stretch our legs. I take off Gran's ridiculous hat and trench coat. It's nice to be somewhere where I didn't have to hide. Gran's three dollars went to a Snickers bar, a bag of Doritos, and a Coke. When I get on the second bus I eat the fried chicken and white bread Gran had packed in my bag, then all of my junk food. I can't fall back asleep, so I pull out the romance novel I packed and try to lose myself in the story.

Aunt Kat had on a yellow scarf just like Gran said she would. But even if she didn't I would have recognized her. She has the same head shape and cheekbones as Gran and my father. She's just a little older and her skin was sunburned in a way Gran's would never be. I wondered if it was because she lived in the country.

"Look at you, gal." She pulls me into her arms. "I ain't seen you since you was knee high to a grasshopper."

Aunt Kat directs me to a navy-blue pickup truck and brings my bag into the cab with us. She keeps up a constant chatter on Route 29, pointing out the shopping center with the Food Lion, the post office, and her beauty parlor. It's dark and I can't see much. I nod and look at the Blue Ridge Mountains, highlighted by the moon. Majestic. Like paintings in the sky. After about ten minutes driving, we turned on a back road that leads past an endless row of cornstalk fields. I even spot a few cows, horses, and pigs.

Aunt Kat lived on fifteen acres of land that's been in the family for three generations. Since the end of slavery, she told me. Gran said that part of the house is hers and that she could come down here and claim it anytime she wants, but I haven't known her to make a single trip down here in the years I lived with her.

Aunt Kat shows me to a bedroom in the back. The few pieces of furniture in the room were old, but dusted clean. I put my bag down on the little wooden chair facing the window, and just like that I feel a tightening in my belly that spins through me so fast I'm forced to sit.

"Baby knew to wait till you got here." Aunt Kat put her hand on my belly and looked at her watch. "Let's see what happens over the next hour. Might be time to fetch the midwife."

Thirteen hours later I'm on a bed propped up with pillows, my feet in brown stirrups that look like they belong to the horse out back.

"Puuuush," grunts the snaggletoothed midwife squatting between my legs. Pats of sweat glisten from the balding spots separating her gray sprouts of hair. I've asked at least three times why I wasn't going to the hospital, and all Aunt Kat said was that this woman would give me better care.

Every time a contraction rips through my body, I feel like cussing. The old lady had already shoved her bare hand and whole arm inside of me, breaking my water and deeming the baby ready. Warm liquid had dripped down my thighs, and was soaked up by the pile of towels propped under my behind.

The overhead light is harshly fluorescent, and there is a desk lamp sitting on the floor at the foot of the bed, which Snaggletoothed is using to see. The wallpaper is a faded mauve color with marching lines of potted plants. A cousin I didn't know rubs a cool towel across my forehead, and I like her because she kept smiling with the same doe eyes as me.

She whispers, "Don't worry none. She delivers all the babies within fifty miles. She betta than the hospital. You go there, they'll cut you for sure." She smiles and then runs her hand across my forehead. I feel okay for all of thirty-five seconds, and then the next contraction ripples through me like a tidal wave.

Aunt Kat is at the foot of the bed reading Bible verses. She's Jehovah's Witness, and prays in a much more subdued way than Gran and her Daddy Gracious friends. I could imagine Gran stomping her feet and catching the Holy Ghost while I was trying to dispel this thing, getting on my last nerve. I'm hot all over and I want this to be over. I pray my own silent prayer. Lord, I've learned my lesson. Please let this be over soon.

"I sees the head." Snaggletoothed leans in closer.

"Grab it," I sass as a cold pain pierces through my belly with a fierceness that has my teeth rattling, so much that I was sure I would swallow my tongue. Oh, I can't die like this. Please, please, please I pleaded with my eyes closed.

"Next contraction, give it all ya got, chile, and this baby be here. Push like you's mad, push."

Fire. That's the only way I can describe the heated pain that comes from below as she pulls the thing's head out, and then lets it dangle between my legs while she sucks the mucus from the nose and mouth.

"Slow and steady," she says, and then yanks the rest of the body out of me.

I don't know what happened after that 'cause the room went dark. Maybe I fainted, but the next thing I knew, the cousin was trying to put a swaddled something in my arms. I pushed her away.

"No, thank you." My voice was weak but stern.

Cousin looked at me with those doe eyes and said, "You sure you don't want to hold her? She's beautiful."

I turned my back. If I didn't touch it then she wasn't real. If she wasn't real, then I could go back to my life in Philadelphia like none of this mess ever happened. Then maybe I'd have a real chance of getting out. If I got out, moved on, I'd be better. Happier. I'd be like the girls on *The Facts of Life* who had their whole lives ahead of them. That's what I wanted. Not to hold a beautiful thing that wasn't mine.

TWELVE

The Restraints

My cell phone vibrates for the umpteenth time against my purse as I stub out my third cigarette.

"Can I get you anything else, doll?"

"No. Thanks." I push a few bills across the bar. My head is light when I stand, but after I roll my shoulders back and fix my ponytail I feel together. The same men who catcalled on my entrance repeat their same tired lines on my way out. I don't even turn my head to acknowledge them as I step out onto the street. The smell of Mc-Donald's fills the air and I wonder if they have a vent or something that pushes the scent in all directions, calling customers to come.

My life is so different than the one I left behind in Philadelphia. How dare Martin call me and dredge all of this up? My cell phone vibrates again when I get inside my SUV.

"Hello."

"Fox, what the fuck? Why aren't you answering your telephone?"

I don't have my answer ready for Preston so I simply say, "I'll be home in ten minutes."

I need to get myself together so I drive across the street to the

CVS. After standing in line while the lady in front of me goes through every coupon in her purse only for them all to be expired, I buy Listerine, Febreze, baby wipes, and Advil. Out in the parking lot, I spray myself down and wipe my face and hands before heading back home.

The door is barely open before Rory and Two are rushing me. "Mommmeeeee." They say it like I've been to war in Iraq and had to hitchhike back home. It's one of the things I love about having kids. They love you in every moment. Even the kids of crackheads love their mamas.

"What are you guys still doing up? It's way past your bedtime."

"Daddy said we could wait for you." Two crinkles that cute nose. *Of course he did. Putting the kids to bed is your job.*

"Let's head upstairs." The baby is in her bouncer. When I pick her up, her diaper sags to her knees.

"You didn't know the baby needed to be changed?"

"Where were you?"

"Answer me."

"Answer me." His eyes bore into me and I stare right back.

"Come on, babies, let's go brush your teeth."

On the way up the stairs Rory waves his hand in front of his nose. "You smell funny."

"And so do you." I pinch his butt cheek.

I close the upstairs gate so that I can put Liv on the floor, change out of my smoky clothes, and bury them in the bottom of the dirty laundry pile.

"Go find a book and sit on the floor," I call to them from the bathroom. The door is cracked so I can hear what's going on while I brush my teeth, and then move the washcloth in the places that need to be freshened. Gran calls that a "whore's bath."

After Liv is changed and clean, I sit all three children on my lap and read a New Age version of Humpty Dumpty by Mark Teague, about a prince who is afraid. They love the story and I take my time acting out all the characters. When I'm finished Rory puts his arms around my neck.

"Mama, can you tell us one of your stories from your head?"

I don't have anything better to do than avoid Preston, so I agree.

"Yes, I'll tell you one while I feed the baby. But you have to get in your bed and keep your heads on the pillow."

"Can I sleep with the girls tonight?" Rory asks.

I nod, and settle into the glider by the window. Liv reaches for my breast. I lift my shirt and unhook the snap on my bra. It's not until she gets the milk to flow that I remember the drinks and cigarettes.

Bad mommy, unfit. Just triflin'.

I don't give her strength, and start in on a story about a leaf that got separated from its leaf family in a storm. When I'm finished, Liv is asleep and Two reaches for a cuddle.

"That was the best story ever, Mommy."

"Many more to come, Two. Now don't get out of this bed or tomorrow there will be no dessert. Good night."

I kiss Rory and tuck him tight.

I head downstairs. Every step fills my belly with dread. Preston is sitting on the sofa. The living room and dining room lights are on. His scratch-offs are sitting in a pile on the coffee table.

"Win anything?"

"Thirteen dollars."

"I can use that for groceries."

"You going to tell me where you've been?"

I ease into the loveseat, opposite from the sofa where Preston is seated, and pull my vanilla throw over my lap.

"Stop with the tight leash, would you?" I snap.

"Leash?"

"Yes, you move how you please. The moment I take some time for myself you're calling the National Guard."

"Because you said you were going to CVS."

"And I did. But I didn't feel like rushing right home. I've been with the kids all day. I needed a break."

Preston stares at me. "Next time, just say that. I was worried."

I flip the covers from my lap, am on my feet, hands on my hips, lips poked out. "Worried for what? I was in the neighborhood, for Christ sakes."

"You weren't answering your phone."

"So fucking what? You guys drain the shit out of me." I move for the stairs, but he's up, pulling me by the waist. "Let go." I squirm but he holds tighter.

"Calm down. What has gotten into you?"

"I'm going to bed, Preston. Move."

"Sit down, Foxy."

"No."

"Why do you have to make everything so difficult?" He grabs my chin and pins my waist to his. "I don't have a problem with you getting air. I just want to know. It's different when I'm out. I'm a man. I can handle myself."

"That's some sexist bullshit." I push away from him but as soon as I break free he's on me again.

"Relax, Fox. Let's make some drinks. It's Friday."

His hand pulls my ponytail loose and his fingers on my scalp calm me.

"Please?"

I untangle myself from his arms and head back to the sofa. He brings me a mixed concoction and then sits next to me. The television is set to the Food Network and we watch *Chopped*.

The drinks, my worries, my week put me right to sleep, and Preston has to nudge me awake after he's secured the house for the night.

"Want me to carry you?"

"No, I'm fine." I get to my feet.

In the bedroom, I strip down to my camisole and panties. Preston is on my side of the bed, reaching for me, smelling me, adoring me. I'm not really in the mood but his lips, his hands are so persistent that I turn my body over to him and let him have his way with me.

Before the fluids dry between us, he's knocked out cold, snoring like sex is a sedative. I'm wide awake. The cigarette craving is back, and I don't know what's come over me.

THIRTEEN

The Colored Museum

Two hours have ticked by on the wall clock and I am still awake. I have gone through three rounds of tapping, rubbed down in lavender oil, counted backward from five hundred, played the city alphabet game in my head, imagined myself sleeping in a peaceful meadow, adjusted my pillows, changed my body position, but still sleep eludes me. Preston's not snoring tonight, but he's breathing heavily, and the air from his nose makes the sheets ruffle. On his back with his head lulled to the side, chest naked, one foot flung from the covers, the other nestled between the sheets. He looks at peace. I watch him, sick with sorry.

Preston is the one person I'd never intended to hurt. The omission of my past just happened. There never seemed to be an opportune moment to bring it up. By the time we were serious and I was ready to shed and share, Preston distracted me with his perfect vision of our future, and I didn't have the courage to smudge his picture even if it was man-made and unauthentic.

. . .

When I met Preston, I was in a play called *The Colored Museum* by George C. Wolfe. It was the first performance at the Theresa Lang Theatre with an all-black cast. Monumental really because the theater was on the Upper East Side of Manhattan, where the rich white folks lived, and people came from every borough to see it. I had minor supporting roles throughout, but my time to shine was in the role of Topsy Washington, and I loved all five minutes and thirty-two seconds of it.

Topsy came onstage in the last vignette, titled "The Party." Do you remember the first scene of Spike Lee's 1989 movie *Do the Right Thing*, where Rosie Perez danced to Public Enemy's "Fight the Power" so hard, you thought she was going to lose a breast? Picture me as Topsy dancing just a fraction calmer, but not by much. My costume was ridiculous. I wore a neon halter top, and a blazer with metal bottle caps sewn all over it. The skirt had little cowrie shells and bells attached, so when I pumped my chest back and forth and threw my hands in the air, I was the music. Dancing, dancing, and dancing until I was sweating and out of breath. Then I stopped, looked out into the audience with a dramatic pause, and said,

"Have you ever been to a party, and there was one fool in the middle of the floor dancing harder and yelling louder than anyone in the room? Well, honey, that fool was me!"

From that moment on I had the room mesmerized as I talked about going way, way, way, way, way, way, way uptown to a party where every black icon you could think of was in the room—Nat Turner, Eartha Kitt, Malcolm X, Aunt Jemima, Angela Davis—discussing things such as existentialism and the shuffle ball change. It was a powerful piece, and when I left the stage every fiber in my body was high. So high I could have just glided back to my apartment and called it a night. But my friend Serena, who was the stage manager, convinced me to come celebrate opening night with the cast and have a drink. When I walked out into the lobby, Preston was standing against the wall looking right at me. I looked back, thinking, have we met before? Then he walked over to me. He was a cute thing—tall, bookish, but handsome. Not the badass boys from Brooklyn that I normally liked. There was something behind the horn-rimmed glasses that said security. Safe.

"Excuse me, Topsy Washington, but could you sign my Playbill?" His left dimple deepened. His accent was south of New York, but I couldn't place it.

Tickled, I turned on my stage charm. "Of course. Did you enjoy the show?"

"Very much. You were fantastic." His eyes drank me in. "I'm not really into plays but my friend's sister, Yolanda, is in the production, so I tagged along."

Our fingers touched as I handed back the Playbill. I didn't care for Yolanda. She played the part of the girl with the egg. I wanted that part and when she got it, she flicked her nose up at me. I stayed away from her after that.

"Felicia, ready?" It was Serena, impatient for her liquor. I motioned to her to give me a second.

"Let me see that Playbill again." I took it from him and wrote my telephone number on it. "So we can continue our conversation. What's your name?"

"Preston, Preston Lyons."

"Felicia Hayes." I extended my hand. "See you around."

The cast and crew went around the corner to the Dive Bar, a favorite hangout for Marymount students on Third Avenue. Serena had to stop at the ATM for cash and refused to go to the Citibank on the corner because she banked with Chase.

"I'm not paying those high fees for taking my money from another bank. It adds up," she scoffed.

So we walked five blocks to the Chase and then back to the bar. When we walked in, Preston was already there. He spotted me immediately, came over, and offered to buy me a drink. I ordered a Jack and ginger. It was my cool grown-up girl drink, the one that let the boys know I could get down like them. We tried to get up a conversation while the DJ spun G Love & Special Sauce, but then he switched to hard-core metal. The white girls ran to the bar top, kicked their high heels off, and danced berserk, as was the norm in Upper East Side bars such as the Dive. It was time to go. I cornered Serena and told her I was leaving. She was wrapped up in the guy who worked the stage lights and waved me off.

"I live down the block. Walk me home?" I shouted into Preston's ear. He took my hand.

Outside, the fall breeze felt good. It was a few weeks before Thanksgiving, and the air had a mild quality to it with no bite. Preston and I walked two blocks down Third Avenue and then cut across Seventieth, heading toward York Avenue. I lived in a dumpy fourth-floor walkup with Serena and another friend. It was a two-bedroom that we converted into a three, by dividing the living room with a curtain and a Chinese screen. I decided when we got to my building that I wasn't going to let him come up. We'd just met, I liked his straight-up demeanor and I didn't want him to think I was easy.

"Want to sit?" I pointed to the bench near the corner.

We watched the headlights of the cars and cabs race back and forth up York Avenue.

"Foxy."

"Excuse me?" I said, lowering my eyes at him.

"Sorry, did I say that out loud?" He looked sheepish. "You just, I don't know. You're name should be Foxy.

My eyes found his, so brown and gentle.

"You have that reddish-brown skin and onstage you seemed so clever, so crafty, so sure of yourself. Made me think, Foxy."

He got all of this about me from a first encounter? I wasn't sure if it were entirely true because there wasn't much that I was sure of and I often felt myself coming apart at the seams. But it sounded good coming from his lips and I bought into it on the spot. On my thigh, I traced Preston and Felicia and drew a heart around it. On our third date, we headed to Spice, my favorite Thai restaurant, near NYU.

It was over crispy basil spring rolls and massaman curry shrimp that Preston trusted me with a part of his past.

"I was raised in downtown Newport News, affectionately known as 'Bad Newz' by the neighbors. Have you ever been to Virginia?"

I willed my eyes to stay focused. "Yeah, 'round Lynchburg."

"Well, the city is basically nondescript urban sprawl—shipyards and ports." What he didn't have to say was violent crimes, drug-addicted neighbors, and fast-food joints on every corner, because all of our black neighborhoods were the same.

"The city got a little fame when Michael Vick's dog fighting made national news. My godmother would see Allen Iverson's mom every weekend spending his NBA money at the bingo."

"Really?"

He shook his head. "What most people don't know is that my hometown is also the hometown of Ella Fitzgerald and Pearl Bailey, but I guess that's for the history books." Preston sipped his Thai iced tea, and I could tell by the way he clenched his jaw that this trip backward wasn't breezy.

It wasn't until our fifth date that he revealed, "I was raised mostly by my godmother, Juju."

Preston's mother, Peaches, was a misguided orphan raised in the group home where Juju worked as the director. Peaches was sixteen when she gave birth to Preston, and Juju took a liking to him. His young mother was in and out of foster care, juvenile detention, and jail for everything from prostitution to writing bad checks to selling drugs. You name it, Peaches did it. None of it stopped her from having children.

After Preston came Patrik, who lived with his grandmother on his father's side, and then a set of twin girls who were raised mostly by their father. Peaches wouldn't let Preston see his father because she wanted him and he didn't want her. When Preston was eight years old, Peaches wanted to follow her new man out to Las Vegas to live.

"Juju always tells me she said, 'You aren't taking Preston more than five miles from me. If you want to go, then you need to sign him over so I can give him a proper home.'" Preston removed his glasses and wiped them with a napkin.

We had just seen an indie movie at the Angelika Film Center. I nursed a latte and we shared biscotti.

"She was gone about six months, and then after that I saw her now and then."

"Juju drilled into me, 'The only way you going to be something is to get out of Newport News, baby.'" He imitated his godmother with a southern drawl. He went on to tell me how Juju wrote letters to local organizations and programs for funding. When Preston entered fifth grade, she got him into an elite private boarding school, Randolph Macon Academy, seventy miles west of DC, on a full scholarship. When he graduated with honors, it was off to Columbia University for his undergrad degree.

I deposited my empty cup, and Preston grabbed my hand as we walked outside onto Houston Street. "What about you?"

"Well," I bit my bottom lip.

Just then, an African American family strolled past us on the street. Mother, father, two boys, and a girl. You could look at them and tell they were all from the same family, strong bloodline.

Preston kept his eyes trained on them and squeezed my fingers. "That's what I want."

"Me too," I confessed, admiring the mother as she held the younger two children's hands in hers while they crossed the street.

"I mean the whole package. One woman to have all of my children, no divorce, no step-anything. I want the holiday card, the summer vacations, and the picket fence."

I nodded for two reasons; first, because I realized as sure as the New York wind was blowing through my hair that if I wanted to move forward with this man, I could never tell him about Martin or the baby. Second, I wanted the same exact thing. It was all I ever wanted since losing my parents at twelve. A redo of childhood, but this time as the parent I could make it right and sidestep all of the mistakes.

When I let Preston up to my apartment that night for the first time, he reached for the zipper of my jeans, but I removed his eager hand.

"I'm a girl who likes to save something for later."

His eyes got big, like a boy being promised a coveted toy. "Like marriage later?"

It hadn't occurred to me to hold out that long before he said it, so I surprised even myself when my lips parted with, "Yes."

"Oh, damn. A virgin. Foxy, I knew you were the real deal."

All I could say to that was nothing.

Preston and I dashed through the winter months like a sleigh on snow, giggling every step of the way. I enjoyed being with him because he liked going to concerts and comedy shows, eating exotic cuisines, and chasing art exhibits throughout New York City. We were at the Metropolitan Museum looking at King Tut's artifacts when he pulled me close to him.

"Growing up, I looked at my younger siblings' fathers or whoever my mother was dating at the time with hunger, asking them to raise me. Love me. Throw the football with me. And I hated being that desperate. With you, Foxy, I want the fairy tale, the old days. Will you be my wife?"

He had dropped down to a bended knee, and my one-and-a-half carat sparkled with promise. It wasn't the most romantic proposal but it promised security, suburbs, and me as a stay-at-home mom, where I could nurture our family close and personal. With tears burning in my eyes I said, "Yes, yes, yes."

Yes, I'll save you from the demons of your past if you save me from mine.

We were married three months later. Preston picked the date. Since I wasn't putting out until marriage, he said he couldn't wait. When Gran found out I was engaged, she insisted that I have the wedding at the Daddy Gracious Church. *Was she crazy?* That was when I decided that it would be a destination wedding in the Bahamas. Gran said, "I ain't gettin' on no rickety plane to see my only grandchild get married."

I told her I'd take lots of pictures and bring back a video. She said she would never forgive me for cheating her out of that moment, but I didn't care. Planning a wedding anywhere near Philadelphia would have threatened everything I built in the past few months with Preston. I couldn't take that chance.

On our first night together as husband and wife, Preston was clumsy with his rhythm, quick and awkward, but when we finished I felt as if I had been washed of my sins. Locked away were the deeds of Miss Hayes. I was now Mrs. Felicia Lyons.

FOURTEEN

The Saturday Fever

Preston is not in the bed when I wake up. The house is too quiet. I check the clock. It's after nine. What's the schedule for today? I scratch my head and sit up in my bed. Two has ballet at eleven. I turn my neck to the right and then to the left to stretch. That's when I hear laughter coming from downstairs. I walk to the top of the stairs to listen. The television is on. I brush my teeth and then head down.

"Good morning."

"Mommeeee." Two runs to me and throws her arms around my legs.

"Hi, sweetie." I lean down and kiss the top of her messy head. Liv is in the ExerSaucer with drool down her neck, soaking through her pajamas. Rory doesn't look my way. His favorite show, *The Back-yardigans*, is on, and he is absorbed. Preston walks from the kitchen fully dressed, with a cup of coffee in his outstretched hand.

"Morning, Fox." He kisses my lips and whispers. "You were great last night."

I blush. Take the coffee. "Where're you going?"

"I've got some paperwork to finish up at the office. It shouldn't take long."

"When are you coming back?" I hate when he works on Saturdays. It's supposed to be family day.

"I'm hoping to finish up and be back early afternoon." He pecks my cheek and is out the door. I want to chase him, make him stay, but I sip my coffee.

"After this show I'm turning off the television so we can get ready."

"Ahh, man, where are we going?" Rory turns.

"Two has ballet."

"I don't want to go."

I pretend like I don't hear his protest as I lift Liv from the Exer-Saucer and carry her upstairs.

The children and I are coming down the front steps of our home. They are asking me questions that I'm not answering because I'm going through my mental checklist, confirming that I have everything for our journey to class. Ballet slippers, water bottles, snacks for the car ride home, sippy cup for Liv, books—and that's when I see her, stop dead in my tracks. You've got to be kidding me.

She's toothy as she moves up my block toward me with long strides. Her eyes hold mine like magnets. They seem to say, *Oh, my goodness, I can't believe I've just run into you out of the blue.* How does this heifer know where I live? She wants something. I can feel it.

You were the one foaming at the mouth over Martin and needed someone to talk with. Should have let sleeping dogs lie. Ain't that what she told you?

I grit my teeth.

"Faye," she calls.

"Who is that, Mommy?" Two plucks her finger from her mouth.

"Oh, my God. Twice in one week." Her glossy lips are on my

cheek. She's leaning her hip into mine, smelling of the same expensive perfume she wore to lunch.

"Shayla. What are you doing at my house?"

"Where you heading?"

"To ballet." Twyla looks up at her.

"Ballet." She widens her eyes at me. "Ain't that something." I have Liv in my arms, Two is clinging to my leg, and Rory is leaning into me, watching.

"They are cuter in person than on your phone." She kneels down so that she is eye level with them. "You can call me Auntie Shay-Shay."

"Auntie Shay-Shay, great seeing you again, darling, but we've got to go. I'll hit you on Facebook." I use attitude to make my point, but Shayla cracks up, shows all of her teeth.

"I need a ride, baby. My car is in the shop."

"Why are you even in my neighborhood?"

"Working." her voice trails. "So ride, yes?" She doesn't wait for me to answer as she struts to my car in her four-inch heels and skin-tight jeans. Where the hell is she going dressed like that on a Saturday morning? I'm wearing the crumpled clothes that I found at the foot of my bed this morning in the laundry basket.

The car is unlocked and I strap the kids in, handing them their books to read on the way.

"We have to read," Rory protests.

I bore my eyes into him to let him know this is not the time. He opens the book.

Shayla slides in next to me and places her high-end designer bag at her feet. I turn the key in the ignition. Drop all of the windows down to let a bit of her out and fresh air in.

"Stop touching me," Rory moans from the backseat.

"Twyla, stop it. Mommmmeeeee."

"Twyla, please keep your hands to yourself. Guys, it's quiet time."

"Mommmmeeee! She's still doing it."

"If I have to say it one more time, no dessert tonight!" I screech, putting all of the venom in my voice that I want to use on Shayla.

"No dessert? I'm scared of you." Shayla starts digging in her purse and pulls out a packet of gum. It's a fresh pack and she undoes the wrapping.

"Here, cuties." Shayla hands a stick to the kids without asking me first.

"It's ten thirty in the morning."

"It's sugarless," she says with her phone in her hand, texting.

"Where are you going?"

"Just drive to ballet. I have to talk to you."

I back out of the driveway and steer my car toward the Garden State Parkway. It's the fastest way from my house to Montclair. Twyla loves to dance, and even though there are three dance schools in the town where we live, I drive her thirty minutes every Saturday to the studio, where the director graduated from Juilliard. If this is Two's calling, I want her to start with the best.

I turn the radio on. Flip from NPR to 107.5 FM. Something pop-like croaks from the speakers. I turn it up to drown out our voices.

"What's up?"

"Brave got locked up last night."

"Who's Brave?"

"My man."

I switch lanes.

"I need to bail him out, but he has the money stashed where only he can get it. I can give it back to you when he gets out."

I don't want to be involved. But I asked the question anyway. "How much?"

"Two stacks."

"What's that?"

"Oh, my God, stop acting brand-new. Two grand. Two thousand dollars. I'm good for it. You know I am."

I cough. Choke. Hold the wheel tight. "I don't have it."

"Faye, come on."

"Shay. Before lunch, I haven't seen you in like forever. Just because you bought me lunch doesn't mean you can show up at my house and start asking for money. Seriously, how do you even know where I live? Why are you stalking me?"

"I'm wicked with information-gathering."

"You're a hacker?"

"That's illegal."

I turn onto Bloomfield Avenue. Regretting my impulse to reach out to this girl in the first place.

"You owe me."

"For what?"

"We don't have to go there now." She gestures with her neck toward the kids. "It's just a loan. I'll get it right back."

I spy a parking space a block away from the dance studio and start backing into it.

"Are you helping me or not?"

"Not."

Shayla grabs my phone from where I keep it in the cup holder and starts punching away. Her phone rings.

"I saved my number for you. Think it over and give me a call." She hops out of the car. "'Bye, cutie-pies."

"'Bye," says Two, all goggle-eyed. She's a sucker for pretty women.

Shayla comes onto my side of the car, where I am now standing in the street.

She whispers, "I need your help. Just like you needed mine once upon a time."

"This is not the same thing."

Shayla winks at me and then gestures with her finger and thumb, call me.

"Mommy, how do you know her?" Rory asks.

"Mommy, what time is it?" Two is clutching her dance bag. "Am I late?"

"We have five minutes, so let's hurry." I drop three quarters into the parking meter. I look up and see Shayla turn the corner.

"How, Mommy?" Rory asks again. Liv is in the front carrier and I grab hands as we cross the busy street.

"Just a lady I knew from before."

"Before what?"

"Before you were born. Watch where you're walking, Rory. Pay attention."

I lead the kids into the dance school. What have I gotten myself into? The sheer nerve of that chick. Where does she get off thinking that buying me lunch entitled her to anything?

We get off the elevator and I lean down to help Two into her ballet slippers. She waves good-bye and bounces into her classroom.

"Can I play on your phone?"

I hand it to him. We sit but I cannot get comfortable. Most of the parents look like they rolled out of bed with fifteen minutes to get to class. They are clutching cups of coffee, fiddling with phones, typing on laptops. I rub my eyes, trying to piece together Shayla showing up at my house. What if Preston had been home? Then what? I'm not giving her two dollars, let alone two thousand. She had better try to run game on someone else because I am not the one.

FIFTEEN

The Sinners Don't Win

We don't go to church, but I try to make Sunday our Sabbath day. No children's classes, minimal running around, I even forbid Preston from leaving us for the office. I'm up before the rest of the house, taking the telephone off the hook in the basement. I also power down my cell phone and toss it in the drawer. Today I won't be interrupted by anyone, not Gran, not Martin, not Shayla. By the time the kids come downstairs I have made a full breakfast; heart-shaped pancakes, fried potatoes, sausage, and eggs.

"Where are we going today?" Rory looks at me.

"Nowhere. It's Sunday."

"Awwww, man. We have to stay in the house for the whole day."

"We can go in the backyard and play."

"I want to go somewhere."

"Eat your breakfast."

Preston walks in the kitchen, wearing his boxers and a long tee. "Smells good. Paper come?"

I point to where I've left it on the counter.

The kids eat, crash their toys, and fall into the rhythm of our lazy day. For dinner, Preston fires up the grill and we eat roasted vegetables, cheeseburgers, and hot dogs. The plastic kiddie pool is filled with water, and the children swim and play. Once they are in bed, I plopped down on the couch next to Preston and zone out on thoughtless television.

I'm up before the sun, in my basement office working my monologue for the Dames audition. There is something about this time of morning when the house is still and the world not fully awake that makes my creativity flow. I type what I've jotted in Rory's notebook and then let it expand. When I write a scene, I print it, read it, and then retype it. I do this several times until I am happy with the piece. The character that I've created is a funny mom who tells the real truth about the behind-the-scenes life of a stay-at-home mom. What I've written sounds good to me. I sure hope the Dames get my humor and go with me on this journey. That's what acting is about, grabbing your audience and taking them on a ride with you. As I rehearse the piece out loud, stage direction, costume, and lighting come to mind.

I haven't had many personal goals for myself over the past few years, but I want my Dames membership. It's been a dream for as long as I can remember to be distinguished as an artist and belong to a group of women who share my ambition for creating art. People I can feed off of and network with to take my career and our family to the next level. These women are the connection to my future, and I'm getting in.

It ended up being one of those rare days when Liv napped late. I was so absorbed in rehearsing that the afternoon got away from me. By the time I arrive at the school, most of Rory and Twyla's friends are gone, so it's easy to get them off the playground and to the house without a fight or tears. My plan is to have them fed, bathed, and in the bed by seven thirty. That will give me an hour and a half to work my monologue before Preston is home and demanding my attention. Friday will be here before I know it and I want to make sure my piece is flawless.

The frozen collard greens that I've taken out for dinner smell stronger than usual, like they were a second away from going bad, but I have a taste for greens, so I hesitate for only a minute before throwing them in the pan. If anything, I'll season them up more than usual.

"Give it to me!" Two shouts, drawing my attention from the stove. They are fighting over a pretzel.

"Here," I say, dropping a few more in front of both of them.

"Mommy, how do you spell karate?" Rory asks.

I spell it. "What are you doing?" I peep at him.

"Writing out my schedule for the week."

"Oh," I say. At six, the boy never stops amazing me.

"How do you spell piano, sparring, and swimming?"

"Rory, sweetie, you have to look it up. The children's dictionary is on the bookshelf."

He covers his pretzels with his napkin and then runs off.

I'm circling the pan with olive oil and my favorite vegetable seasoning by Goya when Two starts pulling on my pants leg.

"Take this off, Mommy."

I look down to see what she wants while trying not to forget what I've added to the greens and what still needs to be dropped in.

"The baby's panties," she says, pushing her doll into my face. "Fix Pamper on." Her face is tight, and I can see the influx of tears waiting to fall. I'm about to correct her English but Rory is back clutching his children's dictionary. "I don't see it."

"Sound out the next letter."

"I did."

I'm pulling clothes off of Two's doll while I look over his shoulder.

"You're on the wrong page."

Two's after-school floodgate is threatening to burst open, so I rub her belly and fix her baby's Pamper.

"Here you are, honey. Take this in the living room so you can play with Liv."

I decide to fry the chicken instead of baking it, since it will be faster. My cell phone dings. It's a text from Sam, our sitter.

So sorry, Ms. Felicia, but I don't have school on Friday. My mom is taking me to New York so I can't babysit for you.

Damn. I try not to panic. Tell myself that it's going to be all right and drop the floured chicken into the hot skillet. The meat and oil greet each other happily. The bubbling of seasoned skin permeates the air. The doorbell rings.

We have an electric bell, so when my neighbor's bell rings, our bell rings, too. So I don't stop stirring the greens. It rings again. The kids flock to the door.

"Who's coming over?"

"Are you going out?"

"No. Back away from the door." I look through the window. It's Shayla. My heart dives.

"Go into the kitchen and color. I'll be right back."

"Coloring is for babies," Rory says with a pout.

"Well, you can watch Liv." I grab her off the floor. Stick her in her high chair and turn the food down low. Again the bell rings, longer this time.

"Faye, open up!" she shouts from the street.

I open the house door, walk across the enclosed porch, kick mismatched sneakers to the side, and grit on her. "What're you doing here?"

"You going to let me in?" She cracks her gum.

I unlock the front door. We stand on my enclosed porch. The house door is wedged so I can hear the kids but she doesn't push me to go any farther.

"You can't keep showing up like this. It's not cool."

"I told you I need to get Brave out of jail."

"Jesus Christ."

"The money is taken care of. The problem is collateral."

I watch her. She flings her long hair over her shoulder and flutters her lashes at me. The bone-straight hair is all hers, but I can tell she's wearing lash extensions. Shayla is naturally beautiful, so the effort she puts in pushes her to beauty queen, movie starlet, rock star status. I'm wearing faded jean shorts and a Gap V-neck perfect tee. My hair is in two braids, parted crooked, Vaseline on my lips.

"Faye, I really need your help." She sighs, gives me the lowered-eyed stare. I guess it was her broad with the blues look, but I wasn't buying it.

"I need you to put your house up so I can get Brave out."

"Bitch, please" leaves my mouth before I could filter it. She looks hurt but I'm not taking it back. The kids are calling me. The chicken needs to be turned. I want this chick out of my house, out of my life. I have enough going on. As if reading my mind, she takes a seat in the rocking chair close to the front door on the porch.

"I'll wait."

I navigate my way back to the kitchen, dodging the backpacks, lunch boxes, and toys along the way. I make sure to close the door most of the way behind me. Didn't want her to follow me.

"What's the matter?" I look down at Two on the kitchen floor.

"Rory took my last pretzel and I'm still hungry."

I gave out pretzels thirty minutes ago. Two knows how to make a snack last. I grab a banana from the basket, peel it, and split it in half. "Here," I said, ignoring her frowned-up face.

Liv beats both hands on the high chair tray. She wants out. Her feet are moving and I have about a second and a half before the storm starts. I turn the chicken and put Liv on my hip.

On the porch, I unlock the door and stand on the front steps. The sun is low and there is a bit of a breeze, like it might rain. I hadn't noticed the white Mercedes-Benz with blood red interior parked in front of my house. Wheels and rims gleam like polished glass.

"Listen, I need you to make this happen for me."

"I can't put up my house for your boyfriend. My family lives here," I say with a hiss.

"It's really not that deep."

"Sounds like it."

"Faye, all you have to do is sign a piece of paper saying that the house is going to be used as collateral. It's just insurance."

"And what if he leaves town? Then I lose my house?"

"Brave ain't going to skip town on you. I'll make sure of it. It's just standard procedure."

My eyes look at Shayla like she has lost her mind.

"Please, Faye, I need you to trust me on this."

"Preston wouldn't let me put this house up for my own grand-mother, let alone some man he's never laid eyes on."

"He doesn't have to know."

I laugh. This girl has really lost her God-given mind if she thinks I'm going to put my house up for her boyfriend without telling my husband.

"The house is in your name only. Preston will never find out."

"How the hell do you know that?"

"I told you, I find out what I need to know."

And she was right. We bought the house in my name only so that Preston could have room on his credit to purchase his office build-ing. But how could she know that? I looked at her again.

"Shay."

She takes two steps closer to me and I can feel her energy shift from honey with a heartache to pit bull with a purpose.

"Faye. Listen. We both know what it is. Right? I know the Mr. Straight Up and Down Columbia dude that you married don't know shit about you. The real you, feel me?"

I take a step back.

"Nothing about where we came from and how far you've gone to get this little-stay-at-home June Cleaver life."

I stare her dead in the eyes. She's so close she's whispering. "I don't want to be the one to bust things up for you. That's really not my objective. All I want is to get my man out. All I want is for you to sign the form so I can make that happen."

My eyes are not even blinking when I stare her down. I cannot believe this is happening. I try like hell not to show fear, but I know Shayla. Bluffing is not in her vocabulary.

"I don't want to have to start singing about the summer of '89 when you were—"

"Girl, stop." My head has gone cloudy, making it hard for me to think. I needed a minute.

"I'll call you tomorrow. Think it over. I know you'll make the right choice."

Shayla swishes her hips down my front steps, touches the handle of her car, and starts it with no key. With her pinkie and thumb she indicates I'll call you and then pulls off.

The spot right above my left ear starts pulsing. I need a cigarette. Preston's car turns the corner. He's home early, and if I needed him he wouldn't have been available. I wave, pull the door, and head back into the kitchen.

"Daddy!" the kids shout, jump from the table, and run to him, wrapping themselves around his arms, his legs, tugging him off balance. When they lose interest in him he comes into the kitchen to me.

"Hey, babe." We peck.

"You mind serving dinner? I need to run to the store for some tampons."

"You on your period again?" He looks disappointed.

"Not yet, but it's coming."

"What's a period?" Two asks. "Can I go with you?"

"No, I'll be right back."

I'm in my sandals and out the door before anyone else can grab me.

People in this town know me. I'm the woman who walks through the neighborhood, always with a baby stroller. Sometimes to the playground, library, supermarket, or just working out. I'm the polite woman who comments on the new flowers blooming in their garden, asks after grandchildren away at school. And I smile, always a smile. When I purchase my first package of cigarettes in eight years from the gas station three blocks from my home, I keep my sunglasses on and don't look at the gas attendant when I thrust a twenty-dollar bill in his face.

I drive five more streets looking for a safe place to smoke, as if it's a joint in my handbag and I don't want the cops to catch me. The baseball field behind the middle school is empty so I park, find a secluded spot on the bleachers, and fire it up.

This cannot be happening. I've worked so hard to carefully construct a future with lots of space from my past, and the gap is closing in on me. First Martin, puff, now Shayla. Puff. I feel like a rat hemmed between a trap and a hungry rattlesnake. Damned if I do, double damned if I don't. Would Shayla have run up on me if I hadn't contacted her first? How had she been getting on in the streets without me all this time? If I sign the papers and her fool of a man who I don't even know skips bail, then I'll lose my house and most likely my husband over this. What kind of name is Brave, anyway?

I light another cigarette and puff it slowly, allowing the nicotine to curl in my throat before exhaling. The sun is going down and the sky holds on to the last light of the day. I slap a mosquito against my thigh and kill it. Why am I even considering helping Shayla?

Because that heifer means business. Growing up, I was always happy to have Shayla on my team because I saw what happened to those who crossed her. There is no way I can let Preston find out about Martin and the baby. Not after all this time. A lump rises in my throat.

Look at you. The one to mess up the happily ever after. Preston has always been too good for you. He should have left you in the gutter where you came from.

The baby wipes and Febreze are still in my trunk. I clean myself up, hide the cigarettes in the bottom of a duffel bag that I keep the beach toys in, and go home.

SIXTEEN

The Something or Another

Mornings are the best time to ask Preston for a favor, so I wake him up with my lips. He rises and moans. We have a good twenty minutes before the kids' natural alarm clocks set off, so I ride him until his eyes roll.

"Nice waking up like that?" The covers fall to his ankles. Our scent is strong in the air. "Coffee?"

"Sure."

I bring two steamy cups back to bed. Five minutes until somebody interrupts.

"Friday is the Dames meeting about me performing at the fundraiser. Sam can't come because she's going into the city with her mom."

He looks at me over the rim of his cup.

"Do you think you can come home early?"

He rests his head on his hand and props himself up so we are eye level.

"What time?"

"I need to leave here by five."

"I have two meetings down in Somerset but let me see if I can push them up."

"Thank you." I exhale.

"Aren't the Dames all rich and snobby?"

"No."

"Yes, they are."

"Well off, maybe, but connected. Me being a Dame will expose us in a way that I think is important. Elevate the family."

"You've already elevated this family. Just by being you."

The grin spills from my face, and I splash Preston with it. "Still, this is important to me, honey, so please, please, make it happen."

He reaches for his underwear. "Whatever will make you happy, but I'm hoping this social climb isn't going to affect our bottom line."

Rory walks in, rubbing his eyes.

"Hey, buddy," Preston pulls him close. While they cuddle, I go downstairs to make breakfast. My monologue for the Dames is running through my head. When Liv takes her first nap, I'll rehearse today. I already have it memorized; all that is left for me to do is eat it, own it, make the piece come alive. Acting has always been the perfect distraction from my real life, and right now I need the diversion.

I'm at the door kissing the children good-bye when Gran calls.

" 'Bye, Mommy."

" 'Bye." I prop Liv on my hip and run for the phone in the kitchen. "Hello."

"Did you hear anything about a superstorm coming to this area?"

"Morning, Gran. No, I haven't."

"That's 'cause you don't watch the news. Don't make no sense that you don't know what's going on in the world."

"I know enough from listening to the radio."

"Well, a storm is coming this weekend, so you need to run down to ShopRite and stock up on some canned goods. Always good to have case the power goes out. You can feed the kids that."

I ain't buying no damn canned goods, but I listen as she rants while I clean up the morning dishes.

"Kids off to camp?"

"Just left."

"Nursing home called. Said your mother's pressure is up. Would be good if she had some visitors."

"Okay."

Gran sucks her teeth. "What I got to do to get you to go visit your own mother? Kidnap you?"

"No, Gran." How do I explain to Gran that I hate seeing my mother in that state? Not knowing if she's coming or going, her not recognizing me, understanding me, knowing me. Plus, I feel responsible for what happened, if I had only . . .

"Well then?"

"I've got a lot going on. The kids are busy with activities and I have a really big audition on Friday for a group I'm trying to get into."

"What bougie mess are you working on now?"

"It's not bougie. It's an art group that will help me with my craft."

"Umph." I can picture her crossing her arms over her breasts and running her tongue over her top dentures the way she does when she's unsatisfied.

"What you need to be doing is looking for a job. All the money I spent sending you to that fancy college, and you sitting up there playing house. Day care ain't good enough for your children?"

"Gran, Liv isn't even walking."

"So. Kids in Philadelphia going to twenty-four-hour day care centers now so they parents can work. Hope Preston don't get tired of taking care of you."

It's the same argument. Gran doesn't think being a stay-at-home mother is a real job.

"I worked all my life. Would be working now if this arthritis wasn't eating me up the way it is."

"How you feeling, Gran?" I say to change the subject.

"Tired. Crystal is wearing me out. Got the feds calling me talking about taking money outta my little check to cover her taxes. Damn girl done let her little girlfriend claim Derell. Turns out Derell daddy done claimed him too. It's just a big mess."

Liv slithers across the kitchen floor and stops in the middle to chew on a rubber bunny. I scrunch up my face at her and shake my head until she smiles.

"I need you to call her and talk some sense into her."

"Crystal don't listen to me. Half the time she acts like she doesn't even like me."

"She'll listen to you. Just call her, you hear? And make it a point to come down here and see your mother. I'm giving you till the end of this month."

Gran hangs up the telephone.

Philadelphia's problems are the perfect way to start my day. Now what was I doing today? Laundry, dishes, change the sheets on the beds, rehearse my monologue, stop at the grocery store, pick up the kids, swimming lessons, and what else? Oh, dodge Shayla until I figure things out.

I count my blessings when I open my eyes on the day of the Dames audition. I'm ready to go in and conquer those women. I get the big kids off to school. Sam has offered to watch Liv for me for a few hours this morning, but I need to be home by noon so she can go into Manhattan with her mom. I scheduled an appointment with my special-occasion hairstylist. The one who charges more but makes my hair light and fluffy. She gives me a layered look and blends my curls. Across the street is the nail salon, and I let them take care of me.

I had a hard time figuring out what to wear. I'm not a member, so I wouldn't dare dress in purple and yellow, the Dames' colors. I settle on a spring peach sundress with a matching three-quarter-sleeve cardigan. It has pep, and the floral prints suggest artsy but in charge. I don't own any new stilettos, so I go for a three-inch strappy peep toe that shows off my French pedicure.

For once I've planned things right. After the salon, I stop at the library for the new Spy Kids movie, and I allow the kids to watch the show while eating popcorn in the living room, before dinner. They are ecstatic by the treat and have not come up the stairs once while I'm getting ready. The digital clock in our bedroom flashes four twenty-one. Preston hasn't called. I don't need to leave until five, but I've decided to check in.

"Hey, babe," I say when he answers.

"Hey."

"Where're you?"

"The Garden State. I don't know what's going on but I'm moving like five miles per hour."

"How far are you?"

"Just passed exit one twenty-seven."

We are exit one forty-two, and even without traffic, that's like thirty minutes away.

"How come you didn't leave sooner? I told you how important this meeting was."

"Sweetie, I canceled my second appointment. I'm doing my best to help you. I'll get there as quickly as I can."

I hang up. A dull ache crosses my forehead. Liv starts fretting. I'm dressed and ready to go. I pick her up and walk downstairs.

"Mommy, where are you going?" Two is out of her seat.

"To a meeting."

"You look beautiful. Turn around?" she says.

Rory is looking at me too, with a twinkle in his eyes. "Who's going to watch us?"

"Daddy."

"Awwww, man, why not Sam?"

"She's is the city with her mom. Need more popcorn?"

"Yes," they both chime.

I'm happy for something to do to keep my mind off of the problem. I want to call Preston again but I don't want to annoy him. I make the popcorn and then sit at the kitchen table, looking over my lines. It's five o'clock. The meeting starts at five thirty. It'll take me at least fifteen minutes to get there. Butterflies are mating little caterpillars in my stomach. All I feel is stretch and pull. My skin starts itching around my forearms. I don't scratch. I wiggle my toes instead, willing myself to be calm. It's going to be all right. I try to get in a round of tapping, but the *damn voice* won't stop haunting me.

You should have known Preston wasn't going to be on time. He doesn't want you to be a Dame because it will take away from you catering to him. He's late on purpose. Believe that.

Damn, I wish she would shut up sometimes. A bead of sweat forms above my left eyebrow. I will not sweat over my makeup. The telephone rings. I snatch it up without bothering to let the number register on the caller ID, willing it to be Preston.

"Where are you?"

"I'll be in Philly next week."

I freeze. "Martin." His name is like a sedative to my anxiety.

"Hey, Young Sister. I haven't been able to reach you lately. Everything okay?"

"Yeah, just rushing to a meeting."

"For what?"

I tell him about the Dames, more to take my mind off Preston being late than anything else.

"Look at you, a woman of class, culture, and substance."

Martin can say the most ridiculous things and my face will blush.

"You gonna come see me?"

"Oh, Martin. What do you want from me?"

"I told you, I want to see you. We need to straighten things out."

"There's nothing to straighten."

"Just say yes." His tongue is thick and heavy in my ear. The butterflies have retreated. It's almost as if nothing else exist but his words in my ears. How can he still do this to me?

"That was a long time ago. A forgotten time. Move on."

"What we made can't be forgotten."

My cell phone rings. It's Preston.

"Martin, I have to go." I hang up the house phone and touch the green button on my cell.

"Preston?"

"Traffic's moving. I'll be there in ten."

I'm going to be late. My first impression on the Dames will be lateness. But what can I do but wait for Preston? I'm not close to the neighbors. I click-clack my sandals down into the basement, take the phone off the hook, and go onto the front porch and wait.

Preston walks in the door at five twenty-five.

"Wow, Foxy mama," he says and whistles.

"Thanks. Kids need to eat."

"What's for dinner?"

"Daddy's choice," I say, allow him to kiss my cheek, and then I'm out the door, in my car, backing out of my driveway before he can ask me anything else. The anxiety knots in my belly. I need to poop. I need to put Philadelphia back in its place. I need to be a Dame, a women of class, culture, and substance.

SEVENTEEN

The Dames

Monroe McKenzie lives at the top of a hill with a sweeping view of New York City. Cars are crammed into her driveway and along her street. I pull up twenty minutes late. The smells of evening dew, dahlias, and daisies calm my nerves. Breathe, I remind myself as I touch the doorbell. It's one of those old-fashioned bells that chime five times at different octaves. A graying woman dressed in white with a black apron answers the door.

"Welcome to the McKenzie home. Come right in."

She leads me to the dining/living room combination, where at least fifty women are comfortably seated, some with small plates in their hands and gold-rimmed goblets. On the center table is a short bouquet of flowers, a tier of three types of sandwiches, and platters of cheese, crackers, and smoked salmon. The food looks picked over. Like folks have been here a while. All eyes are on me. I stand clutching my purse. The expensive bone-colored one Preston bought me for Christmas last year. Now I'm wondering if I should seat myself.

Monroe calls out to me, "Felicia Lyons, so glad you could make it." She moves across the room with the grace of a first lady. Her lemon crepe dress has an eggplant sash, and her hair is long and flowing. "We were just about to get started. Why don't you grab a plate and join us."

I smile politely and thank her. I'm not hungry. Intimidated, but not hungry. I move toward the table as I'm told. Erica Prince is standing there pouring a glass of lemonade.

"Erica!" I shriek with pure joy. Ease washes over me. "I didn't know you were a Dame."

"Felicia!" she throws her arms around me. "This is my second year. I just read on the agenda that you are trying out for the fundraiser. I wish I would have known. I could have given you a quick briefing on the playground," she says with a wink.

"Is it going to be that hard?"

"The Dames are strict," she whispers out the corner of her cute mouth. Her hair is flat-ironed and curled today. She's wearing a white pantsuit with a purple shell. Diamond droplets fall from her ears, and she smells like cinnamon. Not the Erica I'm used to seeing chasing after Coltrane and McCoy.

Monroe rings a small bell. All conversation halts. The women who are standing make their way to their seats. I follow Erica. As I pass Monroe, she hands me a gold-stenciled name tag. The room is seated.

Monroe clasps her hands together and beams. "Thanks so much for coming out tonight, ladies. As you know, our annual fund-raiser is two weeks away. I want to thank the committee for their hard work. To date, we've sold more than one hundred tickets to women in our community."

The ladies clap.

"Thanks to Lourdes Maloney for the beautiful design. I'd also like to thank Priscilla Peony and Tasha Montgomery for securing the Green Lawn Tennis Club in Chatham for the event."

More applause.

"Before we start our meeting, I have five prospective ladies who have joined us to audition their talent. Please stand when I call your name. Cassandra Youngblood, Felicia Lyons, Beatrice Blackwood, Maritza Lovett, and Tina Chang. Dames, please welcome our visitors."

Hands move in unison; most women smile our way.

"We will start with Tina Chang on cello, and while she sets up her instrument, I want to remind the Dames that I'd like you to stay for a fifteen-minute briefing once the auditions conclude. Ladies, you should have all received a ballot; please remember to grade each performance by using the number system one to three." Monroe signals for Tina Chang to begin.

She plays the cello as if she's moving with a classical orchestra. The next performer dances a modern piece that will rival any member of Alvin Ailey. Then the third woman sings opera in Italian and the fourth plays piano while singing half in English and half in French. I can't compete with them. What in the world was I thinking? A BFA from Marymount Manhattan College and one Super Bowl commercial doesn't make me equipped. I am not Dame material. My piece on the overburdened stay-at-home mother is not traditional at all, and my feet go cold as I'm waiting for my name to be called. What the hell is wrong with me? I spend at least half of the monologue on real talk, complaining about the woes of motherhood. This crowd won't get it. My knees knock into each other. I would bite my fingernails if I hadn't just gotten a manicure.

By the time Monroe pronounces my name, I have decided to bow out, give up, I am not embarrassing myself. Why do I want this, anyway? Maybe Preston is right. These women are just rich and snobby. I don't really belong. This whole thing is out of my league.

The *damn voice* taunts. *About time you came to your senses. You ain't built for this. Run, heifer, run.*

I push back my shoulders, and as I'm heading toward the center of the room with my mind on the front door, I'm flooded by this interview I saw on the show *Life After* featuring Bern Nadette Stanis, the woman who played Thelma on *Good Times*. She talked about this beauty contest that she had entered in Central Park, but at the last minute lost her nerve. Bern Nadette told her mother that she wasn't going to do it. Her mother had spent her entire paycheck on getting her ready and forced her to carry through with the contest. At the contest, Bern Nadette met the producer for *Good Times* and landed the role of Thelma, which changed her life forever. I remember her saying, "Don't ever let fear get in the way because you never know what's going to open a door."

My feet stop moving. When I look out, I'm standing in the center of the room. At least a hundred sets of eyes are on me. I run my finger behind my ear for luck, run my tongue across my teeth, stand in the middle of Monroe's living room, and perform my panties off.

I'm the last act, and after thunderous applause Monroe stands, commanding the floor.

"Ladies, thank you so much for giving us your time and talents this evening. It was truly an incredible showing."

More applause. Standing ovation from the Dames.

"Have a wonderful night, we will be in touch. Penelope, would you mind showing them out?"

Penelope, vice president of the Dames, stands and walks us to the door. I shake her hand and smile. Outside I congratulate the other talent and wish them luck. My phone starts vibrating. I know it's Preston checking up on me and I fumble through the small clutch for my phone.

It's Shayla. I let it go to voice mail. By the time I've buckled myself into my car, she calls three more times. Then a text message signal dings.

I'm in front of your house. Wait here for you or meet somewhere else?

This chick isn't going away. I text back.

Meet me at Tanky's.

I don't give an address. Since she knows so much, let her figure it out. My foot is on the gas, and as the neighborhood changes from affluent to affordable, I lose the good Dames feeling.

My package of cigarettes is in hand as I pull open the door. Shayla is posted up at the bar on the backside curve of the U. The Heineken sign flashes above her. Her eyelids are painted in a dramatic cat eye, with the top liner curving toward her hairline. With that tight pony-tail pulling on her skin, she looks what we used to call "chinky."

"Hey, Faye." She waves me over like we are meeting for a girls' night out.

I sit. "What's up?"

"Nothing much."

Our eyes touch. My fingers tap the box on the bar top. I remove a cigarette and put it between my lips. Once it's lit, I pass it to Shayla and then light another for myself. We smoke.

"Jack and ginger, doll?" the same bartender as before asks me and I nod.

"Let me find out you hanging at the local bar," Shayla pipes. "Rum and Diet Coke for me."

I look at her.

"Got to watch this hourglass figure, girlfriend."

I snicker. She has not changed.

"So Faye, girl, what's good? Look at you. Married to a Columbia dude with three kids. You doing it, hon, living that life."

"How do you know he went to Columbia?"

She gives me her chile, please, look. "I told you, I'm wicked."

The jukebox is spinning "Peter Piper" by Run-D.M.C. We both move our shoulders. The beat and lyrics take over, my head snakes, and fingers snap in the air. We are back in Shayla's bedroom as teen-agers wearing our neon T-shirts, K-Swiss sneakers, and asymmetric bobs, looking through *Black Beat* magazines, drinking twenty-five-cent Hugs, and eating Doritos.

"This was my shit." Shayla is out of her seat, swinging her hips. Two men at the pool table stop long enough to grit on us. I turn my head and pop my chest. We move through the entire song lost in our faraway worlds, when life was filled with adolescence. The biggest problems Shayla and I had to worry over then was how to convince the grown-ups to let us go to the Sixteenth Street basement party on Friday nights. Simple and easy. We dance until we are both hot and out of breath. A Jill Scott ballad comes on next.

Shayla takes her seat. "Philly girl on the box, woot-woot."

"Girl, if they played Eve I would lose my mind, up in here, up in here." We both laugh. I swipe my fingers for the sweat that's gathered on my brows.

"How's Gran?"

"Same as always. Calls me just about every morning to give me the update."

Shayla dishes what she knows about our old friends in the neighborhood. The girl had always been dramatic and animated, and I watch like she is a television program. The cigarettes dwindle from my pack, and the ice cubes have melted several times over.

"Why are you doing this to me, Shay?"

She sucks her teeth and looks me dead in my face. "Girl, you always did take shit too personal. It's not always about you. This time it's actually about me. Damn, can I have a chance at the good life?"

I want to slap her. "What the hell does that mean?"

She puffs on her cigarette hard. The smoke leaves through her mouth in a big breezy poof.

"My mother died."

"I'm so sorry to hear that," I say, meaning it. Even though her mother was mean as piss.

"Ralphie is upstate doing twenty-five years to life."

Ralphie is her older brother who always tried to freak me in the closet when we played hide-and-go-seek.

"You've got your *Leave It to Beaver* life." She holds up four fingers and makes the quote signal. "I've got Brave. Brave's got the streets. I need to get him out. It's hard out here. You don't even know."

Shayla motions for another drink. I've reached my limit and chew on the last cube.

"Wanna hear something crazy?"

I turn my face toward her and catch her eyes.

"After all this time, you're the only person I can turn to for help. Ain't that some shit? After what like ten years, you're still the only one, Faye."

Well, that was me—reliable Faye. But growing up she was sure-enough-Shayla. She always had my back. After the thing with my parents, I stayed at Shayla's house for a week because I couldn't bear to enter Gran's house. I wore her clothes, ate her food, slept in her bed. And that wasn't the only time. There were others, many others, when Shayla had to come to my rescue. Fight some girl for me because I was too chicken. Hell, Shayla showed me how to use a tampon, and when I couldn't figure it out she told me to take my panties down and shoved the thing inside of me. She was closer to me than Crystal's crazy ass was, and she never asked for anything.

Preston often said that when pity starts to flow from me, I can never find the plug. I could blame it on the booze, but something happened when Shayla's shoulders dipped defeated, and she looked up at me with her distressed eyes. I saw past the makeup, the cunning shell, and the constant attitude. I glimpsed her soul. She was the same girl I loved. Who I would have given a spare lung to if it meant keeping her alive back when we lived on Sydenham Street. We were two sides of the same coin.

Shayla and I had shared the same dream, to get out. She used her beauty and wit to climb the underworld society. No doubt Brave was the biggest, baddest dude on the block.

"Don't make me beg." She tugged on my arm. Her eye makeup had smeared.

I flag for the tab. The room has a hum to it. The jukebox is silent as it waits for someone to play their song.

"Okay."

"Okay what?"

"I'll help you."

"You will?" her squeal is loud, and the two men playing pool look our way again.

"Yes, but under two conditions."

"Anything for you."

"You better make sure your man does whatever he needs to do. If I lose my house, I will whoop your ass."

Her face breaks into a wide grin. "Oh, Faye."

"And two, don't you ever let the summer of '89 cross your lips again, or I will whoop your ass."

She knocks the top of the bar twice with her knuckles.

"You can just meet me at the bail bond's office. I'll text you the address."

"All I have to do is sign a paper backing Brave up?"

"That's all. And he'll go to court. Trust me. The bail bonds don't play. If he doesn't show they'll have the bounty hunters after him so fast your head will spin. You won't lose your house, Faye."

I've gone stone crazy. My husband would blow a gasket if he knew.

"Columbia will never find out." Shayla does that thing again. "I promise."

One thing I do remember about Shayla is that her promises were next to golden. Unless something happened that she couldn't control.

EIGHTEEN

The Pretending Game

When I get home a Honda Civic is blocking my driveway, so I have to park on the street. I'm annoyed. I pull my phone from my purse and see a text from Erica.

You did your thing at the audition. My fingers are crossed for you, darling.

That puts a smile on my face as I head up the stairs and unlock my front door. The light in the living room is on, and I know Preston is waiting for me.

"Why was the phone off the hook in the basement?" my husband asks by way of a greeting.

"I don't know, maybe one of the kids was playing with it."

Preston looks at me. "Has someone been calling here from Georgia and hanging up?"

My mind flashes to Martin. Nose can't take in enough air, but I keep my face blank. "Not that I know of. I rarely answer the phone unless it's Gran. Too many telemarketers trying to sell something." I turn away from him and slip out of my shoes.

"How did it go?"

"It was fine. I think I did well."

He pulls me to him and then lets go. "You smell like cigarettes."

"Really?" I step back. "One of the ladies I walked out with fired up right beside me."

Preston's eyes find mine. Holds them a beat too long.

When did I start lying to him with such comfort? He releases me and I stumble.

"And you're drunk. Is this what I have to look forward to?"

"What are you talking about?"

"You. It's late. What time was the thing over?"

"Not long ago."

Preston studies me. "It's late, Fox. Let's go to bed."

"No, what do you mean 'look forward to'?"

"This Dame thing, I don't want it to change you."

I flick my eyes. "Who the hell do you think you're talking to?"

"I'm just saying."

"Saying what?" Both hands find a hip.

"I just don't want you biting off more than you can chew. You've already got the kids signed up in more activities than you have time for."

"You don't want me involved in anything that's going to take away from catering to you."

"That's not true. It's just that you need to—"

"How about what you need to do?" I point my finger, fired up. "You put the kids to bed in their clothes, won't change the baby's diaper, and why do I have to lug the trash to the street every damn week?"

"Whoa. Where is this coming from?"

"You don't support me, Preston. You leave me here by myself all day. You can't even watch the baby so that I can go to a freaking audition. How do you expect me to book something?"

"I have to work! How do *you* think the bills get paid around here? With magic money that I just conjure up? I'm up and down these highways every day trying to make money."

He looks at me. "Maybe you should get a job and I'll stay home with the kids."

"You're an asshole."

"You're drunk."

"Fuck you." I push past him and slam up the steps. My face is wet. My head is woozy. I'm overwhelmed. My pretty dress meets the floor, and when I climb into bed it all crashes around me. I wait for Preston's body to sop me up. But he never comes.

I wake up feeling like I went a few rounds in a street fight and the other person got the better of me. The alarm doesn't go off because I forgot to set it. Rory tugs on my arm.

"Mama, do we have camp today?"

"No, baby." I pull his body into bed with me and hug him to my chest. He smells like sleep: harsh breath and slob. It's been a minute since he and I had a chance to cuddle, and I enjoy his bony body pressed into mine.

"Where's Daddy?"

My heart turns over in my belly. "I think the gym. Why don't you go get a book and I'll start breakfast?"

He slides from the bed. I brush my teeth and pretend as I go down the stairs that the room isn't spinning.

The water is on for oatmeal and I'm putting the coffee on when the basement door opens. Preston walks through, bare chest and in his jeans from the day before.

I turn my head when I see him and press down on the seal to the coffee can. He walks down the hall and up the stairs without a hello or a good morning.

You've gone too far.

Whatever. Forget him. He was as wrong as two left feet.

The Actress Is Out

I didn't get the Samsung Galaxy commercial, but I do get to perform for the Dames. Monroe phoned this morning and I am basking in bliss. Preston has been coming home late and leaving early, even on my Sabbath Sunday, so we hadn't had much time to discuss the argument. Since it's been two nights, I'm starting to thaw. For dinner I sear a couple of steaks, with butternut squash and scalloped potatoes. I've wrestled the kids into bed fifteen minutes early, shower, perfume my skin, and wait.

When he's not home by ten, I call him.

"Where're you?"

"Out." I hear music in the background.

"Preston, where are you?"

"I'm watching the game."

"With who?"

"A buddy from work. I've got to take this call. See you soon." He hangs up.

I hate when he does that, when he does not leave space for me to have the last word. As I plug my cell phone into the charger, a text flashes. It's Shayla.

We forgot the mortgage agreement.

What?

Standard procedure. I promise, Faye, I've got you. Please don't panic.

Don't worry she says as I'm signing papers to the home I live in for a man I don't know. I'm too exhausted to debate.

Don't ask me for another thing for the next ten years.

Lol! I won't let you down.

Better not.

I try not to think about this crazy house thing with Shayla as I wrap Preston's dinner in foil, load the dishwasher, suds the pans, rinse out the kitchen sink, and then go to bed. An hour later, Preston slides into the bed beside me. He doesn't reach for me. There is a thick pillow between us.

There is too much toxicity in my thoughts to sleep. I'm up before five, pour a glass of orange juice, and head down to the basement to work on my monologue for the Dames. I've gone through the script countless times, broken the scenes down into beats, and identified my objective. In college, my professors taught the Stanislavski method of acting, Uta Hagen and Lee Strasberg. With their technique, it's not enough to memorize the lines and recite them. As the actress, I must identify with something in the character, use memory and experiences in my own life to bring the piece to life. My acting bible, *Respect for Acting*, by the great Uta Hagen (who trained Robert De Niro), is tattered, dog-eared, and highlighted after years of reading and rereading it. I keep it on my desk to remind myself that I am an actress. Just a glance at the book jars me into transformation, but first I must warm my instrument.

It's important to neutralize my body before I start, create a blank canvas so I can adapt and play. My mouth is open wide and I start by yawning with my tongue hanging out. Breathe. Hum. Breathe. Hum. Open and shut my lips and then jaw jiggle. Shoulders back and forth, hand wiggles. I move the energy through my entire body until I feel nimble and free. I end with a spinal roll, stacking each vertebra on top of the other. Ready, set, go.

CAST OF CHARACTERS

Jocelyn...Stay-at-home mom

TIME: Night—the summer of 2008

SETTING: Upstage area; suggest a closet, with a beaded cock-tail dress hanging from a padded hanger. Peep toe stilettos are on the floor. Downstage is a vanity with an antique and gold mirror. Various makeup brushes, shades, and creams are scattered about, indicating the woman is going out.

Scene

(At RISE we see Jocelyn, early thirties, at the vanity applying makeup. She stops to examine what seems to be a gray hair. She gets closer to the mirror and tries to pull the hair out. It won't budge. Frustrated, she looks out into the audience, as if there is a bigger, better mirror in which to locate and pull out the hair.

JOCELYN

Another gray hair. These kids are gonna have me looking like I'm fifty before I even get to thirty-five.

(She shakes her head; her curls bounce.)

Yesterday things got so bad that I hid in the back of my closet. I'm talking way back. I was back so far that I was behind the tan wool coat that my mother bought me when I was working in corporate

America. The coat that has been covered in plastic for the past seven
years, since I traded in my pumps and suits for a wardrobe of cargo
pants and clogs. My head bobbed against the slinky, black halter dress
that became too tight two pregnancies ago.

(She stands and then slinks toward the floor to demonstrate.)

I squatted on top of the tap shoes that I insist on keeping just
in case. Just in case I wake up one day and have time to take up a
hobby. If I wasn't so damn responsible, I'd have a bottle of hard liquor
hidden here, in a crumpled paper bag to slurp down on days like this
when I feel like I'm suffocating in my own skin.

SCENE BROKEN

I hear heavy feet padding against the basement stairs. It's Preston.

I keep my back to him on purpose, like I'm so caught up that I
don't hear him. His legs are long and in seconds he's behind me,
palming the small of my back. It sends a sensation that pulses through
and melts my flesh. It amazes me every time, this effect he has on me.

"Good morning."

"Same to you." He smells of dried sweat and beer consumed last
night.

"What're you doing?"

I shuffle my papers. "Rehearsing for next Friday night."

"The Dames said yes?"

"Not only did they say yes, but Erica said that I was voted number
one out of all five performers."

"Honey, that's great." He turns me to face him. I give him a stiff
hug.

"I get to perform on the same stage as Audra McDonald."

"Congratulations," he says, and I know by his tone that he has
no idea who Audra McDonald is. "And you were worried. I'm
proud."

"Are you?" oozes from my lips with plenty of attitude.

"Of course I am. Stop that, come here." He pulls me to him and kisses my ear. My engine is revved in a tick-tock. The anger between us for three days has drained me. I lean my body in and meet him so that we can be restored.

"I missed you." His fingers are in my hair.

"Where were you last night?"

"I told you, watching the baseball game."

"You don't like baseball."

"I like beer, and I drank lots of it. That's why I'm heading to the gym," he says with a chuckle. It's a sound that I haven't heard in a while and I gush. We slob some more. He's under my shirt.

"Oh, my," he says, touching my flesh. I'm not wearing a bra. He feels me up. I laugh out loud.

"What?"

"Nothing." I feel him back.

He lifts me, my legs around his waist, arms around his neck, and he walks us to the front of the basement, where the cushiony sofa waits with patience. It's still dark outside but we have no problem finding each other and fitting, like the centerpieces of a jigsaw puzzle.

His head is resting on my breast.

"So much for the gym." I stroke his hair.

"I guess that'll count as my workout."

"What's your fantasy?" slips from my lips.

"I don't know." He thinks. "Maybe you and another girl."

I give him the look like that's not going to happen.

"Why do you ask?"

"I don't know, maybe we need to spice things up a bit. It's only been seven years." As I speak, my mind betrays me. *Martin*.

"You calling me boring?"

"No."

I draw circles on his arms. "It's just you on top, me on top, I'm sure the world of sex has much more to offer."

"Okay, let's get freaky." He untangles himself from me. "You want to get a video or something?"

I slip back into my sleep shirt and shorts and let the question hang. What I want is for him to figure it out. I kiss his cheek.

"I'll go wake the kids."

"I'll put on the coffee."

TWENTY

The In Girl

It's 4:32 A.M. when my eyes pop open. It's finally Dame day. All of my hard work over the past few weeks comes down to my moment onstage tonight. My heart feels trapped in my throat. Lungs are heavy. Hair scarf too tight against my scalp. Bedcovers hot around my waist. My nightgown is bunched and I feel tangled and nervous and something else that I can't name. I roll over and Preston is sleeping peacefully, his bare chest rising and falling. I get up and go check on the children. Liv has kicked her booties off and I slide them back over her cold toes. Preston has the air conditioner set too high. It's a tad cooler than comfortable. Rory has crawled into Two's bed and is curled around her like a lover. It's amazing how much they fight throughout the day and then cuddle and cup through the night.

I settle into the glider and listen to them breathe, smell their sweaty, sleep scents. And I'm all of a sudden overwhelmed with unadulterated love. These are my children. I longed for them before they were born. Carried each of them in my belly, nurtured them in my womb, refused drugs during labor because I didn't want their first breath tainted. Nothing would matter if I didn't have them. I brush back a tear.

From the time I knew what trouble was I wanted my own family, my own children whom I could raise right. Twenty-three-minute television sitcom right. Little carbon copies of me to mold, water, and shelter from what I saw growing up. Rory, Twyla, and Liv deserve for things to be easier. Preston and I have worked hard at giving them a two-parent home, complete with summer vacations and private schools. I want them to live a good, privileged life with all of the trimmings so that they can give their children even more. That's why I want to be a Dame. That's what it is all about. Every generation is supposed to take the family to the next level, and I want to do my part. The Dames not only open the door up for me, but also for our entire family. It's a stamp of approval. It's what I want for them, for us, and I'll perform my heart out today to get it.

The glider eases back and forth and as I watch the tree in our yard sway across the moon. I'm soothed by the thought that I am a good mother. I'm available. I'm present and I work hard. It'll be fine.

I look out the window again, and staring at me from my neighbor's rooftop is a fat black cat. She flashes her tongue at me, then leaps.

My ritual on the day of a performance is to drink hot ginger tea with lemon and honey and be quiet. Preston had agreed to take the kids to camp today so that I can honor my practice. It's easy to stay quiet with Liv, but Rory and Two have been demanding that I answer them all morning.

"Talk, Mommy." Two pulls on my cotton robe.

I look at Preston with eyes that say *save me*. He's bent over the coffeemaker, measuring the grinds.

"Twyla, honey, Mommy has to rest her voice today."

"Why can't she just say good morning." Rory wrings his hands.

"Because Mommy is going onstage today and we want her to be fantastic." Preston pats his head. "Who wants cereal?"

"I do."

"Me too."

Preston pours the cereal. I turn up the volume on the kitchen radio. *Morning Edition* is on NPR, and I listen to the headlines while I finish packing their lunches.

The children and Preston are gone. I'm anxious. The feeling that I woke up with this morning has come back. I can't shake it. It feels like I'm forgetting something very important. I review my props for the performance and go over my checklist in my head. I look around my bedroom for a clue. What is it?

Liv crawls around my ankles. I pick her up and hold her to my chest. She has Gymboree today but we are going to skip it since I'm not speaking. Perhaps I'm just tired. It's time for Liv's morning nap, so I lie down on my side, pull my baby to my chest, and close my eyes.

The ding of my cell phone wakes me up. It's a text message from Shayla.

I'm outside. I need the mortgage agreement.

That girl has the worst timing. I slide away from Liv, prop pillows on all sides of her, and then head downstairs. The painting hanging opposite the dining-room table masks a space in the wall with a safe. Preston is a big fan of old movies where the homes have secret passageways, rooms, stairs, and hidden compartments. When we bought our house he insisted on having a concealed space to store important documents. I work the knob and remove a book that looks like an encyclopedia. It's hollow on the inside and contains our marriage license, the kids' birth certificates, Social Security cards, five one-hundred-dollar bills, and the papers to our home. Preston also has a separate folder with duplicates of everything in case of an emergency, and I reach into that file for what Shayla needs. Once I put the painting back, I text Shayla.

Performance today. I'm not talking. But you better make sure your man goes to court, or else. Don't mess this up.

I open my front door. She kisses me on the cheek and snatches the paper from my hand.

"Break a leg tonight," she squeals, and then heads down my front steps.

The *damn voice* yawns. *You are a damn fool to trust that broad with your house. Her man is a street hustler. What makes you think they ain't hustling you?*

This may be true, but I stow away the reality of it, deadening all feeling that comes along with it. It's done and now I must focus on what's ahead. The Dames.

Preston and the kids are standing in the doorway waving as I walk down the front steps. I'm pressed to get into the car and turn on the AC so that my hair doesn't frizz up. Ten minutes ahead of schedule I back my car down the driveway, then pat myself on the back for making good time. My car is washed and gleaming thanks to Preston. When I arrive at the Chatham Tennis Club, the parking lot is mostly empty, so I have my pick of parking. The foyer is decorated in purple and yellow with flowers. Monroe is standing at the top of the stairs with a flower pinned in her side bun. I can smell its fragrance before I reach her.

"Hi there," I call, lugging my big bag.

"Felicia. You are the first performer to arrive. The early bird gets pick of the land. Tiffany?" She calls and a redhead with a clipboard turns our way.

"Would you show Felicia to the performers' holding room?"

"I have some more props in the car."

"Tiff, be a doll and help her. Thanks." Monroe dismisses us both with the turn of her shoulder. I don't know Tiffany well, but since I'm preserving my voice, I don't make small talk on the way to the car. When she shows me the green room, I pick the corner farthest from the door and start my warm-up exercises.

My lips go out and in. My eyes go up and down.

"Me, me, me, me, me." I start warming my tongue, and then I'm on to tongue twisters. "Peter Piper picked a peck of pickled peppers. She sells seashells down by the seashore. How much wood would a woodchuck chuck if a woodchuck could chuck wood?"

I'm at this for about fifteen minutes before Tina Chang walks in. We smile in greeting and she sets up her cello. It's been so long since I've been in an artistic space that my inner actress is positively aglow. This is where I belong. I'm back with my tribe.

Audra McDonald will sing as the finale, and the stagehands have her locked away in her own special green room. I'm dying to hear her sing live. I own at least three of her albums and have gone to her shows. While I wait for my turn, I watch the other performers from the wings. The ballroom has ballooned with more than 250 women, all dressed in their fancy best. Monroe McKenzie is a talented host, adding Dames of Culture anecdotes between performances and set changes. There is so much talent in the room, I can feel the energy pulsing from every corner.

Black-clad waiters serve a sit-down dinner. Only those who have performed in the first act eat and mingle with the attendees. The rest of us are too nervous to do anything but mark our pieces, meditate, wait. I am up first after the chat-and-chew intermission. So I am seated, cross-legged with my eyes closed, and block everything around me from my head.

"Three minutes until showtime, Felicia," Tiffany calls to me.

I give her a thumbs up. My ribs expand as I breathe in and out, focused on transforming into my character. I take my place on the dark stage. When Monroe introduces me, the curtains are closed, and when they whip back I am sitting at the mirror, cheating stage right. My costume is a full silk slip and nylons. I'm working the blush brush across my cheek. I stop and move in closer to the mirror because I've noticed a new gray hair.

Before I open my mouth, I channel the energy of all of the great stage actresses that have come before me: Phylicia Rashad, Debbie Allen, Alfre Woodard, Ethel Waters, Ruby Dee. I ask for inner strength and then I let my voice rip. I give it my all, and they laugh at the right places and give me those mmm hmms, just as I planned. Three minutes feel like thirty seconds. The applause is deafening and I grin until my cheeks sting.

There is an art to exiting the stage and I bow, torso forward, hands clutched in front of me, big toes aligned and together, count to three, and then rise. As if caught up in a wave, the women move to their feet. They clap, cheer, and I hear a few whistles. I soak it in.

This is it. I have arrived. My invitation to the Dames is sealed. I congratulate myself, grace them with an encore bow, and then bring my face back toward the tables and press my fingers together in humble thanks. That's when I see Preston. He's snaking through the crowd, and I smile even brighter. He couldn't resist seeing me perform, even though the event is women's only.

My love for him pulls my smile even wider, and I'm practically levitating. I take a second encore bow, and when I lift up, Preston is looking right at me. It freezes me. His skin is glazed with rage.

The crowd is still electric, so I take an encore-encore-encore bow to mask my confusion. It feels like too much. When I stand again, he is halfway to me, eyes beaded with anger. I give a final wave and move across the stage to depart.

As I clump down the steps, I'm reminded of a line from Martin Lawrence's movie *You So Crazy*. In college I had whole sections of his routine memorized because I watched it every chance I could. It was funny as hell and one of my refuges. When I reached the bottom of the metal stairs, I am face-to-face with Preston. He has that wild look in his eyes that Martin talked about in his act: that crazy, deranged look of a motherfucker who walks into the club with his pajamas and footies on.

"What is it?"

He grabs hold of my arm and squeezes his fingernails too deeply into my skin. The stagehands are running behind the curtains, preparing for the next act.

"Ow!" I yank my arm. "What's wrong with you?"

"You don't want to do this here," he says with a hiss.

"Do what? Where're the kids?"

"Who the fuck is Martin, and why did he just call my house asking to speak to my wife?" His expression is as black as a skillet, teeth bared but clenched. Then I hear it, his voice echoing throughout the ballroom. I look down and see my microphone attached to my dress and realize that it's still on.

I cough and reach for the off switch. Monroe starts up but I have no idea what she's saying. I drop my mic on a nearby table and cough my way out of the fancy Chatham Tennis Club. When the fresh air blasts my body, I know that everything I've worked for—my marriage, enriching our family, becoming a Dame—has all come crashing down around the toes of my overly expensive pumps. The shoes that never really fit right, but stood for something I bought into.

TWENTY-ONE

The Head-on Collision

"Where did you park?" he says with a growl. I point in the general direction, and he takes off, pulling me along with him.

"Will you let me go? I can walk just fine."

But my plea falls to the asphalt like a heavy raindrop and then evaporates into the concrete. Preston ices me on the walk, and I can barely keep up in those damn shoes. He thrusts open my door and then barks his command.

"Drive straight home. I'll follow you."

Once my key turns in the ignition I realize my mistake. In my nervousness for the event, I forgot to take the damn phone off the hook. But what could Martin have said to Preston to make him this angry? I feel a pang in my stomach. Oh, God, no.

My husband pulls behind me in the driveway, and as I get out of the car he walks up on me, pins me between the side of the house and my open car door. He's unrecognizable. I've never seen him this upset.

"What, Preston? What?"

"You fucked him, Felicia."

"What are you talking about?" Fear singes me.

"You told me I was your first."

"I never said that." My eyes are big.

"What?" He stares at me like he could chew my face off.

"Preston."

He moves away from me. "I can't believe you." His eyes mimic disbelief, then he walks away.

I take off the damn heels. I follow him, feeling as if I have stumbled into a honeybee hive and the stings greet me from all directions.

Sam gets a tight smile as we pass each other on the steps and I hurry inside. Preston has already made it to the basement. I tug off my pantyhose and make it down the steps, clutching the banister to keep me steady.

"Preston, let me explain."

He doesn't stop making a bed on the sofa.

I rush toward him, my hands go for his chest, but he grabs my fingers in midair.

"Felicia, right now I feel capable of knocking you the fuck out. So for your own safety, I advise you to go upstairs and leave me the hell alone." The chill in his voice is palpable, the pressure from his hand rough. I know that betrayal can unravel a man. I learned early on from watching my parents that men are capable of doing terrible things to women when they feel deceived. When the bubble of trust and honesty bursts, nothing is off-limits. And even though Preston has never hinted at putting a hand on me before, I turn and go.

In our bedroom I crumble like flaked-off pieces of a stale cookie. My face is wet and I hug my knees to my chest. This can't be happening. Not after all the hard work I've put into our lives. A small sound escapes from the girls' room, and I'm up. Liv hasn't awakened in the middle of the night for a feeding in months, but I'm relieved to go to her. In the glider, I give her my breast and I beg her to grant me some peace.

TWENTY-TWO

The Aftermath

Three days have passed and it feels like I've been sleepwalking. Preston has slept in the basement each night and hasn't said more to me than what was necessary. Before the kids left for school today, Two tuned in to the tension. Preston was pouring himself a cup of coffee and I was at the counter, bent over their lunches. She grabbed both of us by the hand and pulled us to the center of the kitchen floor.

"Kiss," she demanded.

Preston reached down and lifted her off her feet, tickled her belly, and smothered her with kisses until she couldn't breathe.

I wished it were me.

"Eat up, kids. Don't want to be late," Preston called over his shoulder before disappearing through the hall and upstairs. We don't have a shower in the basement, so he's been dressing upstairs. I followed him up yesterday and tried to talk to him but he wouldn't respond to anything I said.

. . .

On the fourth day of Preston not speaking to me, not sleeping in our marital bed, looking through me like a piece of plastic, I am bent over the kitchen sink, cleaning chicken thighs. I hate chicken thighs because they're dirty, and you have to really get under the skin and slice the film and fat from the meat. At least that's the way Gran taught me. It turns my stomach, but I do it because they are his favorite. It's a let's-talk-please peace offering. I'm going to make curry chicken, so I need to get them in the fridge for a while so the seasoning sets in.

Liv has settled in for her morning nap when I hear the front door open. Preston walks into the kitchen. He smells Preston good, and I want so much to wrap myself in his arms and settle this beef.

"Hi," I turn to him with the stinking chicken in my hand. I know I looked used. My hair is sloppy and pinned away from my face. I've been wearing the same red running suit for three days. I should have put more effort into my appearance, but it's taking all of my energy to stay mobile.

Preston studies me. He hasn't looked at me since Saturday night, and my heart starts to loop. Maybe we can talk now and get this behind us. *I only love you, Preston. I only lied for you.*

"You have to go." He looks at the chicken.

My face slips. "Go where?"

"Away from here. Out of this house, now."

I wipe my hands on the kitchen towel. "What are you talking about?"

"You're a liar, Felicia, and I can't be around you."

"Preston, stop this."

He moves a step closer. "You know what my godmother used to say? If you lie, you steal. If you steal, you cheat. Which means I can't trust nothing I have around you. Including my children."

He is staring at me with eyes so black I can barely see the Preston I've loved all these years.

"You are being ridiculous. Why can't we talk about this?"

He continues on like I've said nothing. "We can do this the easy way and you go peacefully. Or I can throw all of your shit out on the sidewalk and give the neighbors something to talk about. It's your choice, but it must be done before the kids get home from school today."

"You want me to leave my kids?" My voice is strained.

"My mother will be here."

"Your mother? The one who left you to be raised by Juju? That mother ain't doing shit for my kids" I say, like I'm running things.

Preston flinches. I see his jaw working the way it does when his mother issues flare. "Juju is coming, not Peaches."

I sigh a small sigh but I still don't want to leave my kids. He's taken this far enough. I won't. Where am I supposed to go?

I reach for him but he bats my hand away. "Why are you doing this? Can't we talk about it?"

"Talk about this man who you fucked and who has been calling my house trying to get at you. Is that where you were the night you were supposed to be getting Advil?" He steps closer.

"No."

"How about the night you were supposed to be auditioning for the Dames but you waltz in here drunk, smelling like cigarettes?"

"No."

"The movie you so-called saw alone?"

"Will you please stop?!"

He waves his hand in the air. "Felicia, just go. I can't stand to look at you."

"Preston, come on."

"Don't make this harder than it has to be. You have thirty minutes to get out of here or I swear on everything that I own, you will be sorry."

Preston walks upstairs like he is dismissing me. I follow him. "Don't you think you're overreacting? This is insane!" I shout at his back, then I remember Liv and lower my voice. "What the hell did he say to you?"

Preston stops abruptly. We are on the second-floor landing. "Does it matter? I should have known you were too good to be true. Marrying a lying ass actress was the worst thing I've ever done." His face slips. I see the weight of what I've done to him sag heavily on his body as he walks into our bedroom, then the girls' room, and a few seconds later he comes out with Liv, asleep on his shoulder.

My heart pierces at the sight of her. My head is reeling. Can he do this? Is this even legal? I can't leave my children. I haven't even combed Liv's hair today. Preston has lost his natural-born mind.

"Give her to me." She squirms in his arms at the sound of my voice.

"The children will be fine," he says softly, passing me on the landing and down the steps.

"You know what? Fuck you, Preston! Fuck you!" I shout at the top of my lungs. Liv opens her eyes startled and then he rocks her until she closes them.

He calls over his shoulder, "I trusted you and you lied."

With that I run down the steps and shove him as hard as I can. He holds onto Liv, who starts whimpering. Preston puts his arm up to shield the baby and blocks me from coming at him again.

"You were the one who needed me to be all pure white with no past."

"Don't be here when I get back. Mark my words."

"Where am I supposed to go?"

"You could take a long walk off of a short pier, for all I care." With that he carries my baby girl out the front door, destroying our Kodak Picture Perfect family.

I trudge up the steps like I have sandbags in my shoes. My heart feels like it's shattering against my breastplate, and I have to hold on to the wall to keep from crashing. From the top of my closet I pull down my overnight bag. Preston has left me five one-hundred-dollar bills on the bed.

Whore.

I change out of my house clothes and into jeans. Fistfuls of clothes from my closet and drawers go into the bag without order. If I think about it, I won't do it. Then my mouth fills with tears as I realize the kids will think I've abandoned them. There are markers on the desk and I scribble them a quick note.

> *Rory, Twyla, and Liv. Mommy had to go on a little trip. I love you with all of my heart and I will call you very soon. Please be good and listen to Daddy and Juju.*
>
> *Love, Mommy*

I tape the note to their bedroom door and roll myself downstairs. Preston is gone and so is Liv, so the house is absolutely silent. The *damn voice* gets loud, thumping in my ear.

But this is what you've been wishing for. Drive until your car runs out of gas, then walk until you're tired, then crawl until your legs are bloody. Remember? Freedom? Run.

Bitch.

I'm driving in the slow lane heading south on the New Jersey Turnpike when my mobile rings. I fumble for my phone and answer the call, hoping like hell Preston has come to his senses.

"Felicia?"

"Yes?"

"Oh, you don't sound like yourself. It's Ashley at SEM&M. Can you get to an audition today?"

I pull over onto the side of the highway. "Where?" I worry. I'm heading away from New York City.

"It's at Johnson & Johnson on Route One in New Brunswick. I don't think it's far from you."

"Yes, I can do it. What time?"

"An hour from now. Sorry for the short notice. I can e-mail you a copy."

"I won't have time to read it I'm already in the car. I'll get the script when I get there. Thanks." I sit and gather myself. My phone dings. A text message from Erica.

Is everything all right? Call me when you can chat.

I power down the phone.

Route 1 runs parallel to the turnpike. I find it with ease. In the parking lot, I powder my face and pinch my cheeks. When I pick up the script, I see that I'm playing a tired mom whose dog gets into the baby powder and covers the house with it. The part comes easy. I even manage a few tears, which I'm sure is overkill but I give the scene all of my pain.

Thirty minutes later, I'm back in my little Nissan, the bucket of a car that Preston and I bought the first year we moved to New Jersey together. I think about stopping for food, but the last thing my stomach wants is nourishment. As I go through the tollbooth I remember reading something in my women and religion college seminar where it said that there comes a time in every woman's life when she needs to return home.

I'm on Roosevelt Boulevard, riding in the center lane, when I see the red-and-white sign that says "Welcome to Philadelphia, the City of Brotherly Love."

PART 2

Home is the place where, when you go there,
they have to take you in.

—ROBERT FROST

TWENTY-THREE

The Incident

My body has tried to bury the memory, erase it, rewrite it, forget it. Still I remember it like it happened yesterday. My mother, Crystal, and I were in Gran's living room watching a rerun of *The Facts of Life*, that eighties TV show with the girls who went to a boarding school in Connecticut. *The Facts of Life* was my Saturday night must-see TV. I loved Ms. Garrett as the sweet-faced, bun-wearing housemother. I was obsessed with Tootie, played by Kim Fields, and imagined myself entering every room on roller skates, with short shorts and cute striped socks, flashing that innocent give-me-what-I-want smile. Saying her signature line, "We're in trouuu-ble!"

Every Saturday night, my mother brought me over to Gran's, my father's mother, so I could go to church the next morning. Mommy didn't go to service but wanted me to have God.

My father's younger sister, Crystal, is only five years older than I, and stayed up under my mother when she came around. Probably because my mother was pretty and always smelled real good. She wouldn't leave the house without spritzing her skin with that dark purple bottle of Poison cologne she kept on her vanity. Her scent made me think I was eating a plum and plucking carnations at the same time. Mommy had just washed my hair. My Hello Kitty T-shirt was damp down my back from where the towel had slipped. I sat between her thighs while she parted my curls down the middle, slathered a gulp of Blue Magic on my scalp, and brushed my hair tangle-free.

We had finished dinner more than an hour ago, but the smell of fried chicken still clung to the fibers in the furniture. I knew when I woke up in the morning I'd still smell the grease, because Gran always left it out overnight to cool in an old spaghetti jar. Then in the morning, she'd stick it in the back of the fridge for the next time she fried. I was so caught up in my show, Mommy had to yank my ponytail a few times to keep me facing in the right direction. Jo, the tough girl, was arguing with Blair, the spoiled rich one, over tying up the telephone line, when Gran's front door opened and slammed back into place.

His key ring dangled from his finger, and my stomach curled and then loosened. Daddy filled the living room with the smell of tobacco, and I could tell by his unstable footing that something wasn't right.

"Where you goin' all dolled up?" He only had eyes for my mother.

"Daddy, Gran made fried chicken and biscuits," I chirped, pinching my fingernails into my left thigh as hard as I could, distracting myself from that drowning sensation that happened whenever my parents were in the same room.

They were still legally married, but we had been living away from him for almost a year. Most times Daddy would forget that he had lost his claim on her. I could understand why. Mommy was a looker, with a pixie haircut, eyes big like saucers, small ankles, and mocha almond skin that stayed rich and creamy all winter long. Her hips were robust, like she had honeydews in her pockets. When we ran errands on Broad Street, men sitting in plastic chairs while playing checkers would sneak a peek at her behind. Smacking their greedy tongues like they had just eaten a juicy piece of fried croaker, and a bone got stuck in their teeth.

"Franklin, you take your meds?" Mommy looked up from my head, but her clever fingers didn't miss a beat.

"Heard you was sneaking down to the West Indian club with that yella nigga again."

My mother clucked her tongue.

"Punchy said he saw you."

"Punchy can't see with his glasses on." She fastened the last barrette into my hair.

I was too big for ponytails, but my mother said that she didn't want Gran to have to do anything in the morning but get us off to church. So I had to wear two of them, even though, at twelve, I was ready for curls.

"Go on with that mess, Frankie."

"Always knew you were a whore. Black-ass dirty whore," he chanted, covering the length of the room quick as a cheetah cat. So close so fast that I didn't have time to scoot from between Mommy's legs before he gripped her neck like he was choking a chicken. It wasn't the first time I had seen Daddy snatch her up, but this time felt different.

It was his fishing knife, the sharp one he used to gut and clean the porgies he picked up on Friday nights from the Italian market on Ninth Street. And now it was the knife bouncing in and out of Mommy's chest, arms, mouth, throat, skin, life. Blood sprouted from Mommy like leaks in a faulty pipe.

My voice paused at the tip of my lips. The room spun as my mother pushed me out of the way and I moved, dizzy with confusion. Crystal shouted for Gran and then rushed toward my father.

"Frankie, stop!" She pulled on his arm, and his knife sliced her from the base of her ear down to her shoulder blade. It was the sight of Crystal's blood that made him stop. Not my mother's.

Gran wobbled down the stairs in her flowered housecoat, with one side of her hair rolled in pink sponge curlers and the other side flying wildly, a pad of grease oozing from the back of her hand.

"Franklin, dear God. Frankie. Sweet Jesus. Lord have mercy on this house."

And all of a sudden, the television was too loud. Blair going on about the date she had for Saturday. Tootie rolling in on her roller skates. Mrs. Garrett pulling a roast out of the oven. Then silence. And next came the flashing lights of the ambulance, and my mother being taken away.

I'm standing in the middle of the one-way street looking at the brick row home. Gran lived in the second house from the corner. It was how she gave directions.

"Corner of Susquehanna and Sydenham Street. When you come down the block it's the house with the yella awning. Mmm hmm, second house from the corner, on the left-hand side. Can't miss it."

On the day of the incident, my father stabbed my mother eighteen times. She didn't die, but she was never well enough to come back home. Since I was only twelve years old, I was moved to Gran's house, on one of those can-barely-get-your-car-down-the-block, one-way streets that Philadelphia is famous for. Almost as well known as our soft pretzels, hoagies, (which the rest of the world called subs), and cheesesteaks. Not with that Cheez Whiz mess you see on the Food Network. I'm talking about real cheesesteaks, with provolone or American cheese, fried onions, mayonnaise, ketchup, and hot sauce on a long Amoroso roll.

The white paint around the windows and door is badly chipped, and the railing slopes to the right side. I slip my key in and unlock the door. I know Gran's schedule as well as she knows mine. When I step into the living room, I know that dinner is ready.

The house is railroad style, with each room running into the next, and from the doorway I can see the entire narrow house. Gran is reading her Bible at the dining room table. She can see me too, and her face spreads into a smile as wide as the Mississippi River.

"Dinner's on the stove. Made your favorite. Roast beef and mashed potatoes."

"How come you didn't have the chains on the door? You're always complaining about how dangerous it is around here."

"Oh, gal, hush that fussing and go make us some plates. I'm hungry. Ain't had nothing in my stomach all day." She grins, all gummy. She doesn't have her teeth in, which means she hasn't been out of the house today. I lean in for a hug. She reaches back from her chair.

"Go on now." She pushes me away. Never been one for a lot of affection. "Don't put too much roast beef on my plate. Hard for me to chew."

I walk back into the living room and put my purse on the side of the sofa. It's still covered in the plastic slipcover from my childhood. The kitchen is tiny. Only enough room for what's necessary. I rinse my hands at the old porcelain sink that has a deep rusty ring around it. I tighten the knob, but a slow drip still slips from the faucet. Two baby roaches scurry across the counter. I swat at them with my hand and rinse them down the drain. Welcome home.

The dining room table is covered with God knows what. I move a few piles onto the piano to make enough room for our plates.

"What is this stuff?"

Gran moves the potatoes around on her tongue. "Crystal's junk. She keep coming around dumping, talking 'bout she goin' to come back and get it. Never do. I gotta mind to toss all of her mess in the garbage, that girl causing me so much trouble. Got the feds talking about taking my little money to pay her debts."

I fork the roast beef into my mouth and just let the meat rest on my tongue.

"Like butta, baby," Gran teases me, and all I can do is nod my head. Gran's food is real soul food, and it does what it's supposed to do—make me forget my burdens and lighten my mood.

"Whatcha got to drink?"

"You can grab me a beer. There's one in there for you too."

I open the refrigerator and Gran's got a four-pack of Schlitz Malt Liquor sitting there like Preston would have Stella Artois.

I carry two back into the dining room.

"You get me a straw?"

I take it from my pocket and put it with her beer.

We sip. It's some nasty shit, but I like the buzz I feel in my head and I sip some more.

"So why the wind done blown you to my doorstep?"

"Nothing worth talking about now." I sip some more. "What's new around here?"

"You really want to know, hand me my cigarettes." She points.

I have an urge to take one but Gran doesn't know I used to be a smoker, so I sit on my hands. She lights, puffs, cocks her head, and opens her mouth in an O. I watch her movements, longing.

"Done told you about Precious man stealing the washing machine. Well, the cops caught him trying to sell it to one of Precious' friends around the corner for ten dollars. Ten dollars! Can you believe that nonsense?"

I shake my head.

"And it wasn't one of those old machines. It's the new front loader. Blood red. Finer than anything I seen, even better than what Mr. Orbach had downtown when I worked for him. Nice. Ten dollars? That fool done gone stone crazy."

I shake my head.

"I got some papers I need you to look over while you here. Important. Don't let me forget."

The telephone rings.

"Hand me that."

I get up for the cordless receiver.

"No, don't answer it. You know I let it ring three times before I pick it up."

On the third ring, I hand it to Gran.

"Hello."

I walk over to the piano and let my fingers trail lightly over a few notes.

"Praise the Lord, Sister Marie. Oh, I'm 'bout fair to middlin'. You?"

I know Gran is about to start in on a good talk, so I take my beer into the living room and look around for the remote. The yellow curtains with the deep gold patterns still hang from the windows, miniature porcelain cats and horses still on the sill, lamp with the jeweled beads still on the coffee table stand, and a stack of Hallelujah records still on the shelf underneath the record player. Gran's house is frozen in a time capsule. Still the same.

I move to the sofa, and that's when I notice there is no cable box. I didn't know Gran didn't have cable downstairs. When I sit down and flip the channels the only thing on is the news.

Headlines: Gun found at Fels high school; student apprehended. Fire claimed the life of an elderly woman in South Philadelphia. Police are looking for five men in connection with a home invasion and abduction in the Juniata Park section. Eighteen-year-old girl stabbed multiple times in Logan at a house party; she's in critical condition. Five-year-old boy is missing, walked out of his mother's apartment at two A.M.

I turn the television back off and look out the window. Two men hurry down the street. A black-and-white stray cat rests on Shayla's bottom step, licking its paws. Her old house that I used to run in and out of all hours of the day is boarded up, as is the one next door to it. Shayla use to have the front bedroom because her mother thought the back one was bigger. When I look up at the window thinking about all the times we shared, I hope like hell she's got her eye on Brave. If Preston knew that I helped her . . . I turn back in my seat and fold my hands in my lap. Sickness for my real home with my real family washes over me and I use my cell to call the house. No answer. Then Preston's phone, but I get his voice mail. I gulp my Schlitz.

Gran played the Clark Sisters' "Is My Living in Vain?" while I cleaned the kitchen and put the food away.

"I didn't know you went to bed so late," I say, following Gran up the creaky, narrow, wooden stairs. She moves slowly, pausing on each step like she's scanning the ocean floor for a sand dollar.

"Jesus," she says, slapping her thigh. "Help me up the mountain, Jesus."

"Why don't you get one of those stair lifts?"

"Cost too much. My doctor tryin' to get me a prescription for it, but even with that it's pricey."

"I'll help with the payments."

"I'm fine, chile. I like the exercise. 'Sides, your husband's money has to send them children to that old fancy private school they 'tend."

I sigh and let her dig go. We walk down the squat hallway. Gran's bedroom is up front, Crystal's and my room is to the right. When I glance into the space, it appears livable.

"I'm surprised our old room isn't filled to the brim."

"I keep it nice for you, case you ever decide to drop in." She leans heavily on the hall railing and then takes the few steps into her bedroom. Her high-back chair has two pillows, and she lets herself down into it.

"Here, untie my shoes."

I kneel in front of her.

"I manage just fine by myself, but since you here I'm gonna let you be my arms and legs," she says with a wink. "'Bout time you came. Now, you goin' tell me why you here?"

I slip Gran's beige walking shoes off her swollen feet and slide them under the chest of drawers where she keeps her everyday pairs. My heart is like a weight in my chest.

"Can you give me something to help me sleep?" I avert my eyes to the worn-out carpet beneath my feet so that she can't see my fresh pain.

"There's a bottle on the dresser, should be toward the front. Called zaleplon. Just take a half if you ain't used to taking pills."

Gran's dresser top looks like a pharmacy, among the many bottles of pills and dusty perfume vials and bottles.

"You never wear the perfume I give you. These are still in the box."

"Well, what you tryin' say, I stink?"

"No, just trying to be thoughtful."

"Old folks don't want perfume, gal. Next time get me something else."

I fumble around the dresser picking up bottles and then putting them down until I find the right one. I shake a tablet into my hand, remembering the one I stole from her when I took that bus ride to Virginia. I leave the memory right where it stands, and head down the hall to the bathroom. When I lean over the sink, the recollections have followed me. I see my fifteen-year-old self in the tub filled with water when Gran walked in and discovered my big belly. Feel the sting of her belt as it lashed down on my wet skin.

It was just after nine o'clock when I crawl between the sheets of the old full-size bed that I used to share with Crystal before she birthed Derell and they moved around the corner. The sheets smell like Clorox and lavender. The bed is hard, nothing like the pillowtop I share with Preston at home. His name on my thoughts makes the tears swell, and I bury my face into the pillow, willing my nose not to breathe, mind not to think, heart not to ache, feelings not to spill.

Soon enough the aid I swallowed takes over like magic, and I fall into the chambers of sleep.

I'm down ten hours straight. When I wake up my breasts are leaking through my nightshirt. I've missed two feedings with Liv and I'm up, into my jeans and downstairs searching for my cell phone. No missed calls. I dial home. Juju answers the telephone.

"Hi, honey. Preston's in the shower but the kids are here."

I know it's a lie. She and I have never been chummy. She would have preferred that Preston married a doctor or a lawyer.

"Did he tell you to use the breast milk in the freezer for Liv? She's weaning off but she feeds from me twice a day."

"Yes." Her tone is clipped.

"You have to heat it on the stove. If you put it in the microwave you ruin the milk."

"I'm aware, dear. Twyla is pulling the phone. Hang on."

"Mommy." She starts crying. "Where're you? When are you coming home?"

"Two, Two-Two, stop crying, my love." I try to keep my voice steady. I miss her like it's been a month. "I'm in Philly right now helping Gran. I'll be home soon. How was school yesterday?"

Two is easily distracted and tells me about a game she played before handing the phone to Rory.

"Hi, Mama."

He's the only one of my kids who calls me Mama, and it makes the dam loosen.

"How are you, son?" I breathe hard, trying to keep the tears that stream down my face from reaching his ears. We talk for a few minutes and then he asks if I want to speak to Daddy. I hear Preston in the background telling Rory to tell me he'll call me later.

"Okay, sweetie, kiss Liv for me and I'll call you later. You know my number, right?"

"Right."

"You can call me anytime, you hear me? You don't need permission from Daddy or Juju. Just dial my number when you want me."

"Okay, Mama."

"Even when we are not together, I love you."

"I love you more."

I end the call and fall against the sofa. I've never felt more hopeless in my life. I want my family back. This ain't right.

TWENTY-FOUR

The Wind Blows Crystals

I'm sitting on the sofa curled in a ball when the front door is strong-armed opened and in falls Crystal.

"Look what the wind done blown," she huffs, sounding like Gran. "Whatchu doing here?" Her hands find the extra flab around her hips.

"Hi, Crys." I stand and hug her. "What's up with the extra hair?" I flip her baby doll, fire engine–red weave with my hand.

"Girl, this is the style in Philly, you betta get with the program. Where's Mama?" She puts her brown paper bag down on the table.

"She was gone when I woke up."

"Damn. I need to borrow twenty dollars from her so I can pay for my son's school trip."

"Mike-Mike?"

"Yeah. They going to the Art Museum or something."

I slump back on the sofa, shifting to get comfortable against the plastic. Crystal opens her bag, pulls out a twenty-two-ounce of Budweiser, and pops the cap.

"You look like shit, girl. What Honeybear do to you?"

"Nothing."

"Where the kids at?"

"With him."

She chokes on her beer and it shoots in my direction. "What the fuck you do to that man?"

I wipe my chin. "Yuck. Say it, don't spray it."

"Ain't no man keeping the kids in a breakup unless you have messed up big time. What you do?" She is shouting, and I want to put my hand over her mouth to keep her quiet, but knowing Crystal, she'll bite me.

"Faye, you better tell me or I ain't gonna leave you alone. You cheat on him?"

I shrug my shoulders and slump farther into the seat. "He found out."

Crystal is practically in my lap. "Found out what?" We exchange looks. The knowing quickly registers on her face. She leans in even closer, like we're in a room filled with people trying to keep this a secret.

"Martin?"

"Would you move over?" I can hardly get the sentence out of my mouth before we hear Gran's key in the door. "Don't say nothing." I stand and walk to the kitchen.

"Hey, Mama," Crystal sings.

"Crissy, come on and get the groceries for me. They at the bottom of the stairs."

"Why can't Faye do it?" She shoots me a look as I walk back into the living room, wiping my hands on a towel.

"'Cause I asked *you*," Gran replies.

Crystal stomps off down the steps, lugs the shopping cart up the stairs, and pulls it into the kitchen. Gran looks at Crystal's bottle of beer and grits her teeth.

"Ain't it a bit early for a clucker, Crissy?"

"It's the breakfast of champions."

"Gon' put you in an early grave."

"Faye's unpacking and putting away." Crystal points to me and resumes her spot on the couch.

I'm happy to unpack the groceries. It gives me something mind numbing to do.

"Chrissy, go get me a Pepsi. Put it in my red cup and bring it upstairs. I'ma go catch up on my stories."

I hear Gran's slow procession on the stairs while I put the three cans of Carnation milk in the cupboard. They must have been on sale. When I'm finished, I stand over the tiny sink and sponge up the few dishes and let them dry in the dish rack.

As soon as I hear Gran's bedroom door close, Crystal pulls a joint from her jacket pocket and waves it in the air.

"Come in the yard with me."

"What if Gran smells it?"

"What are we? Ten? She'll be into her stories. Come on, chicken."

I follow her.

The yard is narrow. Cinder block walls on both sides block the view from the neighbors. There is an empty plot of dirt, two empty forty-ounces, a bag of trash, and two rusty, folding chairs leaning against the wall. Crystal puts the joint between her lips and unfolds the chairs.

Flicking the flame from her lighter, she puffs until the joint catches, and I can smell the fragrance of grass burning.

"So how'd Honeybear find out?" She passes me the joint. I haven't smoked in years but I don't hesitate to take my turn. Two short tokes and I pass it back. Crystal looks surprised when I don't cough. I push out my chest, feeling cool and accepted.

One more inhale and my mouth runs, like Florence Griffith Joyner in the one-hundred-meter dash, with just as much animation, complete with long painted fingernails and outrageous running suits. I tell her everything from how Martin had started calling the house, to my Dames performance and Preston practically yanking me offstage in front of a room filled with important women.

"I haven't even dealt with the Dames yet. I can't."

"So why did you leave?"

I turned. "He said if I didn't he was going to throw my stuff onto the street."

"Damn, he's mad. Why he so mad, Faye? It don't seem that big of a deal. So your ex called. So what?"

I take one last puff of the joint and then drop it when it burns my fingertips. "He thought he was my first."

Crystal falls out of her seat, jumps up, and starts running around in a circle. "Git the fuck out of here." Her belly wiggles.

"Shhhh." I tug her back into her seat. "I don't want Gran coming down here."

"Mama ain't hobbling back down those stairs until dinnertime, and since you here, she might want room service." She lights a cigarette.

"How you even get him to believe that shit?"

"I din't tell him I was a virgin; I just never told him I wasn't."

The backyard is shaded and cool. I like the floaty feeling that's come over me, and I slide my face toward the sun.

Crystal settles back down. "Remember that time that I tried to burn your hat string to shorten it, and accidentally burnt your ponytails?"

I smile.

"Mama wore my ass out for that one."

"Served you right. My hair was lopsided for two years."

"God shoulda gave me some of that hair anyway. Didn't seem fair that you had so much and I had so little." I suspect that she means more by it than just hair. She touches the scar Daddy's knife gave her.

"Well, you got plenty of it now." I lighten the mood.

"That's right, it's mine. I bought it."

Crystal stands and puts the chairs back against the wall.

"What Mama cook? I'm hungry as a hostage."

"Roast beef."

"Nice. Make me a plate," Crystal orders.

Gran's microwave gets hot fast and I have a chuck of roast beef in my mouth when Crystal picks up the remote and flips to Maury. A woman is on television telling some dude with gold teeth that he is her baby's daddy. The man gets up in the woman's face, and security has to pull them apart.

"How can you watch this?"

"Girl, I was almost on the show. I didn't tell you?"

"No."

"Mike-Mike's father agreed to go, but then changed his mind at the last minute. Fool ain't want to be embarrassed. Mike looks like Bootsy's dumb ass done spit him out."

Crystal keeps yapping, but her voice gets smaller and smaller in my head as I daydream about being in another place. About my reality not being what it is, and then I hear his name.

"Martin. You want it?"

"Want what?"

"Girl, you ain't even listening to me. Got me carrying on and shit. Never mind then." She folds her arms across her mountainous breasts.

I sit up, snapping to attention. "What did you say?"

"Martin is staying at the halfway house that my ex-boyfriend use to be in. He's only going to be there another week or so. The place so overcrowded the transition ain't long. I got the address if you want to find him."

Damn right I want to find him and give him a piece of my mind for ruining my life, again.

"Yeah, give it to me."

Crystal scribbles on the back of Gran's electric bill. She finishes off her beer and then burps.

"I gotta go. My son be outta school soon. I'll bring them around so you can see them. Mike-Mike tall as you. Eating me out of a house and home."

I stare at the address as Crystal shuts the door softly behind her. Then she opens it back up. It's loud as it slides across the floor.

"Oh, you gonna lend me the twenty?"

I sigh and go to my purse. I have the five one-hundred-dollar bills that Preston gave me, a ten, and a five. I can't trust Crystal to bring back my change, so I thrust the fifteen dollars on her and tell her that's all I have. She snatches it up quickly and shuts the front door.

Once Crystal is gone, all I can think about is confronting Martin. He's lucky that I ain't one of those shooting girls. But I can fight. And I will.

TWENTY-FIVE

The Halfway

I manage to sleep through the night without taking the other half of Gran's sleeping pill. Perhaps it was the residue of marijuana in my system, but I sleep eight uninterrupted hours on the hard bed. When I wake, my breasts are engorged and I ache for the feel of Liv against my skin, for Rory's smile, Two's bossy laughter. And Preston's forgiveness.

It's my first shower in three days. Under the warm water I roll my forefinger and thumb back along the edge of my areola until the milk lets down. It spurts against the curtain in a stream. After a few minutes I am relieved, and my breasts retreat to their normal C cup size. My head pushes into the water, and it rains through my hair.

Gran's bathroom is large for the size of her house, but I hate the dated, wall-to-wall orange carpet on the floor. My footprints stay as I pad toward my temporary bedroom. I rummage through my bag for something decent to wear. A black T-shirt dress that stops at the knee and a pair of sling-back sandals. It's the best I've looked in days. I pin my wet hair into a tight bun so that I'm all eyes and face. I even smear on a little mascara, eye shadow, and blush. When I look into the mirror that's still fastened to the inside of the closet, I smirk at how cute I am with just a little effort.

I thought you were going to pulverize him. Why do you care what you look like?

I roll my eyes and head downstairs. In the kitchen, I fix Gran two boiled eggs and percolate the coffee. I haven't used a percolator in years, and it takes me a minute to remember where to put the grinds and water.

Gran's weight shifts back and forth on the stairs long before she appears. When she makes it to the dining room table, I have her eggs and coffee.

"You ain't boil the eggs too hard, did you? Still like mine—"

"Runny, I know, Gran." I toss her my grin.

"Where you heading lookin' so nice? Gonna see your mom at the nursing home?" She lowers herself with heaviness into the seat. "Hate to think about her up there not knowing her family from the nurses. Don't make no sense." She smacks her tongue. I know that she still blames herself for her son turning my mother into a vegetable.

My grin fades. "I have a few errands to run. You need me to do anything?"

Gran reaches into her bra and pulls out a folded piece of paper. "Here."

I unravel and read.

- Pay the electric bill
- Play my lottery numbers: (boxed 50) 5333, 2016, 318, 116, 625 (super boxed) 927
- Go to Sister Marie's and pick up my twenty dollars
- Buy a four pack of Schlitz and some unsalted Planter's peanuts

"When did you write this?"

"Last night. Supposed to be damp today and I don't do so good in cloudy weather. Sister Marie expecting you." She peels the first boiled egg in one long motion, and then rubs it with her fingers to make sure she didn't leave any shell.

"Where's the bill?"

"Hand me my purse."

I get up and see the electric bill on the coffee table with Martin's address scribbled on the back. I hand Gran the bill.

"Whose address is this?"

"That's Crystal's handwriting."

Our eyes meet.

"Here," she digs in her bra and out pops a little black purse. "Put fifty dollars on the bill and bring me back a receipt. The check-cashing center is on the corner of Thirty-Third and Dauphin. Right there in Strawberry Mansion. You remember how to get there?"

"Of course."

"Ain't been here in so long, don't lose your way."

She adds two more stops to the list before I leave.

"And lock your car when you get out. This ain't those suburbs you in."

I navigate my way to the check-cashing center and take care of Gran's electric bill and play her numbers without a hitch. It's Sister Marie's house that has me driving in circles. The sun may not be out, but with the humidity, it feels like ninety degrees. Even with the AC on, my knees are sweating. Frustrated, I pull over in front of the KFC on Girard Avenue and plug her address into the GPS on my mobile phone.

It's late afternoon when I finish Gran's bidding. She's upstairs into her Bible when I return.

"Are you going to church tonight?"

"Naw, I ain't feeling so hot. Pour one of those beers over a few ice cubes and bring me a straw."

After I fetch her beer, I freshen up, retouch my makeup, and tighten my hair. I'm ready for the showdown.

It's cooler outside, but the dip in temperature does not tranquilize my mood. I take Broad Street to Vine, and then floor it on the Schuylkill Expressway. By the time I weave into and out of traffic on Market Street, I have worked myself up in a two-sided conversation, with me playing both parts. I have not been to West Philadelphia in years, and I'm baffled that a halfway house would be a few steps from the University of Pennsylvania's campus. This section of the city has always been a mecca for students, with trendy shops and high-end apartments. It doesn't take long to find a parking space, and I slam my car door to release the pent-up anger. The house is a stone single, with a driveway on both sides and a wide front porch. As soon as I touch the bell, a woman wearing a white blouse appears. I state my business.

"You can wait here. He'll be right out."

When the door closes behind her, I see a gap-toothed man in need of a haircut peering out at me. I ignore him. No time for distractions. There is a rocking chair against the front railing but I opt to stand, then pace. It feels like ten minutes have passed before I hear the door crack open again. I deliberately give him my back then turn slowly, ready to slaughter.

"There she is." Martin's baritone voice sings to the tune of "Miss America." It was how he'd greet me in the alley of the church before we'd sneak away. When I turn to face him, my cheeks have betrayed me, blushing cherry.

Martin is as clean as a bill of health. I don't know how he has managed to dress so well under his circumstances, but he looks almost like he was expecting me. Dry cleaner's creases pressed hard into his navy slacks, white shirt fresh, crisp, opened at the chest. Hazel eyes fastened on me. Martin moves toward me like a man who is used to taking up space, and when he opens his arms, I'm against him.

I have been in his presence for only thirty seconds and already I am gooey, like a chocolate morsel abandoned to the afternoon sun.

"Young Sister." He wraps me up like a present. I inhale to stay grounded, but the aroma of his skin sets me floating. He smells like notes of amber and oak, and it makes me heady.

"Look at you." Martin releases me, his eyes taking their sweet time grazing my body. I feel naked and shy.

"Come." He takes my hand on the front stairs, and we descend together.

Time has been good to Martin. To most men it is, but to Martin it was damn good. His hair had just enough chalk to give him distinction.

"You hungry?"

"I can eat," I say.

"How's Indian food?"

"Lovely."

Martin holds the door open for me at the New Delhi Indian Restaurant on the corner of Fortieth and Chestnut.

"This is one of the oldest Indian establishments in the city. Hope you like it."

"Sure I will."

He shows me to a table in the corner with a view of Chestnut Street, then moves about the buffet like a person who is familiar. I have to look at each dish before I decide on the lamb vindaloo, chana masala, and a few scoops of the palak paneer.

I'm a sucker for fried Indian cheese, and my mouth is filled when the waiter comes to take our drink order.

"The lady will have a rum and Coke." Martin nods to me and I nod back. "I'll have the Coke."

His eyes don't leave mine, and I know in that moment that I will need two drinks to act normal.

Normal, Felicia, normal.

"It's so good to see you, Faye." He leans across the table and squeezes my hand. Oh. The sensation of his touch puddles in my belly, then settles in my groin. I cross my ankles. What the hell is wrong with me?

The waiter drops off my drink and I sip. Martin tells me how he got pinched.

"The last I heard, you were down south helping Daddy Gracious One start up a new congregation."

"Yeah, I was in Savannah but things didn't go as planned. I'm heading back down there in a week to resume my work. I'm really glad that you came to see me, Faye."

"Excuse me."

I stand up from the table, grab another plate, and busy myself at the buffet. I'm becoming swept up in his charm, and I pinch my arm hard to remind myself why I'm here. I work to revive my anger, but when I reach the table his smile makes it disappear like dust.

"Still have the same hearty appetite. Nothing nicer than watching a woman chew."

How does he make eating sound like a compliment? The waiter drops off a second rum and Coke and I slurp.

"Long you in Philly, Faye?"

"Why would you talk to my husband?"

"I didn't say nothing. He was the one jumping bad. But I sure can't complain about the results, 'cause you're here, Young Sister." He reaches for my hand before I can pull away and kisses my fingertips. My hand concedes and he smiles.

"Fine, girl."

The waiter interrupts. "Will that be all?"

I shake my head yes and he drops the check.

Martin places his napkin in his plate and stands.

"Pardon me." He heads toward the men's room. I finish my drink. The waiter is hovering around our table, so I reach into my purse and peel a bill from the five hundreds that Preston gave me. By the time the waiter returns with my change, Martin strolls over.

"You didn't have to pay, but thanks, Faye." His hazel eyes touch mine as he helps me from my seat.

We walk out of the restaurant onto the busy street. The sun is sinking in the sky, giving off a beautiful orange and pink hue. We round the corner, and there is a trumpet player tearing up the Rihanna song that's played every five minutes on the radio. The air is cool enough for a light sweater, but my skin is tepid. Our conversation jumps around, and before I know it, we've walked seven blocks and are standing in front of an apartment building.

"Come in a minute?" he pulls a key from his pants pocket.

"Whose place is this?"

"A friend." He holds the door.

"I better get going. Gran will worry if I'm out of her sight for too long."

"Just a minute."

"No, it was nice—"

"For old times' sake. Please, Faye."

"I guess I can come in for a minute." My voice is soft, timid.

"Man, you really like making a brother beg." He leads the way and I follow.

The apartment is pass-through basic and smells clean. Martin gestures toward the couch and then disappears into the kitchen. When he returns, he hands me another rum and Coke and offers me a cigarette. I know what happens to me after three drinks, and I opt to focus on the cigarette. When I place it between my fingers, he leans in to light it.

I exhale my thank you. He fires up one for himself and then turns to me through the smoke. "So, Young Sister, what have you been doing with yourself?"

I had already told him the bones of it on the phone, so I add in a few years of college life in New York City for color.

"I played a few gigs in New York," Martin ashes. "I wonder if it was around the same time." We go back and forth but our time in New York City doesn't match.

My cell phone starts ringing. I clunk around in my bag until I find it. Home flashes on my screen. I stand.

"Hello."

"Hi, Mama."

It's Rory. The spell is broken. "Honey, hang on for two seconds, okay?" I push the mute button. "Martin, I have to go."

He's on his feet, walking me to the door. "Promise you'll come back tomorrow evening. I'd love to make you dinner."

I undo the locks and turn the knob.

"Beef or chicken?"

"Beef." I call over my shoulder.

"Rory, sweetie." I shove the phone against my ear and he's crying.

"I miss you so much. When are you coming home? Daddy won't tell me," he whispers.

"Soon, baby. Where are you?"

"In the closet. I didn't want Grandma Juju to know I was calling you."

"Why?"

"Because she said I can't call you every time something doesn't go my way."

"What happened?"

"She yelled at me because she told me to make up my bed and clean my room. I did, but she said it wasn't neat."

My heart burst. I want to get into my car and drive home. I want to hug him. "Rory, do you trust Mommy?"

"Yes." He whimpers.

"Just be a good boy and listen to Daddy and Grandma Juju. As soon as I can come home, I will. Write me a letter."

"I don't know the address."

"Do you have a pen?"

"No, I'm in the closet, remember?"

"Okay, write the letter. Tell Two to draw me a picture and call me tomorrow with a pen so I can give you the address. I love you, sweetie, even when we are not together. Don't ever forget it."

"I love you more." He hangs up.

TWENTY-SIX

The Mountains Are High

The tears fall freely on my drive back to Gran's, and the effect of the alcohol wearing off adds to my torment. What type of mother am I to leave my cubs?

But Preston told you to go.

So fucking what? I'm no better than—

Your mother?

Shut up.

I take Belmont Avenue through Fairmount Park, drive past the plateau, the spot Will Smith describes with fond memories in his famous song "Summertime." It was where the famous "Greek Pic Niks" used to take place every July. Gran would never let me go, because before the weekend was over someone always got shot and some girl got raped. Crystal went behind Gran's back and would come home with long tales, and rolls of 35mm shots of the freakiness that went on.

I put my blinker on, turned onto the Strawberry Mansion Bridge, and then over to Cumberland Drive. It's easy to get from West Philly to North Philly through the park, and when I make a left onto Ridge

Avenue, I see the Dell Music Center. It makes me think of my mother, and how she used her pretty to get us into the amphitheater to see Diana Ross perform. My mother, Lanette Hayes, was always a great flirt. So when she opened her eyes fully, turned them onto the burly man at the gate, with her Louisiana accent exaggerated, he was a victim of her will.

She balked, "Some horrible man pushed me down on the ground, held his hand to my throat, and then snatched our tickets." She ran her fingers through her hair with her bony wrist, like she was pulling herself together.

"Come with me, ma'am," said the man wearing the black security polo. Mommy kept squeezing my hand as he escorted us past all the people and up to the front row.

"For your troubles, ma'am."

Mommy patted his wrist and gave him her eyes again as a thank you.

I was so close to Diana that I could see her Adam's apple bob. She sang all of my favorites, "I'm Coming Out," "Missing You," "Love Hangover." My mother lost her mind when she sang the theme from *Mahogany*. "Ain't No Mountain High Enough" was next, and that's when she tugged on my ear and whispered,

"Ain't no mountain high enough to keep me from you, baby. I'll always be here for you. Never forget it."

Two weeks later she was taken away from me on an ambulance stretcher.

Dauphin Street leads me all the way to Fifteenth, and then I have to come back around to Sydenham Street, since it's a one-way. As I lock up my car, I'm rubbed with how this separation will damage the children. I've worked so hard to make them issue-free by watching them with hawk eyes, giving them all that they need. And now this will be their issue. My mother was a liar, and now so am I.

I push open the front door. The house has a hum to it. Gran is already in bed. I want to call Preston, but I'm afraid of what hearing his voice will do to me, so I take a Schlitz from the fridge and carry my phone out to the front steps. The steps are smooth and cold against my dress. The street is quiet. None of the kids that I grew up playing with live here anymore, except for Precious down the street. But we don't have anything in common, haven't since I fled. I instant-message Preston.

How are we going to do this?

Two minutes later he replies.

You're a liar.

And you're perfect? The kids miss me.

I know.

I want to come home. We need to talk. Call me.

That's not a good idea.

I'm angry.

Why are you acting so over the top?

Our whole marriage is built on a lie.

I'm coming home.

Please stay where you are, for the children's sake. Let's not make this ugly. I'll call you when I can. Good night.

I stare at the phone until my vision is blurry and then power it down. The tasteless beer is finished and I feel restless. I suddenly wish Crystal had left me a joint. My mind finds Martin and calms. It was amazing how for just those few hours that we were together my discomfort had retreated. He has the same ability he had when I was fifteen. Underneath Martin, in the back of the car, in his bed, the sting of losing my parents disappeared. The potholes were filled and I'd forget that my life was a blistering sore, if only in those moments.

TWENTY-SEVEN

The Runaround

Angst chased me all night in my dreams. I woke up feeling like I wanted to stay with the bedspread over my head until the nightmare that was now my life lifted. The only reason I threw my legs over the side of the bed was because I didn't want to answer to Gran. She had a dislike for lazy. My hands cup my breasts. Liv's milk didn't come in as heavily as before, and I know it's because I'm drying up. I'm an old prune. I can't think about anything but home, and I bite my knuckles in attempt to get myself together.

But this is what you wanted. Freedom.

Not like this.

I throw on a robe and head downstairs. I dial the house, but it rolls to voice mail. I leave a message for the kids. My voice is a fake cheer.

"Hi munchkins, it's Mommy. I miss you guys and I hope you have the best day ever. Please don't forget to put your toys away and brush your teeth. Call me tonight so I can sing you a bedtime song. Love you."

I try Preston's cell phone but he doesn't answer. Why won't Preston talk to me? How the hell are we supposed to work things out? I hear Gran on the steps and I chase away my feelings by percolating her coffee and boiling two eggs.

"Morning."

"Hey, Gran," I call from the kitchen. When I carry her cup and plate into the dining room she is sitting in her chair, pressed out and polished.

"Where are you going all dolled up?" I ask. She's wearing a red button-down sweater with a feathered broach, her hair is in pin curls, and she even has on blush and lipstick.

"To the doctor's office. And then this evening Mr. Scooter coming by to take me to the All You Can Eat Buffet. They just built a new one up on Roosevelt Boulevard."

I hand her the brunch I've made.

"No eggs for me today, just the coffee with no sugar and a lot of cream. I don't want the doctor to say my cholesterol is too high. I'll save all of my eating for the buffet." She laughs, and I see that she's put her teeth in. Gran looks pretty and happy today, and I borrow a little of her sunshine and force a smile back.

"You ready to talk yet?" She looks through me like I'm made of Plexiglas.

I shake my head no.

"Always been like that, walking round here like you ready to bust. Ain't good. Better when you get stuff off your chest, gal." She gives me her Gran look.

I shift my weight.

"Planning on going to see your mother?"

"How are you getting to the doctor's office?"

"You going to take me. So run along and get dressed. Should be dressed anyway, it's almost ten."

Getting Gran to the doctor's is no easy feat. I'm driving the Nissan, which is ten years old and low to the ground, so just getting her into the car is an ordeal. When we arrive at Temple University Hospital, she wants me to drive her to the front and then meet her upstairs, but she doesn't tell me where upstairs. Then, of course, she doesn't answer her ancient flip phone until I call for the eighth time.

"Where are you?" I'm exasperated.

"Gal, I thought something was wrong. I told you fourth floor." And she hangs up without saying good-bye, like I'm inconveniencing her.

My thin blouse clings to my sweaty skin, and I am flipping through *Lucky* magazine when Gran shuffles out. She is smiling and the doctor is behind her.

"This here is my grandbaby. Down from New York City. She's an actress. Had a commercial run in the Super Bowl."

"Oh, you're the one your granny is always bragging about."

I go pink and take Gran's arm. "Nice meeting you." I stretch my hand. His is chapped and calloused.

"See you in six weeks, Ms. Hayes."

As we walk out, I look back to make sure we haven't left anything, and everyone is looking at me. I bet they are thinking, *is she really famous?* I smile as big as I can, and let them wonder.

In the elevator, Gran leans against the back wall.

"Are you tired?"

"No, just catching my breath from all the poking and prying. I'll be fine. I need to make a few quick stops before we go home."

Of course she does, and I wonder again how she does all of this when I'm not around.

By the time we get home, the sun has meandered to the other side of the street. Gran and I have only been in the house for five minutes before the front door drags across the wood floor. Crystal walks in, singing.

"Friday night, just got paid."

Behind her are my young cousins. They've sprouted up like cornstalks. I hug them both and try ruffling their hair, but Crystal's oldest boy is taller than me.

"How old are you now?" I eye him.

When Derell answers, his eyes smile same as when he was a boy. "Just turned twenty-one."

I slap my hand across my forehead. Damn, time flies.

"Mike-Mike just turned eight, not that you sent him a birthday gift," Crystal snares at me. "You can give him a few bucks now. I mean damn, Faye, don't be so cheap. He's a kid, for Christ sake."

"Crystal, stop all that mess, you hear?" Gran calls from her spot at the dining room table.

"Mama, why you always taking up for her?"

"Girl, hush, I say."

Crystal crosses her arm over her big breasts and stomps her foot. Her weave needs combing, and her jeans are too tight because her gut is wiggling under her red shirt.

"Why you running round here in them little clothes?" Gran asks.

"I be back for Mike on Sunday. I packed his church clothes. Derell just stopped in to say hi to Faye. You listen—"

"Where you going?" Gran holds onto the dining room table and lifts herself up.

"I axed you on Monday if Mike-Mike could spend the whole weekend."

"No, you didn't. I'm going out with Mr. Scooter in a few minutes. I wasn't expecting him till Saturday night, same as always." She looks at me.

"I have dinner plans, too."

Crystal looks back and forth between us. "Well, Derell, you goin' have to hold it down until Gran get back. Mama ain't gonna be out long."

"We might go to the casino afterward," Gran reveals, lowering herself back down.

"That's cool," said Derell. "I didn't have plans."

Gran huffs. "Y'all can stay, but don't be tearing up my house."

Derell moves his cap to the back and leans into me for a hug. "Nice seeing you, Faye. How long you here?"

"She 'ont know," Crystal answers for me.

The boys head down into the basement. I haven't been down there, but I assume that's where their video games and other boy toys are. I'm sure it's the coolest place in the house because Gran still doesn't have an air conditioner. The one fan blowing out hot air and one fan blowing in cool air aren't working, and I am a sticky mess.

"Mama, you always keep Mike-Mike for the weekend for church. Don't get new 'cause Faye's here."

"I'm going up to take a shower. Gran, have fun."

She looks like she wants to say something, looks at Crystal, and then holds her tongue. Crystal has flopped down on the sofa and is watching a talk show.

When I come back downstairs, Gran is gone. Crystal looks me up and down.

"Where you going all dressed up?"

"I'm not dressed up. Just dressed," I shoot back.

"Excuse the hell out of me." She rolls her eyes. "Well, give me a ride."

I pretend to be bothered but really I don't care. Crystal is the only woman close to my age that I've spoken to since coming to Philly. I don't feel comfortable calling my mommy friends back home because what am I going to say? My husband kicked me out? Melanie and Erica have texted me, but I haven't responded.

I unlock the car and Crystal climbs in. Before I can pull out of the tight parking space, she is blasting Power 99FM.

"This my song." She waves her hands in the air to some gutter hip-hop that I wouldn't even work out to, but she knows every word.

Here's the thing that drives me mad about the new wave of rap. Don't get me wrong; I can Harlem Shake, Swag It Up, and Chicken

Noodle Soup with the best of them. But the rap that's popular now isn't saying much of anything. There is no story to the music, like when Big Daddy Kane, Salt-N-Pepa, Nas, DMX, and my girl Eve got on the microphone. You could strap in and enjoy a story, get your money's worth. Now the MCs can't even rhyme, and literally I mean rhyme. Michael Kors doesn't rhyme with Michael Kors, Nicki Minaj. That's called using the same word twice. Perhaps she could try rhyming it with pores, oars, doors even. I'm just saying.

"Where are you going?" I ask Crystal once I pull onto Seventeenth Street and pass my alma mater high school, Engineering and Science, at the corner of Norris Avenue. I'm looking at the school like I hadn't seen it in years, and Crystal snickers.

"Yeah, it's still standing. You remember my girlfriend Leefa?"

I nod. She was Crystal's bestie growing up and lived on York.

"Your snootie ass school wouldn't accept her daughter. So she's going to Dobbins Tech in the fall."

I try not to crinkle up my nose at that. I wouldn't send my enemy to Dobbins High School. I remember when we used to play basketball against them and I was terrified that a fight would break out and that we Engineers were going to get our butts whooped. We were known more for our brains than brawn. Dobbins was the opposite, and I can bet the chicken coop that things have not changed.

"Temple buying up everything 'round here. When Mama kicks the bucket and leaves me her house, I'm going to sell to them. Take that money and move down to Richmond, live in a phat house, and start over."

"That's your plan?"

"Yep, that's my master plan. Everybody ain't got no Honeybear like you."

"Whatever." I suck my teeth. Crystal pulls out a pack of banana

Now & Laters and tosses me one. I smile at her for remembering they are my favorite.

"I ain't rushing Mama to the grave. I love her old ass, but when she goes, I'm selling and going too. I've got it all planned, picked out my neighborhood and all."

"Where are you going now, Chick?" I ask her again.

"Where are *you* going?" she asks me again.

"None ya."

"I know you going to see Martin, Miss Fast Ass. You better not be fucking him." She looks me up and down.

"I'm married."

"Ya man ain't come get you yet? He must be mad as a hot tub filled with piss. Damn, how you mess up with a guy like that?" She fiddles with the radio station again. "Wish I could get a man to let me stay home and take care of the damn kids."

It's just like Crystal to marginalize what I do. "That's a twenty-four-seven job. And I audition, too."

"You ain't book nothing since that Super Bowl thingy, and what was that, like five years ago?"

"Two."

"That's what I'm saying. Your ass had it good as shit. Make a right here on Girard Avenue and take that over to Twenty-Second Street. White people done bought all of this up now. Push the black folks out quickly."

I turn onto the block Crystal tells me to, and then onto a side street that hasn't been gentrified in the least. This is, of course, where she's going.

"Right there." She points and is taking her seat belt off before I can get to the curb. "Thanks for the ride. Be good."

Crystal bangs on the door with her fist. A man in a running suit with his eyes half shut and a cell phone glued to his ear feels her booty as she passes him in the doorway. They close the door without looking back.

TWENTY-EIGHT

The Raging War

I get back on Broad Street, taking that to Market. My ring finger itches. Maybe I shouldn't go. I weigh it over in my head, but in the back of my mind I know that I am going. It's Friday night and I don't feel like spending it calling Preston and him not answering, worrying over my children, sulking over home, sitting in Sadville.

When I get to the front door of the apartment, Martin's standing in the doorway with beads of moisture in his hair. His soapy scent draws me in. I go for a hug, but Martin dips his face and kisses me square on the lips. I don't back up or frown fast enough.

"I shouldn't be here."

"Young Sister, I believe in life we are always exactly where we're supposed to be."

"Even prison?"

"Especially prison."

The front door is at my back. Martin stands so close that we are breathing the same air. Just like in the alley way back when, he clouds my ability to think straight.

"I suspect you know a little about that yourself."

I flash to my daily schedule. Every moment tied down to the perfection of my family's life. Moving sometimes as if I'm sleepwalking, but keeping the kids on schedule, never losing pace. Everything for everyone else, nothing left for me.

"I know I promised you a meal but I had a late start. I've ordered takeout. Rum and Coke?"

"I actually prefer Jack and ginger."

"Then you're in luck."

He leaves me for the kitchen. It's not until then that I become aware of the Marvin Gaye album playing in the background. Right away my mind starts comparing real men versus hood boys. I bet the guy Crystal went to see is playing some of that gutter garbage that we listened to in the car, nothing that caresses the spirit and ears. It's Marvin Gaye's voice that carries me to the sofa and allows me to consider removing my sandals. Marvin's voice settles my back against the cushions, allows the tension in my neck to subside, and puts me at ease, not Waka damn Flocka.

"Where did you get a record player from?" I ask. He hands me my drink.

"Some things don't go out of style. I've ordered from Ms. D's. Have you ever had it?"

I shake my head.

"I get the feeling that you don't come home too often. What keeps you away?"

"The memories."

His arm is hung over the sofa, and his fingers make circles on my bare arm. The sensation rushes my blood to the surface. I sip, letting my eyes take a slow stroll up and down him. Martin is comfortable in his skin. The stint in jail certainly didn't wash away his "it" factor.

"So what brings you to Philly now?"

I gaze at him. My eyes are three-quarters closed. I'm in that space of partially here, partially there. My brain's not churning. I'm not thinking about right or wrong. He must have played an oldies greatest hits album, because Al Green's "Love and Happiness" spins, and I feel that Philadelphia soul hit me. I've missed this.

"You are still so beautiful, Faye." He takes my chin in his hand and turns my face side to side. "What happened here?" He traces a thin scar on my cheek.

"When my son was two we were playing in the park and I got scratched with a branch. I was trying to keep him from falling and wasn't looking where I was going."

I'm thirsty.

"I haven't danced in so long. Will you?" He holds his hand out to me. I hesitate, but he pulls me up without me giving an answer. We sail to the middle of the floor, where we sway. There is no awkwardness between us as we glide to the music.

Martin sings "something that can make you do wrong, make you do right" in the same key as Al Green. Our hips stagger toward each other to the tune of the tortured ballad. The horns, bass, and keyboard leap off the turntable and beat inside of me.

"Be good to me and I'll be good to you," he croons at the base of my ear, and I'm glued to this place where nothing else matters. Martin brushes my lips. Before I can object, we are kissing.

His mouth is warm, like just-baked banana bread, and I ooze like peach butter. Martin's hands are in my hair. His eyes are on mine, holding me, caressing me, begging me to allow him to release my pain. I try to resist the tug but I feel him pulling forth his Young Sister while tossing aside the woman I've labored to be.

The delivery guy at the door breaks our rhythm. He taps the bell again and Martin looks down at his feet. I understand and move toward the sofa, reach into my purse, and pull two bills from the dwindling five hundred. Martin carries the food into the kitchen and sets it on the counter. I start for the couch, trying to regain myself, but he catches me in his arms and pulls me to him.

"I love this song."

We dance some more.

My body presses into his chest, and his arms swallow me whole. Bill Withers sings "Ain't No Sunshine," and we cling. I hold on with desperation, like a drowning woman clutches a life raft. That's when I hear the rain, thrashing in thick drops against the windowpane. Martin rocks me and then dips my head. I feel the bulge swelling in his pants. Instead of moving away, my midsection digs against his, and I have to repress the moan. My nipples stretch and strain.

"What do you want, Faye?" His breath heats my neck, and his fingers pull the rest of my uncombed hair down my back. My breasts arch toward him and I know in that moment I have come for my dose.

I am entangled in the same web that he caught me in when I was fifteen, sneaking out of church while Gran was down on her knees praying for my salvation. Martin is the medicine to my pain. He's my remedy. I open my mouth to him and he claims me, like he did when I told him how my father died. Inhales me, like he did the first time I visited my mother at the nursing home and she didn't recognize me. Holds me, like he did when I felt lost and misunderstood. And now that my husband doesn't want me, won't let me see my children, Martin kisses me like he wants nothing more than to make it all go away. And it does.

I drink until I'm tipsy. My clothes melt away. I am oblivious to anything but this moment of sweet, succulent sensitivity. In the middle of our makeshift dance floor, Martin's stout fingers are under my dress, plunging between my lips. I climb. He keeps his fingers there for longer than I can stand, and my suppressed heat airs out.

"Still so juicy, Faye." He's hoarse.

My legs are wrapped around his waist. He carts me to the back bedroom. The queen bed smells like Ivory Soap, and I am against the pillows, spread-eagled. His knees hold me in place as his fingers resume their sweet crawl while his tongue massages my ear. My body dances, escalates, bucks to the beat we share as I feel a quickening light me up. I gasp as the pleasure overtakes me.

"Yes, baby." He dabs my sweat but doesn't let me rest. I haven't caught hold of reasoning before he has stuffed himself into a condom and into me. My pelvis tilts to greet him and welcome him home.

I read in a trashy novel once that the first girl to sleep with a man right out of jail is the lucky one because he's pent up. I wonder if that's what was happening with Martin, because for a man thirteen years my senior his stamina and endurance rival that of a seventeen-year-old. His body buckled around me and squeezed, pressed and pulled at my misery until I am free. Then he stands me against the wall, drapes one leg over my ass, and pounds me until we are both drenched and I feel sweet and pulpy.

The music has stopped. Martin lights a cigarette and hands it to me, then another for himself. The satin sheets lay lazily across my stomach. Too tired to do anything but look at Martin and enjoy the moment of being with a ghost.

"Faye, I need something." He drapes his arm across my waist.

"Not today. Let this just be about me." I puff hard on the cigarette before putting it in the ashtray on the nightstand. My fingers are in his chest curls when I doze.

When I'm shaken awake, my first thoughts are of Preston. Then I see the curly chest and remember I'm with Martin. The sleep has broken the trance, and the realization that I, Felicia Hayes Lyons, has just crossed the line and am an official adulteress creeps in. I think of the woman in the book *The Scarlet Letter* that I read twice in high school, and when I sit up in the bed, it feels like I have a big A tattooed on my forehead.

"I have to go, Young Sister. There's curfew." Martin's leg touches mine and I move away from him like he's fire.

What have I done?

I'm frantic, moving covers, looking on the floor. *Where are my panties?*

I storm off into the living room. They must be on the floor. Martin calls after me.

"Faye," he says my name softly. "Come here."

"I have to go." I'm shoving my unwashed parts into my underwear when he walks in. He's wearing pants but his chest is chiseled and bare.

"Faye, stop." He's standing next to me, pulling me into his arms. His touch calms me. I relax against his nakedness and pause. He grabs my chin and holds my eyes to him.

"No one has ever meant what you mean to me. I'll protect you and our secrets."

TWENTY-NINE

The Other Side

In the Nissan, I can smell Martin everywhere, feel him everywhere. It's as if he has seeped into my pores and reclaimed me. I
can't remember being this sore, since losing my virginity in the back
of the car.

The bars and restaurants are closed for the night, and there aren't
many cars on the street as I make my way back to North Philly.
When I slip into Gran's house, I fall into my bed without showering. I sleep for the first time since I arrive in Philadelphia with no
substances or aids. But guilt is a cognitive emotion that can sometimes be born slowly. Like the first moments a fetus takes hold of
a woman's belly; she doesn't know the tiny dot is there but it is
growing.

By morning, the remorse is so large in my throat I can barely eat.
I have a guilt hangover. What have I done? I've missed my morning
call to the kids and by the time I ring the line, Preston answers the
telephone.

"Hello," I say and then look down at my phone to make sure I
have the right number.

"Hey." Preston's voice is distant.

"Hey." I'm not prepared to talk to him and my mind goes blank of what to say.

"The kids left already for their activities with Juju. Rory tried calling you last night but you didn't answer."

"I went to a movie." The lie rolls from my tongue.

"Living it up."

"Making do. I want to come home."

"No."

"Why're you punishing me?"

Preston sighs deeply. "Honestly, I'm not sure what to do with you."

"What to do with me?" my voice rises. "Preston, I am still your wife. Stop making this more than it is."

"I don't trust you. For all I know you could be sleeping with the dude right now."

I blink in succession.

"You could have been seeing him through our whole marriage. Why didn't you mention you had a man?"

"Preston, haven't you had women before me?"

"Yes, and I've mentioned them. Sadly, you didn't think to pay me the same courtesy."

"Oh, stop it."

"I didn't marry you with you thinking I was a virgin, did I?"

"You believed what you wanted to believe."

"I believed what *you* wanted me to believe. I've got another call." He hangs up in my ear.

I hold the phone for so long my knuckles ache.

THIRTY

The Sunday Truth

Gran is playing Hezekiah Walker in her bedroom. I have never heard this song before, but a connection happens in the soul. The beat feels like silk on my skin, in my ears, and pumps my heart. When my eyes open, I do not think about anything going on in my life. I just feel the words reach down for the aches in my heart. My shoulders start moving and my feet are on the floor. I don't censor myself, and my hands fly in the air. My fingers snap and my neck twirls from one side to the other. I'm so wrapped up in the magic that I don't hear Gran until she's in the doorway.

"Every praise is to our God. He is merciful. God is your healer, your deliverer. Bathe this child in your blood, Jesus." Gran stomps her foot and shouts, "Hallelujah!"

The power continues to move through me. Gran is all worked up and puts her hands on my back and prays over me some more. I go with the flow, with the rhythm, with the moment, and when she says "Amen," I feel peace. Gran gives me a pat.

"That was just a prelude. Wait till you get to church. It ain't like you remember. The young folks done took over." She chuckles.

"I'm not going to church, Gran."

"Baby, ain't nothing like fellowship to lift you up and away from that devil. You see how that music moved you? You'll really feel the presence of the Lord in the sanctuary."

I haven't stepped foot in Gran's church in almost twenty years, and no matter what that song made me feel, I'm not breaking my record today.

"I can't, Gran. I have some errands to run."

She sighs, reaches down into her bosom, and pulls out a crumpled list. "In that case, I need you to ride up to the Acme on Red Lion Road. They have Perdue chicken breast on sale for a dollar ninety-nine a pound. Can you read my writing?" She hands me the list.

I nod.

"The money will be under the flowered place mat on the dining room table downstairs."

"Okay."

"Soak the chicken in some salt water to get the blood out and I'll do the rest when I get home. Ms. Marie gon' carry me to church."

My mind drifts to Martin and the other night. The aftertaste of sex colors my cheeks.

Gran catches me. "What you thinking 'bout?"

"Nothing."

She peers at me again. The corners of her lips frown and then she turns out of my room, humming to the gospel hymn coming from her bedroom. Shame seeps from my skin. I've broken my wedding vows, and my family is split at the seams. It's my fault. Grief weighs down on me like mud. When I hear her lower herself into her chair, I walk down the hall and start the shower. The water runs good and hot before I pull the curtain back and step in. It's too warm but it seems right to suffer.

As I move the cloth over my belly, I remember Martin's touch. The way he moved against my body. That man sure knows how to make a woman feel unforgettable. I up the water even hotter and plunge my head under the stream. I've crossed the line, and if Preston doesn't come to his senses soon I'll be miserably worse.

Martin is leaving after tonight and I've promised to see him one last time. It's wrong, but he said he had something important to tell me. While I'm out shopping for Gran, I'll buy something cute to wear for our goodbye.

I spend the late morning doing Gran's bidding and then stop at the Macy's on Cottman Avenue in the Northeast. On the sales rack, I find a cute skirt and low-cut top. Satisfied, I drive down Roosevelt Boulevard, the same boulevard that brought me into Philadelphia a few days ago. I'm overwhelmed by an eerie feeling. What if this is it? What if Preston never lets me come back home? What if I'm banished from my family forever?

Then they'll grow up without a mother just like you and look at how that turned out.

This has to blow over. Preston can't keep this up much longer. My family needs me.

Of course he can. What's so special about you? And this is what you wanted. Freedom. Remember?

I turn up the radio and drown the *damn voice* from my head.

When I get back to Gran's, Crystal is asleep on the couch. The floor creaks as I walk into the dining room, and she looks up.

"Thought you was out."

"I was and now I'm back."

"Were you with Martin?"

I drop the bags on the floor and turn my body toward her. "No."

"Well, when you see him, tell that fool he still owes me twenty dollars."

"What are you talking about?"

"He was supposed to pay me fifty dollars for your number. Only gave me thirty. Tell him I want my twenty."

"You did what?" I move back into the living room.

She yawns and scratches her nose.

"Crystal, you sold me out for fifty bucks?"

"Girl, stop your whining. I needed the money."

I am almost stunned. Almost, but it's Crystal, same old tired-ass, catty, jealous, stupid, stinkin' Crystal.

"Do you know how fucked up this is?" I'm loud. "My marriage is cracked, he won't let me see my kids, I'm stuck here with you, and—"

"Just the way it would have been if Mama ain't choose you over me."

The front door slides across the living room floor. My knees buckle and I glue my hip to the piano to keep me from snatching out Crystal's weave and eyeballs.

"Praise the Lord," Gran says. I'm not sure if she notices the tension, but she starts chatting us up about the sermon. Crystal picks up the remote and turns on the television. My chest heaves in and out.

"You do what I say?" Gran eyes me.

"Yeah, the groceries are right there. I'll be back," I tell her.

"You having dinner, aren't you?"

"I need some air."

My purse is on my shoulder and I walk out the front door. I can feel my pressure pulsing in my ear, and if I don't keep moving away from Crystal I will do her damage. I pull away from the curb and speed down Gran's little street. The Nissan carries me over to West River Drive, where I park and then walk. The weather is hot, but the humidity is low for a Philadelphia summer day. There is a pleasant gust of air coming off the river, making it a perfect day for outside activities. People are jogging, on Rollerblades, riding their bikes, pushing baby carriages, laughing, talking. Across the Schuylkill River,

I gaze at boathouse row, which consists of about fifteen boathouses that have been there for more than a century. At night the boathouses are lit and beautiful like a Christmas tree. My father brought me down here once, for the Independence Day Regatta. I remember the cherry water ices and salted pretzels we ate. He let me take pictures with his camera. I still have the picture that a woman offered to snap of us. He had his arm around me and I looked startled by his affection.

Truth is I didn't know my father well enough to miss him. He spent most of my life out at sea. I used to daydream about him, though. From snatches of overheard grown-up conversation, I'd picture my father on something like a slave ship. In cramped conditions, damp clothing, little to eat, showering for weeks without hot water, worrying over my mother, and writing countless letters that she'd glance at but never take with her to bed.

My parents married quickly, right before he was shipped out to sea with the navy. I was already swollen like a grapefruit in her belly. I heard her tell Aunt Shelly that she only married him for the benefits.

"In case something happened to him at least my daughter would be taken care of for life."

Their relationship was mostly long-distance, through paper correspondence and a few months out of the year when he was home. After serving for ten years, the navy wouldn't accept his reenlistment because his behavior had become erratic, and he had been diagnosed with stress-related paranoia. That's when he became my mother's problem. They had given him a low-level job at the Philadelphia Shipyard, and he worked early mornings. When he was on his medication he was fine, but when he wasn't, that's when the trouble would begin.

His sun rose and set on my mother's lips, and he couldn't get over her. He'd come to our apartment on Eighteenth and Susquehanna and throw rocks at the window in the middle of the night to get my mother's attention, and then he'd sing his love to her in front of the whole neighborhood.

In the beginning, Gran didn't take my father's mental illness seriously, and said stuff like he'd come around, he'd get over it, give him some time. But time only made it worse. It wasn't until the day of "The Incident" that she saw with her own two eyes how bad it was, and by then it was too late. Crystal got caught with his knife trying to protect my mother and I stood watching like a mute.

I twirl blades of grass between my fingers and try to be soothed by the water and the picturesque view, but that damn girl has ruined my mood. I can't understand why Crystal has to be so selfish. She has always been envious of me. It started even before I moved in with Gran. When my mother was around she would include Crystal in most things, but it was never enough. I often wondered if Crystal was a little touched, like my father. Not a full bottle missing from the six-pack, but maybe a few sips, because her behavior has always been irrational.

One time when she was in high school, she beat up a girl so badly with a soda bottle that she had to be rushed to the emergency room. Why? Because the girl supposedly rolled her eyes at Crystal. She was expelled from more high schools in the city than I could name, and found trouble without effort. I had my one snag, but for the most part I did things right. I learned my lesson but I pay for that mistake every single day. Just because she can't see my scars doesn't mean I don't have them.

THIRTY-ONE

The Last Dance

On my drive to Martin, I let the window down and the fresh air in. The full moon is radiant against the backdrop of night. My mother used to say that the moon ruled my moods because I am a Cancer. Who knows if that's true, but agitation is definitely crawling under my skin. I soothe myself with thoughts of seeing Martin for the last time. I've abandoned my plans to be especially cute tonight, because I don't want to go back to Gran's and risk running into Crystal, so I'm still wearing jean shorts and the V-neck shirt I slipped on this morning. I stop at Ms. Tootsie's on South Street and order takeout. There is a vial of perfume in my purse and I dab my throat, ears, and wrist, slap a little gloss on my lips, and fluff my ponytail.

When I tap the door, Martin opens it. He kisses my cheek and then hands me a drink, Jack and ginger ale.

I sip, tasting the extra Jack. "You trying to get me drunk?"

"Just trying to make you happy."

"I'm a mean drunk."

"Oh, then give that back," he teases. "Did you eat?"

"No, but I brought us some fried chicken from Ms. Tootsie's." I hold up the bag and then carry it into the kitchen. He follows me.

"Thanks, but that's not what I crave, Young Sister." Martin pushes his hips into me, and the drama of my day evaporates. The kitchen is small, barely enough room for two. His hands kindle me. I am pinned between the countertop and his manhood. He talks shit into my hair.

"You like that?"

I don't answer. It's our game. Martin has always known what brings me pleasure, and before I know it his hand is inside my shorts. One finger stretches my thong as the others go to work on softening me. With his free hand, he unzips his pants, and his belt buckle clunks against the linoleum floor. I can't help it, and the sound heightens my anticipation. He shoves me onto the counter. My head bobs against the cheap cabinet. Martin smells like freshly chopped wood, and it's heady as he plays my body with his fingers, touching each note until the pleasure rips through me.

I cry out.

"That-a girl."

My foot is on his shoulder, and when he rams into me it takes my breath away. We find our rhythm and flow. I rest my hands behind me and let him do all the work. This is why our tryst works. Martin has allowed me to just receive, when I'm used to giving it all. With him I don't think, prepare, plan. I just take and it makes me float. When I finally come down, it's hard and heavy and we are soaked in my bliss.

Martin rolls the condom off and steps out of his pants. He lifts me and carries me to the bed, where we spoon. This is all I want, peace from the drama of my real life. A freshly lit cigarette passes between us.

"Young Sister." He says my pet name with such care, I curl catlike into his arms. I feel beautiful and strong. Goddess-like. His fingers move lower and start making circles on the small of my back.

"I need a favor."

I breathe heavily.

"My youngest child, Antwan, is sick." His voice trips. "Really sick. He needs a kidney transplant."

I turn to face him. Annoyed that he has reminded me of his life outside of me when I would prefer to stay in our little bubble.

"I'm so sorry to hear that. How old is he?"

"Thirteen, and he has been dealing with this for a while."

I slide my hips away from him. "What do you need?" I'm sure as hell not about to give up a kidney.

Martin runs his fingers through his wavy hair. "I need to find our child. I need to see if their kidneys match."

I sit up in bed. So this is the something important he wanted to discuss with me.

"We've tried everything. He's been put on the national list, but his kidney is different than most. It's a genetic thing called PKD. We've been through everyone in the family. Our child is the only hope left."

He tries to punctuate his news by looking deep into my eyes, but he can't because I'm gazing over his head at the tiny bedroom window that faces the alleyway. I'm remembering my gas range at home. When I turn the knob to ignite the flame, I'd hear that *tick, tick, tick, tick* sound until the fire caught. Then in a split second, the ember would spark bright orange and yellow with a tint of white at the tip, ready to lick anything that comes into its wake.

Martin dropped that feel-sorry-for-me bullshit into my lap, and now I am the stove. I ticked, ticked, ticked. Swirled and sweltered until my skin felt balmy. The bedcovers absorbed my heat until they felt like they were cooking my sweat.

"So that's what all of this is about?" My words entered the room softly. "All of this fucking, and 'Faye, you mean so damn much to me'?"

"No, you do." He starts to plead, but I kick the covers to the floor and detach myself from the bed. The combustion surged through my body, and my brain added more wood to the fire.

"You want to talk about our child? Where were you? Huh, Martin? I was fifteen and pregnant and you let me go off and have the baby by my damn self. You never checked for me."

"I didn't know where you were."

"Bullshit. I saw you."

He looks at me.

"I came to your house. To tell you I was pregnant. To ask for your help. You walked right by me, pretended not to see me. Like I was disposable. Like I didn't matter. You left me to deal with it by myself."

I see a quick blink in his eyes that lets me know he remembers. He opens his mouth. "I don't know what you are talking about."

"Bullshit."

"Faye, please calm down."

"After I had the baby I went to the same high school that you used to pick me up from when you wanted some ass, but you never came."

"They would have thrown me in jail."

"Well, you should have thought about that before you stole my virginity in the back of a damn car."

He moves to stand, but my internal thermometer has reached three alarms. My look is like a dragon shooting flames, and it makes Martin stumble. All of the sudden he seems embarrassed to be naked and reaches for his pants. He lights a cigarette.

"Where's the child, Faye?" Back to smooth. He has recaptured his composure.

"Fuck you."

I move around the bed and he cuts me off at the doorway. His fingers are on my shoulders.

"Where is the child, Faye?" His eyes are desperate. "Answer me."

"Our baby died." The syntax comes from a place so deep I don't recognize my voice. A piece that had been anchoring me just flew from my throat, and now I'm off balance.

I stagger out of the bedroom and back into the kitchen for my clothes, snatching articles off the floor. And this time, when I can't find my panties I dress without them. I'm at the front door when he recovers from his shock and calls my name.

"Faye, I'm sorry. How? How did it happen?"

"Like you care."

"Don't leave like this. Come." He holds out his hand to me but this time I don't go toward him. I run like hell.

When I crash open the glass door of the apartment building, I am a disheveled sight. I skid out of the parking space and drive to the corner of Forty-Eighth and Market Street. At the red light, the heavy tears stream. I can't see the car in front of me so I turn the corner, pull into the Wawa parking lot and kill the ignition. My body convulses, and the sorrow secretes from the countless Band-Aids I've stitched on. It's the first time I have even thought of that baby as being my child. Like Rory, like Twyla, like my little sweet Liv.

When I was in it, I was so filled with guilt and shame that the baby dying was a relief. I moved on like it never happened because it released me of the agony of making such a costly mistake. A baby would have chained me to Philadelphia, and I would have ended up like Crystal—baby daddies, dead-end jobs, manipulating the system, living off of Gran. Or like Shayla, chasing that street hustle, fast money, always having to stay one step ahead of the game before the rules changed. The baby's death was my ticket out, my second chance. I took it and didn't look back.

THIRTY-TWO

The Low and Lonely

I am a lump in the bed, tightly curled into the fetal position with my back against the wall. A woman who abandons her own child is crud. Rory, Twyla, and Liv deserve better; that's why Preston took them away from me. I am not worthy of being called a mother.

Ghetto trash. Always have been, even when you were pretending to be more.

The voice is right. She has always been right.

Damn skippy, I'm right.

Gran pulls back the covers.

"Gal, get up. Ain't you gon' eat something?"

I hear but I don't answer her. My voice no longer lives in my throat. It left me for someone more suitable. I pull the sheets back over my head.

"What's wrong with you?"

She waits for me to respond, and when I don't, I feel drops of wet on me through the covers, probably holy water. Then she wobbles away. Rain has been falling, and the bedroom is gray. I don't even need pills to sleep; sadness makes me sleep, and I welcome the black cocoon. It feels delicious. It feels like death. It feels like I have sailed over the brink and capsized.

The hours puddle into days, and the days spill into each other. I'm not sure if it's Tuesday or Friday when the vivid dreams start happening. I see slaughtered cows in bathroom stalls. I'm peeing on a lion cub in the toilet. Panic starts building and I realize that the cub is growing underneath me in the toilet bowl, rising out of the commode. I run from the stall but I can't move as fast as I would like because I haven't pulled up my pants. When I reach for the bathroom door handle, the cub is now a fully grown lion and it is on my heels. I make it out of the bathroom and then push the door closed behind me and hold it with all of my might in place. The beast is contained. It doesn't catch me.

Gran is back. "Here, sit up and drink this, girl. You need some strength."

I shake my head no.

Please let me suffer, Gran. Just let me die like this.

"You want me to call an ambulance?"

I nod no.

She shuffles off and I can hear her praying all the way down the stairs and into the dining room. Then I hear a cat meow in the alley and another respond. Sirens whine as they race through the streets, but I can't remember if it's police, ambulance, or fire engine sirens. I went to St. Martin de Porres School until eighth grade. Whenever the nuns heard the sirens of an ambulance, and they could always tell the difference, we had to stop what we were doing and pray that the passenger arrived safely and stayed alive. Maybe I should pray.

Dear God, please strike me down. *Pretty please, God, strike me down.*

More dreams happen. I'm running in every dream, always running, always exhausted, always trying to break away before I am caught.

Then I hear a faint sound. Tiny little pitter-patters on the steps and then in the hallway or maybe it's outside. The bedroom doesn't have a door—Crystal knocked it off the hinges a long time ago. Everything blends. But the tip-tap continues and gets closer. It's on my shoulder, my head, stealing my covers. The little sweet presses continue, and I wonder if it's a dream or if I've gone stone crazy, like my father.

Then I hear the loveliest word in the English vocabulary.

"Mommy."

My eyes flutter open.

"Mama."

They are here. My children, my babies have come to me. They jump on me, climb into bed, cover me, grab for whatever piece of me they can muster.

"Mommy, Mommy, Mommy, Mommy." Two makes a song as she snuggles under my chin. Her hair is in messy braids. Rory is under my arm and Gran hobbles in, handing Liv to me.

"This one sure is heavy. Could barely get up the steps with her."

My breasts swell at Liv's touch. My voice is still gone, so I smile at them through clear tears.

"Mommy, you're not happy to see us?" Two stares up at me.

I clear my throat. The sob frees my vocals. It comes out hoarse. "Yes, of course I am." The backs of my hands sop the wetness from my face.

"So why are you crying?"

"Because I'm so happy to see you."

Rory offers me his shirt. "Here, Mommy, wipe your face." My sweet boy. I do as he says.

Leaning my back against the cool wall, I position myself so they can all fit into my lap. And then the chatter begins as they catch me up on all I've missed in the two weeks we've been apart.

"Guess what?" Two grabs my face. "I took my bathing suit to school and we got in the sprinklers."

"Really."

"Can I have a bikini?"

"No."

"Morgan has one. Please?" She pleads.

"I don't want to go to karate anymore." Rory pulls my arm tighter around him.

"Why?"

"Because."

I ruffle his hair.

"I want you to take me. Juju doesn't know how to make quesa-dillas. She forgets the sour cream."

The conversation continues like this, in a random sequence, with the children cutting each other off.

"Shut up, Rory." Two swipes at him, but I stop her.

And it's almost like being at home.

THIRTY-THREE

The Children Feel Like Christmas

From the rickety wooden stairs, I can smell batter, butter, and bacon. My heart is doing flip-flops, anticipating Preston's long arm draped over my grandmother's sofa, the other hand at work on his cell phone. The kids crowd me as I walk, but I let them. At the bottom of the stairs I look into the living room. No Preston.

Gran has made her famous bacon bit pancakes. I've never given my kids pork, but I get them settled at the table. My ears strain for Preston's voice in the kitchen or even the basement. The kids lap up the bacon pancakes like it's the best thing they've tasted in the world.

"Where's Daddy?" I serve myself a helping. Gran stands in the kitchen doorway with a bowl of grits.

"He said he'll be back tomorrow to get us," Two reports. "He said we can have a sleepover."

"I'm just glad he came when I called." Gran moves toward the table.

"You called him?"

"I had no other choice."

"Gran."

"Are you coming home with us tomorrow?"

I give her my best smile and say, "Two, sugar, let's just enjoy the moment."

"Who wants grits?" Gran has the dish over the table.

"Not me." Two crinkles that cute nose.

"Only Liv eats grits, Gran."

"Mommy, Gran's pancakes taste better than Daddy's." Rory talks with the food falling out of his mouth.

"Rory, you know better," I scold. But I can hardly talk because I'm not doing much better than him, shoving forkfuls of pancakes in my mouth while holding Liv in my lap.

"Preston left the big car for you and took the little one." Gran hands me the keys. "Said you needed the car seats."

"What else did he say?"

"Nothing else. You need to go shower." Gran wags her hand in front of her nose and smiles at me. She has her teeth in, must have put them in for the kids.

I head upstairs with Rory and Two on my ankles. In my bedroom I give them some old dolls to play with and then text Preston. *Thank you.*

A few minutes later he responds. *I'll pick them up tomorrow at three. Why didn't you wait for me?*

I check for his response in between taking my shower and combing my hair but there is nothing. From the looks of it, Two's hair hasn't been washed in what smells like a month, so I put her under the bathtub faucet before combing her hair into three lovely ponytails.

"Mommy, where are we going?" Rory asks as I dig through the bag that Preston sent for snacks and diapers. He's packed twenty Pampers for overnight but no baby snacks. I knew he couldn't do this right without me.

I check my phone again; he still hasn't responded, and I decide to forget him and focus all of my attention on my babies.

"It's a surprise," I say, making my eyes bright.

"Chuck E. Cheese?" he asks.

"Absolutely not." We say so long to Gran and head out the front door. I tell them both to settle in to their car seats and enjoy the ride. We pull up to the Please Touch Museum, which is no longer the rinky-dink museum that my mother chaperoned my third-grade field trip to. The museum has recently relocated to historic Memorial Hall in Fairmount Park, and the building is stately and massive. I glance at the kids in my rearview mirror, and I can tell by their faces that they are not sure if they should be excited or pout.

"Grab Twyla's hand," I call to Rory while strapping Liv's car seat onto the stroller. The line is long, and I can feel Rory and Two's excitement build as we wait to pay our admission. The five hundred dollars that Preston gave me have dwindled, so I pull out my Amex and cross my fingers that he hasn't closed my account.

"Thank you." The women slides four metal pins with the museum's logo across the counter and I breathe a sigh of relief.

"Let's go." I pump my fist in the air like a pirate.

"Where to first?" Rory is bouncing on his heels.

"Let's start with the first exhibit and work our way through." We make a day of it. The kids go crazy in the Rainforest Rhythm section, and we spend most of our time exploring the sights and sounds of the jungle. The exhibit is noisy for Liv, so I kept her safe in the front carrier, where I snuggle her close and tickle her feet.

"Look, Mommy," Two calls to me. She is beating the conga drums. To make her laugh I do a little shoulder shimmy and shake my hips like I'm African dancing. Rory has run across the room with a boy he's just met and together they spin the giant rain stick. My heart is light and free. I dance with Two as a few kids pick up drums. Then we all play the forest marimba with a pair of mallets. Next, we pile into a dugout canoe and pretend to paddle down a river. I'm hot and sweaty when we finish but I feel alive, a feeling I've missed.

Once I have everyone strapped into our SUV, I text Preston and invite him to join us for dinner at TGI Friday's on the Benjamin Franklin Parkway. At the stoplight I hear my phone ding with a message from him.

I'll see you tomorrow at 3 p.m.

I bring my attention back to the children, trying hard not to let Preston get in the car with us and spoil my good mood.

I'm surprised when we step into the restaurant and don't have to wait for a table. As soon as we're seated, Two starts wiggling.

"I have to go bathroom."

"Me too," Rory adds. "Can I go in the men's room by myself?"

"Absolutely not."

"But Mama, I'm big enough."

"Rory, please," I say, leading everyone to the ladies' room. When we get inside, I make Rory hold Liv while I take Two into the bathroom and scoop her over the toilet.

"Don't let her touch anything," I call to Rory.

After gathering my troop, we head back to the table. The kids order chicken fingers and French fries with honey mustard. They are happy and distracted. Liv doesn't leave my lap. Her tiny fingers curl into my neck, and she snuggles her face against my chest. When I try to put her in the high chair so that I can eat, she whines and I take her right back out. I can't believe how big she's gotten.

"Can we have dessert?"

"Let's go back to the house and see what Gran has for us."

Gran is still downstairs when we walk in the door.

"Did you guys have a good time with Mommy?"

"Yes," they say in unison.

"Where did you go?"

Two gives a full account, while I take Liv to the sofa and change her diaper.

"Gran, do you have a special treat for us?" Rory asks.

"I think I can find something." Gran slow-foots it into the kitchen. She comes back with a plastic container and bowls.

"Is this ice cream?" Two holds her spoon to her mouth.

"Sure is."

"This is so good." Rory talks with the ice cream slurping around on his tongue, and I shoot him a look. "Sorry," he says, and swallows.

"It's homemade," Gran says. "Your mother never made you kids no homemade ice cream before?" Her hands find her round hips.

"No, never." Two swallows. "Do you have an ice cream maker?"

Gran chuckles. "No, baby. Gran does things the old-fashion way." While Gran chats with the kids, I go through the bag Preston sent and gather their pajamas. None of the pieces match and he didn't pack Two a clean pair of underwear, or socks for Rory.

"Let's go Pudding Pops."

"Five more minutes." Two puts up five fingers.

Who did she get that from? "No, now."

I take the big kids upstairs while Gran gives Liv a spoonful of ice cream. Once I have Rory and Two in their pajamas, I tell them to sit on the bed so that I can go back downstairs and get Liv.

"But we're scared." Rory looks at me.

"Scared of what? I'll be one minute. Stay together."

"No, Mommy."

"Okay, count to fifteen and I promise I'll be back. Ready, go."

I dash for the baby and back up the stairs before they finish.

"Will you read us a story?"

"Did you bring books?"

"They're in the car," Two tells me.

"Okay, so I'll make up a story. But first go brush your teeth."

"Scared," says Rory.

Honestly, Rory is afraid of his own covers. I walk them down the hall with Liv on my hip while they brush their teeth. Water dribbles down the front of Two's pajama top.

"Uh-oh, I'm wet."

"It's hot, you'll dry fast. Gran doesn't have air conditioning."

"I want to sleep next to Mommy." Rory pushes Two out of the way.

"We're all sleeping together." I stop the argument before it reaches a brew, and then start the story. Tonight I can't think up an original so I tell them the story of the three little pigs.

We sleep on top of each other, but I am awake. Listening to their ragged, puppy-dog breathing and smelling their sweaty scents, willing the morning to stay far away.

But it comes, like it always does. The kids are all teeth and smiles.

"What's for breakfast?"

I don't hear Gran moving about so I assume it's my turn to cook.

"Let's go downstairs and see."

I put the television on.

"Can we watch *Nick Jr.*?"

"Gran doesn't have cable."

"What does that mean?" Two asks.

"It means you have to watch *Sesame Street*." I put on channel 12.

"Awwww, man. That show is for babies." Rory pushes back.

I ignore him and head to the kitchen with Liv in my arms. I decide to make oatmeal for everyone, even though I know they'll complain. The clock is racing against me. It's already eleven thirty when the breakfast dishes are cleaned and put away.

"Can we go outside?"

My stomach shuffles a dull but constant churn as I worry over our separation.

"Put your shoes on."

The kids don't have any toys, so I walk them through the neighborhood for some fresh air.

"How come there's trash everywhere?" Rory asks as we walk up Susquehanna toward Broad Street.

"Because people haven't learned to stop littering."

"It smells funny," Two notices.

"Whenever you travel you will experience different types of environments."

"What's 'envi-o-met'?"

We walk and talk. The humidity is low but the sun is high. When we pass a water ice stand, I stop and buy them each a treat. I carry them back to Gran's and we drip them all over the front steps. Gran produces some chalk and the kids make pictures on the sidewalk. Time whips around the clock, and before I know it, I have to start packing their things. My movements feel heavy as I prepare for Preston to take my children away.

Gran's house is too small and too hot, so we are back on the front steps eating banana slices and grapes when the Nissan pulls onto Gran's block.

"Daddy!" Two and Rory shout together and I lean over the baby bag and pull out the wipes.

"Let me clean your hands and mouth."

"Mommy, please come home with us. Please, I beg you." Two has her hands in the prayer position and I pull them apart and swipe them with the wet wipe.

The car rests in a space a door down from Gran's house. It's the same spot we parked in when I brought Preston home the very first time to meet Gran. I watch Preston. My eyes are starved for his presence and I note every movement he makes. Turning the wheel, opening the car door, the first glimpse of his foot as it hits the tiny Philadelphia one-way street.

Preston smiles at the kids, but his effort to ignore me only gets him across the street. In front of me, he's forced to make eye contact that I nag and pull and suck on until he drops his eyes.

"How are you, Felicia?" He says my whole name, formal, like he's a collector picking up a debt.

"Better. You?"

"No comment."

"Would you care to stay for dinner? Gran is frying chicken. Thighs." My voice tilts toward him with hope. "She's soaked them all night in buttermilk."

His face softens a bit. "As tempting as it sounds, we need to get back. The kids have camp tomorrow. Rory has a project due."

My head hurts. "How come you didn't bring it? I would have helped him."

"It's cool," he says breezily. "Come on, kids, give Mommy a kiss."

"Mommy, I want you to come." Two stands, her feet spread apart, face determined.

"No," Preston answers for me. "She has to help Gran."

My heart rams into my lungs and I run my finger over my nose to remind myself not to cry. I've made it easy by having their clothes at the door. I do not want them in the middle of this.

Preston grabs the bag and tells the kids it's time. Rory wraps his arms around my neck, Two around my waist. I'm already holding Liv in my lap. Preston looks away. Then Rory cries, Two cries, Liv cries, like they are all wired to the same tear system. I pull them all in close to me. My tears are folded behind my lids and I will them not to trickle. We will have all night to bask together at my pity party. Tomorrow, too. Maybe forever.

"I'll be home soon, guys. Okay, please be good."

"But I don't want Juju. I don't like her," wails Two.

"Me either. I want you, Mommy. I want you." Rory holds me so tight I almost tip over.

Preston stands with a lost look on his face. I take pity on him, hand the baby to him, and take both kids by the hand.

"Sweetie pies, I'll be home soon. Very soon. You trust me?"

They nod.

I lean in closer and whisper in their ears. "I promise." I kiss them each ten times on the lips, and then I do the same thing to Liv. When I lift my head from the car, Preston is standing next to me. I can smell his familiar scents. Dove soap mixed with the Caliente man body butter I bought him from Pooka Pure and Simple. He knows what that body butter does to me and I wonder if he's sending me a mixed message. Or worst, teasing me. I close the car door.

"You smell nice."

"It just happened to be in my travel bag from the trip to—"

"Vermont," I finish. It was our anniversary getaway a few months back without the kids and we stayed holed up in the king-size bed and jet tub the entire three nights. "Seems like ages ago."

"I don't think I want to be married anymore," he blurts.

My breath catches. "What?"

He holds the key to the Nissan out to me, and an envelope. I can see the color green peeking through the thin paper with his assistant's curvy script spelling out Felicia Lyons. Delivered like I'm just one of the others on his payroll.

As the items travel from his hands to mine, our fingers touch. Neither of us moves. I look up at him and he's looking at me. The lovely man I fell in love with, the face that I could spend my day gazing at, is a jumbled, broken mess.

"Why," he says. It's not a question, more of an acknowledgment. He gets behind the driver's seat, starts the car, and pulls away. The kids are frantically banging on the back window and I stand in the middle of the street waving until he gets to the end of the block and turns the corner.

I can't bear going back inside my hot prison, so I walk in search of the answer to the question he didn't ask.

THIRTY-FOUR

The Reason Is Not the Answer

I move west on Dauphin until I reach Eighteenth Street. Eighteenth runs me into Diamond, and I pause in front of the Church of the Advocates. It's one of the most splendid churches I've ever seen and the best American example of Gothic revival. The lavish architectural sculpture, stained-glass windows and flying buttresses seem more appropriate for a little village in Europe than North Philadelphia, but that adds to the promise and beauty. It's the only cathedral of its kind built specifically for the working class, and Gran has been a big fan of how they have served the community for decades.

As a girl, whenever we passed the church, she'd tell me the same story about attending the church's first ordination of women. "It was a moment in history. Eleven women became priests for the first time ever in an Episcopal church. "'Fore your time, gal. Back when we women had to fight for every little thing." She'd pat my head.

Little did Gran know but I was still fighting, just in a different way.

I keep going on Eighteenth Street until I reach the corner of Norris, where I run into my alma mater, George Washington Carver High

School for Engineering and Science. My fingers curl around the chain-link fence, and I pull myself as close to the school as I can get. Wonderful memories of jumping double Dutch until my hair turned back kinky, eating hot dogs and soft pretzels from Pop's food cart, starring in the drama club's production of *Grease* as Patty Simcox, hiding books on my lap, and reading during class when I didn't feel like paying attention. The images swerved through my head as fast as a motion picture.

On my first day as a freshman, I sat in the auditorium on wooden pews for ninth-grade orientation. Our principal, Dr. Travis, peered out into the audience and said, "Look to the person on your left. Look to the person on your right. One of those students will not be at graduation with you."

I didn't think she was talking to me. Not even after I left school at the end of tenth grade with a bogus doctor's note saying that I had pneumonia, but was really hiding out, waiting on the baby. I missed two months of the school year. When I came back from Virginia worn, heartbroken, and childless, Dr. Travis's prediction of graduation echoed in my head, serving as a constant reminder that the odds were stacked against most of us. I became determined not to be a statistic.

Not long after graduating from college, I had a role in a short documentary film directed by an NYU film student. The short was intended to bring attention to the poverty cycle of African Americans and was shown at a film festival during Black History Month. The production highlighted the cycle of poverty and why it was so rampant in the black community. I remember the data like we shot the script yesterday.

Seventy-three percent of African American children are born out of wedlock and raised in fatherless homes. When there is no father in the home, children are more likely to grow up below the poverty line, receive a poorer education than their counterparts, and eventually engage in criminal activity. I'm sure this could be traced back to slavery, but the filmmaker didn't connect those dots. He focused on a more seeable culprit called welfare.

The rise of welfare in the 1960s contributed greatly to the demise of the black family. A mother received far more money if she was single. When the woman married, her benefits were reduced by 10 to 20 percent. This made illegitimacy affordable and acceptable in the community. The three most vital components one needs to rise above poverty are education, marriage, and work, and when I met Preston I was more than ready for the upsurge.

I walk up Norris toward Temple University, still seeking to understand why I omitted my truth from Preston. It was those broken pieces inside of me. Those shards of secrets that only stopped speaking when I'd swallow down a happy pill. The *damn voice*. I was afraid that if Preston saw my scars, knew I was a damaged damsel from North Philly whose father tried to kill her mother, got pregnant at fifteen, had a baby in secrecy, and then spent her entire adulthood like none of it ever happened, then he wouldn't love me. Would not want me. Then he wouldn't take my hand so that we could jump over the broom and off the cliff into another world where things were possible, pretty, and had the potential of being perfect. I had already rewritten my history with gaping holes that I filled along the way. Preston was the one who pushed me to the finished product with his flawless ideas of family, and I don't pretend to blame him, because I wanted it too. I had already experienced the other side.

Gran left a plate of fried chicken and collards in the oven for me, but all I want to do is sleep. In her bedroom I find the bottle of sleeping pills and instead of taking a half, I take a whole one. When I wake up the next day I have a sleep hangover, so I take another one. The bed is my comfort, and I cuddle in the leftover traces of my children. As I drift, I hear a man's voice calling out to some woman named Tammy. It reminds me of the commotion my father would cause standing outside of our apartment window, calling for my mother.

I hear a siren in the distance and think of the nuns praying at my old school. The pill takes over and I can't keep my eyes open. It feels nice. Manette. Mom. Mommy. A smile creeps onto my face and I let go. Relinquish myself to the pull of the tide, sleepy water washing over, pulling me back. Way back. Far back.

Mommy and I are sitting on Gran's front steps, the marble and white ones they don't make anymore, the ones Gran used to make me scrub with a hand brush dipped in Clorox and water until they sparkled clean. The renters couldn't care less about the debris that blew up and down the street or the syrupy carbonation that spilled from kicked-over Coke cans.

Mommy and I are sitting three steps from the bottom. Her Poison perfume elbowed its way up my nostrils and put me at ease. She is brushing my hair so softly the bristles barely touch my scalp, and I am eating a freeze pop. Green, my favorite flavor. I was such a nervous child, always on guard, anxious to be the buffer between my mother and trouble. Her fingers in my scalp always soothed and reassured me.

"You know, Sweet Potato, it's not your fault what happened to me." My mother always called me Sweet Potato.

"It is, Mommy. It is my fault. All my fault," I answered in my little smoky voice. It held a quality to it that led most people to believe I could sing. But years in the children's choir proved that I could not. The choir director stuck me in the back, as far away as possible from the microphone.

"You were a little girl. It wasn't your job to protect me."

"But I just stood there and let him hurt you. I didn't even save Crystal. That's why she hates me so much."

Mommy took a section of my hair and twirled it with her fingers. "Can Twyla save you?"

"She's only three, Mommy."

"I know you felt like a big girl, but you were only eleven or twelve, baby. Your daddy was sick. There was nothing you could have done to save me."

She pulled the comb through my hair and it felt like she was dragging out a weight wedged into my roots. I wanted to see her but she kept me facing forward, looking out onto the tiny street. "Stay still, honey, this isn't the time to be tenderheaded."

I took another slurp from my freeze pop.

"Crystal getting stabbed by your father wasn't your fault either." The teeth of her comb scratch my scalp, and she yanks the comb forward. A heaviness lifts from my head.

"Your father committing suicide. Well, that was the city's fault." My head tilted backward as she ran her bare fingers through my hair and then wrung out the ends like she was trying to extract water.

"Martin was your pain medicine. I don't agree for many reasons, but I understand." The coconut oil that she would purchase from the health food store was massaged between her fingers until it liquefied. Then she let the oil drip down to her fingertips so she could knead the oil into my head, soothing all of the tender spots she had created by pushing and pulling.

"The baby, Angel." She whispered the secret name I had given the child. "Let that go."

Somewhere a church organ started the beginning of a song. Mommy pulled at a tangled knot in the nape of my hair that didn't want to budge. But she didn't give up. She held the piece tightly and worked the comb over small sections, piece by piece, until the hair flowed.

Then braids started going through my hair two at a time, like she had four hands instead of two. "Let it go and enjoy your chance at better. A better life, baby."

The organ was playing something fierce, and Mommy, who could sing, started humming while she worked. A church song. "Amazing

Grace." I always loved that song but it seemed I only got to hear it on TV or at funerals. Mommy hummed it, nice-like, happy-like.

"And Preston." I tensed. Then saw some of my hair float down the steps. I was pulled from that space with Mommy by the sound of a bird pecking on the windowpane. It was so insistent that I cracked open my eyes. A beautiful white bird was sitting at the window and looking at me straight through the fan. It held my eyes, moved its head, and flew away.

THIRTY-FIVE

The I Don't Know What

"Cut it all off," I said, sliding my butt into Mr. Stanley's barber chair. Once the bird woke me up, I realized that I had exhausted all of the sleep in my body. There was none left, so I showered and ransacked all of the leftovers in Gran's fridge. Once my belly was full, the decision on my hair was made and I half jogged to the shop.

Mr. Stanley has been the neighborhood barber since I was a little girl. His corner barbershop on the corner of Sixteenth and Dauphin is the one staple in the changing neighborhood and, in my opinion, should be declared a historical landmark.

Mr. Stanley was much older than he was in my memory, but the first person I thought of when I made my decision to chop my hair off. I was surprised that he even remembered me.

"'Course I remember you, Faye. Used to cut your daddy's head before . . ." His voice trailed. "You have beautiful hair, girl. Ladies running over to the Ko-reans to buy hair to look good as you. Why you want to do that to yourself?"

"Mr. Stanley. If you don't cut it, I will."

After a long grunt, he drapes me with a cape, fixes the television on one of those talk shows Crystal always watches, and pulls a pair of scissors from the barbercide green liquid.

"All this hair," he mutters while cutting.

"I'll pick it up and donate it to cancer patients."

Snip, snip, snip. My hair fell around me and I could feel the weights that Mommy pulled in my dream drop to the ground. When I walked outside into the sunshine I felt light and amazingly free.

THIRTY-SIX

The Sift and Shift

It couldn't be put off any longer. Gran had gone to Saturday afternoon service with Sister Marie and didn't say what time she would be back. So that she wouldn't worry, I leave her a note on the dining room table.

I'm dressed in the cute skirt and top I bought to wear for my good-bye with Martin. The clothing still had the tags on them. I brush a little blush onto my cheeks and slide a pink-stained gloss over my lips. When I open the front door, the sky is overcast with clouds, and a dim gray hovers. I consider going back for an umbrella but I don't want to turn away from my destination for fear I may lose my nerve. I pad down the front steps.

"What the hell did you do to your hair?!" It's Crystal, yelling from the corner. I stop and stare.

"You know hoes goin' be callin' you a ball-headed bitch now."

I flick my hand in the air at her and start moving toward my car.

"Just kidding, Faye. Listen, I need a ride."

"I can't."

"Why? You going to see Martin? It's on the way."

"No, I'm not." I suck my teeth. "You need to mind your business sometimes and learn how to stay in your damn lane." I do some serious eye rolling as I turn away from her.

"Come on, Faye, seriously. It's important. It's just a few blocks away."

When I unlock the car, she gets into the passenger seat.

"Thanks. Make a right onto Fifteenth Street." She starts fiddling with the radio station. I push her hand.

"I'm not listening to your crap."

"What's wrong with you?"

"Nothing."

We drive in silence.

"Turn onto Cecil B. Moore. Right there, I'm going to Lamar's."

"You're going to a bar in the middle of the day?"

"Yeah, I heard Ronnie was in there with this trick from down Twenty-Ninth Street. Come with me. I need backup." She starts climbing from the front seat, and a switchblade falls out of her back pocket.

"Crystal, I know you aren't carrying a damn knife. Aren't you too old for this?"

She tucks the blade in her back pocket and starts moving toward the door. I contemplate pulling off. Fighting in a damn bar over some two-bit boy was not on my agenda today. Still, for Gran's sake, I un-buckle my seat belt, feeling obligated to make sure Crystal doesn't do anything stupid. I follow her into the cavernous beer garden. It is dark and bluesy on the inside, with a long bar and a few tables scattered. An early hit by Nas and Lauryn Hill plays.

In the back, I see the same guy who felt Crystal's booty when I dropped her off last week. He has on sunglasses and is posing with some girl against the jukebox.

"What the fuck is this?" Crystal is up on them both, weave swinging.

"Nothin', baby." He reaches for Crystal and holds her in his arms before she can reach into her back pocket. "She ain't nothing, Boo."

"What you mean, I ain't nothing." The girl snakes her neck at him, her bra straps peeking from beneath her purple top.

"Yo, chill." He grabs Crystal's hand and they move toward me and the other end. I guard the front door like I am the police. Crystal bumps the girl with her shoulder. The girl looks like she wants to say something, but it's easy to be intimidated by Crystal. Everything on her is meaty.

"This my niece, Felicia."

"Hi." He looks me up and down, eyes lingering a bit too long. I look away. I've been down that road with Crystal, her man trying to get at me. I didn't need that drama today.

"Niece?"

"Yeah, don't ask." She links arms with him.

"I'ma go."

"All right."

"I can't buy you a drink?" asks Ronnie.

I crinkle my nose and shake my head no.

Outside, I am happy for the fresh air. How could Crystal still be stuck here, doing this? Where were her children? She was never going to change, and it made me want to scream.

Back in the Nissan, I plug in the address on my phone's navigation system and start heading toward the Schuylkill Expressway. I used to have to catch the C bus to Center City, and then the 125 bus. It took forever to get out to Valley Forge that way. Driving is much more convenient, and the hum of the highway relaxes me after that ordeal with Crystal. India Arie's latest hit croons softly from my radio, the windows are down, and the breeze swishes away the nagging dread of what may come.

Valley Forge Homes has always been an intimidating brick building for me. When I was younger, I was scared to death to walk through the sliding glass doors. It tore me up to see my once beautiful mother as nothing more than a space-staring shell. The other patients scared me, too, nodding, scratching, and talking to themselves. It made my stomach hurt, like I could throw up the salt and vinegar potato chips and butterscotch Krimpets that I devoured on my way. Each time I returned to Gran's heavy with grief, I vowed never to go back. I didn't want to see my mother like that, unable to communicate, walk, go to the bathroom unassisted, or feed herself. But Gran insisted that I go, every second and fourth Saturday of the month, and that's what I did.

The Nissan eases into the parking lot, and I take a hefty breath as I remove my key. Surrounding the perimeter of the buildings are well-manicured shrubs and bushes sprinkled with coconut petunias, vibrant dahlias, and bursting marigolds. My mother lives on the third floor. A young woman with a braided bun stands at the front reception desk. She greets me with a smile, clear braces.

"May I help you?"

"Manette Hayes."

"Sign her name and your name here." She points to a sheet for visitors. "Give me one second." She moves to a file cabinet.

"You also have to sign here."

"What is this?"

"It's a record of all the guests visiting a particular patient."

I write my name on the ledger. My eyes scan over the names before mine. I recognize Aunt Stella, my mother's girlhood friend, and Uncle Jessie, her favorite cousin, but there was one name that I don't. Kita Reeves.

"Thank you." The woman takes the ledger from me. "You can go right up."

Who is Kita Reeves?

On the elevator I stare up at the ceiling as the car creeps to the third floor. I haven't been here since Twyla was born. When the doors open I pass the nurses' station but don't recognize any of the staff. The corridors cling to the same smell. Cooked cabbage mixed with disinfectant.

I check the common room first, and find Mommy sitting in front of the big bay window. Her back is slumped and her neck is lulled to the side, as if it is too heavy for her head. Her ponytail is long, but her hair lacks luster and shine. It is mostly gray. She seems thinner than when I saw her last. Weaker. I watch her from the entryway for a while, unable to move toward her. Then she turns her head and looks right at me. My heart takes off. She recognizes me.

"Mommy." I take the few steps toward her. She looks at me, eyes on my eyes.

"Mommy. It's me, Faye."

Then she looks away, and her eyes glaze over like she wasn't seeing me at all. I pull up a chair next to her and stare out the big window with her, trying to push away that unflattering feeling of desertion.

An afternoon soap opera is on the big television hanging from the wall. Three women sit at the table, playing cards. Most of the others are covered in knit blankets, nodding from their medication. Mommy and I sit side by side for a while, neither of us moving. I touch her hand, move in closer, and before I know it, I'm chatty. I share each of my children with her, describing them down to their birthmarks and quirks. I tell her about the dream I had last night about her combing my hair. The whole while, I'm stroking her veiny hand. Her skin is cold, and I adjust the throw over her lap. There were older pictures of the kids in my wallet, and I hold them up to her face. She looks and then looks away.

"Mommy, I know you are in there. I know you came to me in my dreams last night."

Her fingers are limp and lifeless. My nose dribbles, and I wipe it with the back of my hand, trying not to feel sorry for us.

"Time for chair yoga and meditation." A woman with coiled black hair and dressed all in white is standing in the doorway.

"You can come, too." She directs her voice at me with a smile. Her skin is creamy, her eyes emerald green and inviting. I can imagine lying down and resting in those eyes.

Mommy's head bobbles as I wheel her to a conference room on the right where the woman has led us. People in wheelchairs sit in a circle and two attendants stand in the corner. Candles are lit and I can smell something burning.

"What's that smell?"

"White sage. It cleanses the energy in the room."

The place did feel good. Cozy, even. The nursing home with all of its odors and smells evaporated. We had been transported someplace else.

"Welcome to chair yoga and meditation. I am Shira."

I detect an accent but can't place it. I like her immediately.

"Today we are going to focus on grounding our energy. So place your feet as flat on the floor as you can and then push your bellies forward." She demonstrates.

A lady wearing a black wig and a T-shirt that says "World's Greatest Nana" rolls her neck and shoulders with agility to Shira's command. I wish she were my mother or that my mother were her. I adjust the blanket on Mommy's lap, feeling an overwhelming need to protect her. I move a hair from her face and kiss her cheek. I've missed her.

At least half of the patients keep up. The man sitting next to Shira moves to her rhythm with a grin that makes him look like he thinks he is her teacher's assistant.

"Wonderful, Sam," Shira praises him. His face lights bright.

Shira rests her hands on her heart and starts humming the sound *Om*. We join our voices with hers. Then she pulls a bowl and a wooden stick from under her chair and starts playing this amazing tune. It hums and vibrates deep down in my soul.

"Close your eyes, dear ones, as I lead you into meditation. If there is anything that you are still holding on to, let it go. This is a place of healing."

I inhale, allowing my lungs to expand.

"Let's try breathing with our eyes closed and going deep within our bodies for five minutes. Enjoy."

My mind rests. Before I know it, Shira is standing in front of me.

"How was it?"

"It was great. I needed that."

She extends a card to me. "I teach class to able bodies tomorrow night. You should come." She gives me a hug. She feels like the Holy Spirit.

I roll Mommy back to her room. There is a brush on her table, and I brush her hair until it shines. She has a knot at the back of her head, and I make a mental note to ask the nurse about it. A bottle of Poison is on her dresser, and I spray a dab onto her wrist. Her arm twitches and then her mouth curves. I wonder if the scent brings any memories to her mind. I make a mental note that when I return to bring her a fresh bottle. Maybe I'll even bring Preston and the kids with me.

There is a jar of cold cream on her nightstand, and I warm the lotion between my palms and then massage her face, fingers, and feet. I hum "Amazing Grace." She says nothing, looks at me sometimes, but most often just stares at the wall. I work at peace, not expecting anything from her. Instead I bask in her presence. I hum children's lullabies as I work because I can't stop hearing my children's voices, Mommy, Mom, Mama, Mommeeeee.

THIRTY–SEVEN

The Cleansing

The next night I drop Gran off for evening service. She had already gone to morning and afternoon services, came home, had a little dinner, and then back for some more.

"Gran, you haven't had enough?" I say, helping her from the car.

"I gots lot to pray on. Family all shook up." She leans against me hard as she pulls herself to her feet. "You ought to come with me, do you some good."

Not happening.

"I'll come back and pick you up."

"Gal, the only way out of this is the Lord."

I turn to her with a smile that lets her know that I don't want to be disrespectful, but I'm not going. Gran huffs but acquiesces.

The address that Shira gave me happens to be a few blocks north of the church in what they now call the Arts District of Philadelphia. It is a storefront dance school, and I find easy parking right in front. When I walk into the building, the smell of white sage resets me.

From the small lobby I hear laughter drift from the right. I walk in that direction and see a door that opens into a large studio. The room is half filled with people sitting on the floor on top of fluffy pillows, Mexican serape blankets, and yoga mats.

Shira is kneeling in the center of the room, playing a bowl. Her heavy hair is pulled in a loose bun off her face. Her green eyes are on me.

"Welcome, Felicia," she calls, but her fingers never miss a step as she twirls a mallet around the rim of the bowl. The vibration of the bowl unthreads me. Barefoot people pour into the room behind me. That's when I realize that I need to remove my shoes and leave them outside.

"Thank you," Shira says to me when I return.

We all sit in a large circle. Shira taps the bowl three times and then places it back on a metal plate. I can still feel the vibration encircling us. My spirit is alive. The smells, vibe, energy were unlike anything I've experienced before, but it all felt necessary for where I wanted to go.

"Tonight I want to talk a little about finding your purpose."

The room stilled. Most sat crossed-legged with their eyes closed, so I did the same thing.

"There is something that we have all been put on this earth to do. Purpose. We all have a purpose. My purpose is to motivate. What's yours?"

Her question rolls around in my head like a loose pebble. Beyond being a mother and Preston's wife, do I have a purpose? I can't really say acting, because it's not like I'm out pounding the pavement trying to make it happen. More like waiting on a call from my agent, hoping she can make it happen.

"Now, let's begin our meditation together as one." Shira takes a long pause. "As we go into the meditation, I am going to put some questions out into the Universe. Who am I? What do I want? What is my purpose? How can I serve?" Shira words swaddle me like a soft scarf. I feel warm and present.

"Don't worry about the answers to the questions. Just let them drift out into the Universe. The answers will come when you need them." She falls silent. "We will do a twenty-minute meditation. I'll watch the time for you. Enjoy."

I thought I would be fidgety, but twenty minutes felt like three. Shira hit the mallet against the metal bowl. Her husky voice slithered into the room, gently pulling me from the state I was in.

"Begin to bring your awareness back into your bodies."

I opened my eyes and looked around the room. Faces pasted with the same dazed, orgasmic look. I grin.

"Thank you, dear ones, for coming. Go in peace." She bows, and the people in the room start moving slowly toward the door. I take my time getting to my feet, not wanting to break the spell. My hands fall through my very short haircut. I stretch while trying to remember the last time I felt so centered.

"Felicia, don't leave," Shira calls to me.

I sit back down. It takes about five more minutes for her to clear the room, and then she smiles at me. Her walk is tall even though she is petite.

"How was it for you?"

"Nice. Like a bubble bath."

"Are you in a rush?"

"No."

"May I give you a reading?"

"What do you mean?"

"Come, I'll show you."

Shira leads me to a tiny room off to the side of the dance studio. The entrance was covered with colorful sarongs that I have to move aside to enter the space. I am instantly reminded of a Catholic church. The room smelled strongly of frankincense. Or was it myrrh? I remembered the scent well from when the priest used to shake the censer at the start of Mass. When I was at Catholic school we went to Mass a few times a month.

Shira sits cross-legged on a thick, silk pillow. There is a small table between us. I kneel on the other side. She reaches underneath for a black velvet bag. She pulls the drawstring and out comes a stack of cards.

"These are tarot cards. They are meant to give you some guidance." She shuffles the cards and then hands them to me. "Shuffle until you feel your energy in the cards. Until you feel compelled to stop."

I immediately thought of Preston, how much fun we always had playing cards at the kitchen table. Listening to Pandora radio. Me drinking wine. Him some crazy-name beer. Those nights were lovely and always ended in hot, rude lovemaking, and I push my knees together to discourage the feelings that stir.

"Okay." I place the cards in front of Shira.

"Now split them in three piles from left to right. Wherever you feel the natural break."

I do as I'm told. Shira turns over cards until I see three rows of three. She looks down at the cards for a few beats and then starts talking. Her voice sounds different. Deeper, fuller, and even huskier.

"This is your foundation, your past, what you've been sitting on," she says, referring to the bottom row. "This is what you are going through now," she points to the second, "and this is what's most likely to occur if you continue down this path."

My stomach is knotted with anticipation. I've never done anything like this. Gran would be knit and tangled if she knew. But I need this and eagerly lean forward. Shira studies the cards for a while, her eyes almost trancelike as she starts speaking.

"You've been going through a very rough, trying time. But I see here that the worst is over." She points to a card with a person laying facedown with swords piercing his back. "This is the eight of cups. It signals that you need to turn away from something or someone who has been unhealthy in your life. It could also be a behavior or way of life. Once you turn your back completely, the transformation will begin."

She moved to the second row of three.

"This is the tower card," she explained. "You have built your life on ego, and such grounds are unstable. This card symbolizes being broken down to the barest element so that this time, when you build up, you build from the core of your being. This is the hangman, and it's in reverse." She ran her thumb along the card. "This means that you've been feeling restricted in your life, confined. You need to get in touch with these feelings so you can release yourself. It is time to live from your core, not from the peripheral. That's why this transformation seems so challenging."

She picked them up, shuffled, and gave another spread.

"This is called a Celtic cross." She flipped a card over and continued. "Here's the challenge," she said. "The challenge is you. You haven't forgiven yourself for something that happened in your past. Whatever it is, you need to let go." She flips a card and then places a card on top. The card has a picture with cups, a rainbow, a husband and wife with their arms wrapped around each other, and kids dancing.

"Looks like a family tie, tragic, something that you need to wash out of your system. You've been deceptive. But that doesn't have to be the end. Wash it out of your system and make amends. Once you do that, see here?" She flipped another card, the nine of pentacles. "Look at this. The clarity starts to flow. This card means that you can have the life you want, with all the trimmings. But you have to start moving forward."

Tears are in my eyes.

Shira picks up the cards, stacks them back into one pile, and then places them back in the velvet bag. Her eyes are still low, almost hooded.

"I'd like you to lay down here on the rug and I'll give you a Reiki healing to cleanse your aura. It won't hurt."

I do as I'm told.

"There is a strength in you that wants to come through. I'll do my best to clear the blockage."

Shira appears with another velvet bag. This time she shakes three small crystals varying in color and size and tells me to close my eyes. I do, and then soon I'm somewhere else. Floating.

I'm not sure how much time has passed when I hear Shira singing my name softly, and then I hear the beautiful song of the singing bowl and my eyes are open. I feel like fresh air.

"Bring your awareness back to your body gently. I'll go get you some water."

When she returns with a Dixie cup, her face has a filmy shine to it, like she had run up a flight of stairs.

"What did you do?" I sit up, feeling a little unstable.

"I cleansed your chakras and balanced you. You were very clogged. Be sure to drink a lot of water and pay attention to your dreams for the next seven days. Usually a cleansing is followed by strong images, even premonitions and warnings. Will you come to class again?"

"Yes." I thank her and lean in for a hug. "That was wonderful. I tap, but I've never experienced anything like this before. What do I owe you?"

"First session is free." She smiles and I hope I can see her again.

THIRTY-EIGHT

The Fan

I walk to my old car feeling brand-new. That was the most wonder-ful gift I've ever given myself, and I feel a little skip in my step. The windows are rolled all the way down. When I turn the radio on, my favorite Michael Jackson song is playing, "Don't Stop Till You Get Enough." I sing, shake my shoulders, and do every dance I can manage while driving a car. When I pull up to the church, I'm happy to see that Gran is standing outside with two of her church sisters, Ms. Marie and Ms. Evelyn.

I get out of the car. "Hi there." I wave.

"Faye, it's good to see you, girl. What in the world have you done to your hair?" Ms. Evelyn motions for me to come over and give her a hug. I do.

"Just something different."

"Well, if anyone can pull it off, it's you. How are the kids?"

"Fine. Getting big."

"Well, you take care of yourself." Ms. Evelyn pats my arm. I squeeze Ms. Marie and then take Gran by the hand. She lowers her-self into the passenger seat. Her breathing is heavy.

"Gran, you're breathing hard. You want me to stop for some water?"

"I'm all right. Just praised the Lord with all I had. So much to pray on."

I slide behind the wheel.

"I took the papers down to discuss my will with you. I'm going to call Chrissy over tomorrow to tell her. She ain't gonna like it one bit."

"Why?"

"I'm-a leave the house to you and make you power of attorney over what I have. It ain't much, but it's something."

"Gran—"

"Let me rest my eyes. I'll show you everything when we get to the house. Every time I look at you, can't believe you chopped off all that pretty hair."

"I needed a change." I protectively run my hand over my head.

"A change would have been a press and curl. That what you did is drastic, girl. Women cut their hair when they desperate. You talk to Preston?"

"Go on and rest your eyes, Gran."

I pull the car onto Broad Street and take the slow way from South Philadelphia to North with easy sing-along music playing on the radio. Gran dozes, which gives me a chance to think over some of the things that Shira said in my reading. *What do I want? What is my purpose?*

When I park in front of the house, the front door is wide open. Gran doesn't have a screen, so you can see clear to the kitchen.

"What the devil?" Gran hobbles up the stairs. "Crystal?"

"Yeah, Mama." I can hear the substance.

"Why is the front door like this? You know Precious had a cat run into her house the other day. And it took two days to get the darn thing out."

"I was hot."

The television is blasting a reality show. When I walk into the living room after Gran, one girl on the show throws a glass of red wine on the other girl's white dress. They start fighting.

I close the front door.

"Where y'all been? What you best friends now? Going to church and whatnot like two peas in a pod? Always been like that. Always leaving me out."

Gran moves heavily into the living room. She leans on her cane. "Don't start no mess."

"Mama, why you always taking up for her?"

Gran sinks into her favorite dining room chair, the one that's between the living and dining rooms so she can see both ways.

"Ain't 'bout sides. It's 'bout what's right." She pulls at the bobby pins in her hair and unpins her wig.

A forty-ounce of Old English sits between Crystal's legs. She clutches it with both hands. "What about me, Mama? I wait on you hand and foot while this hussy is away living the good life."

"Hussy?" I interject.

"Hush, Crystal."

"Why I got to be quiet? I saw your little will." Crystal flings her words at Gran like marbles.

"Why you in my stuff?"

"Ain't fair that Faye always gets everything."

"Stop it, Crissy."

"I'm tired of playing second to her."

Gran sighs, like she has the burden of the whole family on her collarbone.

Crystal takes a long swig from her bottle and snarls. "You fucked Mr. Orbach to get her into that fancy college in New York City. You didn't even try to get me into community college."

"Crystal!" I'm exasperated. "Don't disrespect your mother like that!" I shout.

"Mind your damn business."

"And you watch your mouth in my house. 'Sides, you ain't cared nothing about school. Too busy chasing those boys," Gran mumbles. "Fast ass."

Crystal jumps to her feet, spilling a slurp of her beer on the floor. "Fast? Faye got pregnant right behind me. You always favored Faye and I'm yours. I'm your child. Why? Just 'cause your crazy son tried to kill her mama?"

Gran slams her fist on the table. "Cut it out."

"You ain't never want to talk about that. Sweeping Faye's stuff under the rug but letting mine hang all out. Now she gets the house I grew up in and I get the crumbs as usual. Faye don't even need the house. That's bullshit, Mama."

"Girl, if you don't watch your mouth—"

"Faye's mama was a whore, and the apple don't fall too far from the tree."

"Who you calling a whore?" I turn my head and push my chest forward.

"You. A stank-ass whore, at that."

"You better stop it, Crystal," I say, fists balled.

"Mama, bet you didn't know that Faye been sneaking around with the old man who got her knocked up in high school. You smuggle her off to Virginia in the middle of the night to get rid of her baby, and then it's like nothing happened. You ain't do that when I got pregnant with Derell."

Gran looks at me with disbelief. I look away.

"That was different."

"Only difference was that it happened to me!" Crystal screams at the top of her lungs, and the framed photos on the piano shake. I consider moving toward her to calm her down, but then I remember her pocketknife, so I stay near the steps.

"You can give Faye this old funky house. I don't want it anyway." Crystal swings her bottle as she slams out the front door. I close it behind her and lock up. My new and cleaned aura is back to being muddled.

"Go get me a beer."

I look in the fridge and grab the last Schlitz Malt Liquor. I place it in front of her with a red straw.

Gran reaches for her package of cigarettes. Her fingers shake. I take the package from her and then flick her lighter, holding it until the tip burns brightly. She nods her thanks and motions for me to turn up the fan. It's already on high.

"Crystal got the devil in her, same as her father. Tsk. Can't do nothing with her when she goes off like that. All you can do is try not to feed the fire."

"Gran, you don't like Corona or Heineken?"

"Stuck in my ways, gal. 'Sides, neither one of those give me my buzz. Just makes me piss every five minutes."

I sit down, across from Gran at the dining room table and fiddle with the end of the tablecloth. The motion calms my nerves. Crystal's energy still owns the air. The telephone rings and breaks the silence. I wait the required three rings and then ask her if she wants me to answer it. Gran shakes her head no.

"I've always felt responsible for you, Faye, baby. Since you was a little girl. Come 'round here with your mama. Had to have you sleep in my bed. My first grandbaby. I died a little on the day Franklin tried to kill your mama. Broke my heart into a thousand pieces. I knew then if there was anyone I could save, it would be you. They say as long as you save one, well, that's all you can do."

I twirled my wedding band around on my finger. I missed my family, my safe space where none of this ever mattered.

"Then you got yourself into that mess." She drags on her cigarette, and the mess comes out in two syllables instead of one.

"I died a little bit again. But I vowed you was gon' make it. I wasn't gon' lose you to these Philly streets. These streets can swallow you piece by piece until there ain't nothing left. Chile, I done seen it."

She takes three drags on her cigarette and inhales sharply. "That's why I sent you down South to have the baby. At the time it felt like the only way to give you a fresh start."

"Gran, we don't have to talk about this. The past is the past."

"Orbach did give me the money for you to go to college, paid your tuition for all four years, but it ain't what Crystal thought. Me and that white man had been lovers for years." She cracks up laughing and shows all of her dentures.

"What?" I crack up, too.

"Since his wife passed. You know she died of some type of throat-swallowing problem. We took up with each other and it was a real romance. He was sweet as pie."

My eyes are big like buttons.

"Yes, honey, I have lived my life and then some. Been around the block and seen more than you'd ever know." Wickedness played on her face.

She stubs her cigarette out and then reaches for her Bible. Rubber-banded to the back is a folded paper. She removes it and slides it across the table.

It's the birth certificate for a baby girl born on June 13, 1989. Behind it is a handwritten letter. The ink is faded and edges of the yellow lined paper are frayed. I let my eyes move over the paragraph.

Gran talks while I read. "She lived for five days. When I talked to your Aunt Kat, she said the cousin who took the baby told her it was sudden infant death." Gran brought her Bible to her lips. "Just let this give you some closure, gal. Move on and take care of your family. They all you got."

THIRTY-NINE

The Light in the Tunnel

I take the papers from Gran and carry them up into my little hot box of a room. I stare at them so long my eyes cross and glaze. Five days. God gave me a second chance, and what am I doing with it? I think about Shira. What do I want? What is my purpose? How can I serve? I slip into the bed and lay on my back. The papers that Gran gave me are on my chest. I imagine those healing crystals that Shira used retuning my body. I search for peace. I search for that brand-new feeling. I'm ready to move on. But first I need to rest.

I close my eyes but my stomach is queasy. It's not long before I'm sitting up in the bed with the covers around my waist. Sweat is all over me. My cell phone is ringing. I've left it on the living room table again. I scoot out of bed and run toward the sound. Preston's name is flashing across my screen and I say hello a second before it rolls to voice mail.

"Felicia, it's Preston."

"I know." Why is he being so damn formal this time of night?

"Um, Rory . . ." He pauses.

"What? What happened to him?" My voice is seven octaves higher than usual.

"He isn't in his room. I've checked the whole house. I thought he was hiding. I know I put him to bed."

I toss the phone in my purse. Write Gran a quick, sloppy note. It's not until I get into my car that I look down and realize I'm in my pajamas.

PART 3

Although I can't live inside yesterday's pain, I can't live without it.

—TOPSY WASHINGTON FROM GEORGE C. WOLFE'S

THE COLORED MUSEUM

FORTY

The Five-Alarms

I've watched the sky go from gray to pink, and now the sun is blar-
ing right at me. The traffic on the New Jersey Turnpike is bearable,
but I'm only a few minutes before rush hour, so I foot the gas to stay
ahead of the congestion. I'm hot, so I turn on the air conditioner.
I'm cold, so I turn it back off. I'm restless but confined to the width
and length of the driver's seat in the Nissan. I switch to 1010 WINS
for an update, but it's filled with static. Panic pumps through my
veins. I need a cigarette. I flip to a classical music station in an attempt
to calm my nerves.

My cell phone chimes from the passenger seat next to me and I
feel for it with one eye on the road, hoping with everything in me
that it's Preston calling, having found my son.

It's Shayla. I let it roll to voice mail. I can't deal with her right
now. But she had better have my house secured. My hands shake
against the steering wheel. Calm down, I tell myself. A car accident
wouldn't be good right now. Rory. My sweet son. My only son. I
remember when I found out I was pregnant with him. I called him
little L. Preston and I didn't find out the sex but I knew he was a

boy. I knew he would be a rambunctious boy. When he was a tod-
dler, I remember one mother at a playgroup commenting on how
much energy he had because Rory was curious and into everything.
A smile crept on my face when I responded, "God knew what he
was doing when he paired us together." God did know what he was
doing, and my sweet baby has to be okay. I switch lanes.

The traffic is next to nothing after exit 9, and I push the Nissan
just above the speed limit. It doesn't take long for me to get to exit
11 and then hop off the turnpike. The Garden State Parkway is also
empty, so I gun it for home. Preston hasn't called back. No news has
to be good news. Please.

Our home looks the same as I pull in to the driveway. When I get to
my front door I realize that I don't have my house key. I lean on the
bell and wait. Preston opens the front door and then walks across
the enclosed porch and unlocks the second. His head is held low and
his eyes don't reach mine. When he moves to let me in, I hear his
breath cinch.

"Your hair?"

I run my hands over my short do. "Have you found him?"

He shakes his head.

"Did you call the police?"

"I was waiting for you."

"Are you kidding me? He's six, for Christ sakes. He could be halfway to New Hampshire." I push past Preston and walk into the
house. It's quiet. The girls must still be asleep. The kitchen is tidy
except for a package of bacon thawing on the counter.

"Call the police," I order.

Preston has crumbled against the banister. Crisis always turns him
to powder. It's been my job to handle emergencies in the family, par-
ticularly kid calamities. When Rory came down with croup, I had to
rock him. Twyla jammed her finger in the door, I had to drive us to

the hospital. Preston doesn't do well with trouble. But that's why I'm here. That's why my name is Mommy. I put on my cape and start moving through the house. I grab the cordless phone and call the police. I tell them the little I know and they say they are on their way.

"Where did you check?"

"Everywhere."

Preston is following me on the stairs. I walk into Rory's bedroom and look around to see if there is any sign of him. His Spiderman sheets are tangled and pulled back, his blue pillow pet is on the floor. I move the covers around.

"Where is his brown plush dog?" I look at Preston. He looks back at me. It's almost as if he didn't hear me. I talk slow and loud so that my words will sink in.

"The brown plush dog that he has to sleep with. Gran gave it to him three Christmases ago. He even drags it into the girls' room when he sleeps with them."

Preston's face is blank. "I don't know."

I open the closet and then get down on my knees and reach all the way into the back, but all I feel are his old shoes. I go into the girls' room. Man, I've missed them. Their breathing is rhythmic, like they are dancing together. I peek into the crib and Two is wrapped around Liv. They look like conjoined twins. I think about pulling them apart but I don't want them to wake up. Not yet. I search their closet but it's so narrow that if Rory were hiding in there I wouldn't have to look hard. Our bedroom is next.

"Did you look under the bed?"

"Yes."

I look again anyway; nothing but Preston's shoes and the vaporizer. In our closet, I find the familiars.

Where are you, darling? Did you leave the house?

On the stairs, I feel Preston's heat as he moves behind me. My pulse is as quick as it gets. I'm in overdrive. *Where is my child?* I head to the basement.

"You look in all of the storage areas, Preston, and really look. Get a flashlight."

Preston opens his mouth to say something but then bites his tongue. I'm being bossy, but so what?

I check the bathroom, the laundry room, under my desk, and in the space where Preston keeps his tools.

"Rory, Rory, where are you?" I call his name. I crawl around on the play area rug, looking behind boxes of puzzles, as if he could really fit with his plush dog in such a tight space.

"What the fuck, Preston?"

He's standing, looking at me on the floor.

"How the hell do you lose one of our children?" The hysteria has reached my voice. I'm no longer Mommy-in-control. I'm Mommy-maniac.

"I've been getting home early, cooking dinner, and putting them to bed myself. I put Rory to bed last night. We talked about submarines. He wanted to know if people in submarines could breathe or if they need oxygen tanks. It was a ten-minute conversation. I checked on the kids again before I fell asleep in the basement." He sits on the arm of the sofa.

"When I came up for my middle-of-the-night check, the gate was open and I couldn't remember if I closed it or not and . . ." his voice trails. "Rory wasn't in his bed."

"You forgot to set the alarm?"

"I thought I did."

My hands go to my face and I rub my eyes. I don't want to start blaming Preston but I want to blame Preston.

This would never have happened if I were home. But there is no time for the shoulda-couldas. I have to find my son. I head upstairs, into the kitchen. Preston is behind me. The telephone starts ringing. I walk to the wall unit and peek at the caller ID.

"It's Juju. When did she leave?"

"A few days ago."

I walk to the refrigerator and open it. Preston answers the telephone. I pour myself a glass of apple juice before it clicks in my mind that I don't like apple juice. I drink it anyway. Gas bubbles are crashing against each other in my belly. Where are the fucking police?

Preston hangs up the phone and asks me if I'd like coffee. I nod.

I hear movement upstairs and I sprint up the steps, two at a time.

"Mommy." Two says my name loud enough and close enough to Liv's ear to wake her.

"Hi, Pudding Pops." I lift them both from the crib, one on each arm, and carry them to the glider. I've missed this chair. "How did you sleep?"

"What happen to your hair?" Two sticks her pointer finger in her mouth and starts tracing my face with her free hand. Liv is squirming in my lap. She doesn't seem to know which emotion to go with, happy to see me or mad that I've been away.

"I cut it."

"You look like a boy."

I smile at her. "Two, we can't find Rory. Does he have any new hiding places?"

Her eyes get wide.

"Yes."

"Where?"

"He likes to hide in your bed."

"I've looked there. Where else?" I'm staring at the extra door in the girls' bedroom and realize I haven't checked the attic.

"Does he go into the attic?"

"Sometimes. But he's scared of the spider." I stand up and put Liv back in the crib. She starts crying right away. I give her a toy rattle and tell Two to stay with her. The attic steps are narrow and steep. When I reach the top it all looks the same. A mess. I've needed to sort the kids' clothes all summer, but it's always an extra twenty degrees warmer in this part of the house and I've been avoiding the job for weeks.

"Rory," I call his name softly. "Rory." I throw back all of the crawl space sliders and peek in, calling his name. He's not up here. I hold back tears.

"Was he there?" Two is crawling out of the crib.

"Does he have another hiding space?"

She thinks. "I have an idea. Follow me."

It feels fruitless to follow a four-year-old, but I'm at my wits' end and I do it. As we turn in to the hallway Preston is on the steps with a cup of coffee stretched out toward me. I shift Liv onto my other hip and take it.

"Thanks. I just checked the attic." Then I shake my head. "Maybe you should call next door or knock on the neighbors' doors or something. We should be doing something. How long does it take for the police to get here?"

His shoulders sag, but he doesn't move.

Two goes into the bathroom and pushes back the shower curtain. "Sometimes he hides in the tub when we play hide-and-go-seek." She looks at the entire tub, like if Rory was in there she might miss him. He's not.

"Mommy, I have to pee-pee." She starts dancing from one leg to the other. I put my coffee on the sink and hand Liv to Preston, who is right behind me. I pull Two's pajama pants down and sit her on the toilet. We all wait as she pees and washes her hands.

"Oh," she says. Then she opens the bathroom closet door. The shelves are deep, with sheets, towels, and bins of toiletries. On the bottom space is where I store the oversized bathroom rugs. On top of the rugs is a lump of ill-folded towels. They don't go there. Two pulls the towels away and there is Rory, curled with his plush dog and fast asleep.

"Ta-da," she presents him with her right hand.

"Rory," I say his name. "Rory, sweetie." The tears fall without fanfare. "Baby, wake up."

"Mom?" My name is soft on his lips. "Mommy." He slides from

his hiding place. "Mama!" He kicks at the pile of towels and scrambles from the floor. Rory throws himself at me so hard I hit the wall, but I don't let him go.

"I knew you'd come back. I just knew it." He holds me tight.

"You cut your hair?"

"Yes."

The doorbell rings. Must be the police.

"Son," Preston calls his name, "I've been looking all over for you." He takes him from my arms and hugs him. His back convulses in silent tears that will never be shed. "Why're you in the closet?"

Rory jumps down onto the floor and then lowers his face into my knees. "Because I wanted Mommy."

FORTY-ONE

The Sweetness of Home

I make oatmeal for Liv, bacon and toast for Two, and an egg sandwich with cream cheese for Rory. Preston declines my offer to make him breakfast.

"Can I drive the kids to school?"

He nods.

We aren't really talking to each other, just what's necessary to navigate through the situation. After warming up his coffee, he slips upstairs. I can hear the shower running. The kids are seated at the table, rattling off all that I've missed.

"Mommy, guess what?" Rory has cream cheese in the corner of his mouth. "I stayed on the green for the entire week so today I get to pick from the surprise box."

"Really?"

"Yes. I'm going to pick the red car. That's what Jeremiah picked last week."

"Good job, honey." I rummage through the cabinets, looking for snacks to put into their lunch boxes. Once we are finished downstairs, we head up to wash faces and teeth, and get dressed.

"I'll see you guys later." Preston stands in the hallway and the children run to him for a hug.

"Have a nice day," I call from the bathroom sink.

He mumbles his thanks, locks the gate, and trots down the stairs.

My phone vibrates from the back pocket of my jeans. I wonder if I worried Gran. When I look at my phone, it's a New York number.

"Kids, go sit in your room and quietly read a book. Rory, take Liv." I close the bathroom door.

"Hello?"

"Felicia?"

"Yes."

"Hi, it's Ashley calling from SEM&M. Sorry to call so early. I know you have children so I figured it would be fine."

"Yes, of course."

"Good news. You booked the Johnson & Johnson commercial we sent you on a few weeks ago."

"Wow. Really?" I pump my fist. "That's incredible."

"Congratulations. They're working on the shoot date, but it may be in a week or so. I'll e-mail you all of the contract information. Is your fax still the same?"

"Yes."

"Great. I'll be in touch with more when I have it. We are really excited for you. Johnson & Johnson have been looking for a repeat mom to appear in a string of commercials. Fingers crossed that you'll be their girl."

"Yes, that would be wonderful. I'm over the moon. Wow. Please keep me posted."

I hang up and scream. The kids come running to the bathroom.

"Mom, what's wrong?"

I open the door. "I just booked a commercial."

"What does that mean?"

"I'm going to be on television."

"Can I do it with you?" Two's eyes widen with hope.

"We'll see, honey. Let's get going to camp."

I grab Liv and usher the other two down the steps. Johnson & Johnson. That has to be a national. Commercials pay well, but a national is like hitting the jackpot. Ching-ching. A repeat series, nothing but net. Maybe my luck is about to change. I lock the front door. Then on the bottom of my steps it strikes me. I went on the audition before I cut my hair. Man, I hope that isn't a problem. I scratch my scalp, knowing that it could be.

I drive through the neighborhoods as they change from tightly woven to the sprawling suburbs. When I pull in front of the red schoolhouse, Erica is standing on the curb with McCoy on her hip, saying something to a tearful Coltrane.

"Felicia. Girl, where have you been?" She looks me over. "Wow, love the hair."

First compliment I've received since I chopped it.

"Thanks." We do a side hug, since we are both clutching kids.

"You just dropped off the face of the earth," she comments.

"It's been crazy."

Two clings to my free hand as we stand at the sign-in table. When the teacher reaches for Two and Rory, they both grab a leg and refuse to go.

I lean in and whisper, "I will be back to pick you up."

"You promise?" Rory looks at me through his lashes.

"Pinky promise, with cherries on top and a squirt of whipped cream."

"Oooh, can we have that when we get home?"

"We'll see."

I kiss Two's cheek and she grabs her teacher's hand and starts skipping down the driveway.

Erica is rocking McCoy on her hip, her red hair catching the sun. "You in a rush? Want to stop for coffee?"

"That sounds good."

I strap Liv into her car seat and follow Erica's SUV to the bagel shop on the avenue. After feeding our meters, we cross the street. The place is crowded, but we manage to order. I have an egg and cheese biscuit, Erica a BLT. We sit near the window facing the busy street, adjacent to the big fish tank. The colorful fish, aquarium beta flowers, and sunken treasure pirate ship will keep our babies entertained.

"So, how have you been?" I ask.

"Honey, we haven't heard from you since Preston pulled you out of the Dames fund-raiser. I haven't seen you at school. You don't text back. And when I called the house some older woman kept answering. What, are you outsourcing?"

I manage a dry chuckle and my brain clicks over how much I should share with Erica. There is a difference between Mommy friends and real friends. I haven't known Erica long enough to move her up a category, even though she is my favorite mother at the school. When I open my mouth, I struggle.

"Things are fine. I just had to go Philly and help my grandmother with a few things."

Erica tilts her chin. "Is it serious? Your husband marched in with the thunder, girl."

I hesitate. "Yeah . . . she's fine. Preston tends to overreact sometimes."

"So why were you gone so long?" she pushes. I swirl my stirrer around in my latte, feeling emotions well up that I want to keep down low.

"Well, I hadn't been home for an extended period of time since college. It was a nice break."

Erica looks me over, than turns away to feed McCoy a crust from her plate. "You were fine without the kids?"

"Preston's godmother stayed with them."

"That's nice, I guess."

I take a bite from my sandwich. The Havarti cheese is gooey and warm, just the way I like it. I feel like Erica isn't buying my story. I'm scared to say more, so I eat.

Erica sips her coffee. "Well, I'm glad you're back. I've been thinking about a playdate at the Turtleback Zoo. That playground should keep the kids occupied."

"The weather is perfect for it. Count me in." I reply and then steer the conversation toward her. I listen to her qualms with her mother and Warren's traveling schedule, thinking that I would trade my problems for hers in a shake of a lamb's tail. Liv starts fussing, so I pull her onto my lap. Three teenage boys enter the shop talking loud and being rowdy. Liv watches their every move.

"I went to a meditation class in Philly. It was the best experience ever. I'll have to find one locally."

"There's a class on Friday mornings at the center where I practice yoga. I'll e-mail you the link. I hear the class is life-changing, but I'm always on with clients Friday mornings. It's the day everyone wants an update on their campaign," she says, referring to her business, which reminds me.

"I almost forgot to tell you, I just booked a commercial."

"Really?"

"Johnson & Johnson baby powder. I'm pretty sure it's national."

She spreads her lips into a smile. "That's wonderful. I'm so happy for you."

"Thanks." I dab my mouth. "It's been a long time coming."

"Did you get anything in the mail from the Dames?"

"I literally got back this morning."

"Oh. Monroe is so secretive about the vote. She notifies everyone through the mail. As soon as she realized that we were friends, she's been asking about you every chance she gets."

"Really?"

"I hope things go your way."

"Well, it's done now."

"It'll be fine. I'm sure." Erica plugs McCoy with his pacifier.

I check the clock. "I better go."

"Me too, but before I forget, Warren won an All-Star music award. So we're having a party. You and your hubby must come."

If Preston and I make it that far. I smile and tell her, "We'd love to."

FORTY–TWO

The Decision

When I return home, I can smell Preston's scent everywhere. I think about what I did with Martin and how often in just a few days. Guilt starts to bubble. I go to the phone and dial Gran.

"Chile, why you leave here in the middle of the night?"

"Preston called. He thought Rory was missing."

"Oh, Jesus. Where'd you find him?"

"Asleep in the bathroom closet. Curled up with that brown plush dog you gave him for Christmas."

Gran chuckles. "You shoulda took a picture of that. Something to show him when he get grown."

"I was too relieved to do anything, really."

"Well, you keep yourself at home. No matter what Preston says. 'Nough time done passed. It's time for you two to figure things out."

"Gran . . . I just want to say thank you for everything. I didn't realize how much you sacrificed."

"Children never do. Good Lord made it that way."

"Well, thanks. I appreciate you."

"You can thank me by keepin' your hind parts at home. Don't

want you comin' back to Philly no time soon. Maybe I'll make a trip up there to see you."

"That would be nice."

"I'll call you tomorrow when the circular come."

She hangs up.

Liv slithers into the kitchen and I pull her to me, snuggle my nose in her neck, and enjoy the weight of her against me. Her hair has grown wild, and she giggles while clutching one of my earrings in her tiny hand. I shift her and remove the pair before she can yank and cause me pain. By the time I finish cleaning the kitchen and decide on a menu for dinner, it's time for her nap. The tub of formula Preston has been giving her is on the counter. It's weird for me not to breastfeed. I have never given my children formula before, but I follow the instructions. Liv doesn't seem to mind, and sucks the bottle down. I hold her in my lap and let her put her hand down my shirt for comfort. Before the bottle is empty, she's fast asleep, and I'm glad to see she's still on schedule. I carry her upstairs and put her in her crib. As I gaze down my eyes start to water.

All at once everything that has happened hits me. The branded A sits heavily on my forehead, and I scratch at it until a layer of my skin clogs my fingernails. How could I have been so careless with Martin? I deteriorated so deeply inside of myself that I never stopped to think of the consequences. What if Preston found out? I don't have a lie big enough to explain why I did it. He'd never understand.

I lean against the wall, throbbing. The regret makes me wish that I could step outside of my own skin. Maybe a hot bath is what I need. I force myself into the bathroom, where I start the water. Mechanically drop in two scoops of chamomile bath salts and three drops of lavender. Then I add a generous amount of Calgon, because I love how the water turns blue. I need the blue to take me away. The steam from the water warms the bathroom, and I close the door to keep it toasty.

I open Preston's closet. The clothes that he needs me to take to the cleaners are hung toward the back, and I run my fingers over his linen shirt and bring the collar to my nose. I imagine how he moved through his day in this shirt, unconcerned with me. Hating me for shattering him at his core. I take the shirt and bring it with me as I lay across my bed. The pillows are neat, too neat. And when I bury my face into them searching for Preston, I smell floral and talcum powder instead. Juju.

Clean sheets are in the linen closet, and I replace the soiled with fresh ones. The tub is nearly filled, but the water is too hot, so I stop the flow and go back to my bed and wait. The ache won't stop pulsing inside of me. The remote is on the nightstand and I flip on the television. *The Wendy Williams Show* is on. I used to love her radio show, but now I rarely get to watch her talk program. I don't watch much of anything but I lay back, happy for the distraction.

Wendy introduces Kyle Richards from *The Real Housewives of Beverly Hills*, who has a new book out. Wendy notes that in the book, there is an interesting perspective on cheating. Kyle flips her long black hair and smiles like a Hollywood starlet.

"I say if you cheat on your spouse once, keep it a secret." The remote slips from my hand as I sit up. Is she talking to me?

She goes on to tell the story of a couple she knows where one had an infidelity and never told. "It was a one-time deal, and the couple is now more than happily married. Personally, I think you should deal with it yourself and with God."

Deal with it myself?

I head into the bathtub and let the water scorch my skin. It's still too hot, but I deserve it. Preston has his faults but he's a good man. I cheated repeatedly with Martin, not just once. I was like an addict for what that man had.

It was the little girl hurt who reacted to Martin. It wasn't your heart. Forgive yourself and move on.

The *damn voice* never has anything positive to say and I let her thoughts wash over me. The tears leak from everywhere. I remember when I tried to drown myself in the tub, pregnant with Martin's baby.

You need to let it all go. Just like your mother said. Let it all go. You've been given a second chance. Take it.

I know the *damn voice* is right. For once, she really is right. Nothing matters more to me than my family. I have to get over my past, including Martin, and get things back on track. I decide that I won't tell Preston. I'd take the affair to my grave. It wasn't right, but he wouldn't be able to handle it. Not after all that has happened. Maybe I wasn't the innocent virgin he thought he married, but I am still a faithful wife in his eyes. I can't take that away from him. It's all we have left. God help me.

My reunion with the children after school is all shouts and glee. I grab our Friday night pizza and wings, cupcakes and ice cream for dessert with whipped cream.

"This is the best day ever," Two says.

Rory puts his arm around me. "I'm glad you came home."

We are sitting on the living room floor. I'm painting Two's fingers and toes while the movie *Rio* plays, and Liv is in my lap. When the movie ends, they beg for another but I don't give in. I read three bedtime stories and then tuck them in.

"Can I sleep in here with the girls?" Rory asks.

I tuck him into Two's bed, then I rock in the glider and softly sing every lullaby I know. When Rory starts that heavy breathing that's borderline snoring, I sneak out. I take a long, hot shower. Even though I soaked earlier, I can't seem to get clean enough. At some point the sin will subside. My hair is damp and I squirt a little leave-in conditioner to give it a shine. My favorite body mist, Dawn by Pooka Pure and Simple, is light and clean, and I spray it generously on my neck and the balls of my wrist. My silk camisole and matching pants feel good on my skin. I'm so happy to be around my familiars and away from Gran's, I could do a somersault.

Preston is home. I didn't hear him come in but I can feel him. Barefooted, I pad downstairs. He's not in the living room. When I walk into the kitchen, I see the basement door slightly ajar and hear the television on. The wooden door creaks, announcing me before my footsteps do. Preston is slouched in the middle of the leather sofa. His tie is hanging from his neck, his shirt unbuttoned to his waist, his stomach flat, and his shoes are kicked slightly to the left on the Persian rug.

"Hi," I say.

"Hey."

He doesn't look my way. He's wearing new glasses. The rims make him look like a black Clark Kent.

"I made meat loaf. Your plate is in the microwave. I can bring it down if you like."

"No, thanks." He raises his Stella Artois and sips.

When Preston and I first moved into the house I was pregnant with Rory, and this space used to be Preston's "man cave." As the children came, more of their things started to migrate down and it became a second playroom. I'm not sure what Preston has done with the toy kitchen set, strollers, and such, because the space has resumed its smoky charm.

I'm sitting on the bottom step, afraid to go any farther without a personal invitation. A pile of scratch-offs are on the coffee table in front of him.

"Win anything?"

"Twenty-two dollars."

"Why are you down here?"

"I can't sleep in our bedroom."

"Why, Pres?"

His eyes are on the television. I'm not sure he's heard my question. I open my mouth to repeat it. But he cuts me off.

"You look like you've lost weight."

"I hadn't really noticed."

His eyes find mine. "The haircut makes you look younger."

"Two said I look like a boy."

His eyes leave me.

It's raining outside. Big petals crash against the windowpane. Chills come over my arms and I see goose bumps.

"Preston, I'm sorry."

He says nothing.

"Honey, when are you going to talk to me about this?"

"What do you want me to say? I forgive you for allowing me to believe that you're someone else?"

"I'm the same person, Preston." I stand.

"Do you know how fucked up it is to believe your wife saved herself for you only to discover that—"

"I had a life before you. With a beginning, middle, and lots of ends."

He doesn't look at me. The wind blows a draft, and I'm shivering.

"May I use your blanket?" I walk to the love seat where he is sitting and ease into the seat next to him. I wrap myself in the afghan before he can answer.

Preston sits, stiff like a board.

I'm sick on the inside. Worried over what I feel I'm being pushed to do to save my marriage. There is no other choice. If nothing else, it's time to set myself free. I wrap my arms around myself in a hug.

"Preston." His name feels like home in my mouth. He looks at me sideways. I fold my feet underneath me. "Once my mother was taken away from me and my father died in prison, I was alone in the world. I had Gran and sometimes Crystal. My friend Shayla, who you've never met. But for the most part, I felt alone. I loathed myself. I thought I was unworthy of love because my parents left me."

"Felicia—"

"Let me finish. I started seeing a man at church. Martin."

Preston shifts away from me.

"He was older and suave, he knew all the right things to say to a young girl who was dying on the inside. I gave him my virginity in the backseat of a car. Thought we were in love. Thought we'd live happily ever after. When I wound up pregnant, he was nowhere to be found. Gran shipped me down to Virginia on the Greyhound, alone, to have the baby with relatives I didn't know. I delivered the baby in a back room with a midwife that had scaly skin and missing teeth. When they told me it was a girl and asked if I wanted to hold her"—my voice cracks—"I turned my back. If I didn't hold her, then she wouldn't be real and I could go back to Philly with a real chance of getting on with life."

"Wait. You had a baby?"

I shook my head and willed the tears to heel.

"A baby, and you never told me?" Preston stands. "What else have you been hiding from me?"

"That's all." I pinch my thigh.

"I don't even know you." He drops his head in his hands and starts rubbing his face.

I pull the throw around me tighter and catch the tears in the corner of my eyes before they fall. Preston looks at me and I can't read his thoughts.

"How come you never told me this?"

"It was the lowest point in my life. I was ashamed. It was easier for me to bury it and pretend like it never happened."

"Where is the child?"

I lower my eyes. "Dead. Lived only a few days."

Preston beats his fist on his chest. "You should have told me."

"You wouldn't have asked me to marry you. This is all about your picture-perfect idea of family."

"No, this is about you lying, Felicia. Boldly deceiving me."

I drop my head. Preston sits down on the arm of the chair. I wish he would sit closer and touch me. "Why can't we just move on?"

"Because."

"Because what?"

"Because I don't know if I was in love with you, or the idea of you."

My fingers feel the sting of his words and I tuck them between my knees to keep from slapping him. Anger rushes to my skin's surface. "How could you say that? We've had seven good years of marriage, Preston. I've been good to you."

"Our whole foundation was built on a lie. Can't you see that? I don't trust you. Honestly, this is a deal breaker for me, Felicia."

"Fuck you, Preston."

He stands while backing up, like I've got something he doesn't want.

"That's all I've been thinking about since you've been gone is how to split up the assets and what to do with the kids."

"I just bared my soul to you," my mouth mumbles.

"Don't turn this around on me. This one is all you." He glares at me. I glare back. I don't see even the tiniest glint of hope in his eyes.

"Fine, then. I'll give you what you want. I'm done. Draw up the fucking papers." I walk up to him and shove him with all of my might. He stumbles but barely moves. I stomp up the stairs and then slam the door as hard as I can.

I run upstairs, lock the door, and crawl into my bed. A poem I wrote for Martin, after I watched him drive away with that woman, chants in my head.

It struck me like an accident.
It hit me like a ton of bricks.
It made me realize, it made me understand.
It's over.

There was nothing left for me to do but accept it.

FORTY-THREE

The Crude Truth

My eyes flutter open with Two crawling into bed. It's the weekend, so I have time to adjust to the kids' schedule and my new singleness.

"Mommy, what's today?"

"Saturday."

She thinks a minute. "I don't have school?"

"No."

She bounces on my bed, and her face breaks out into a huge smile. "Yes." She pumps her fist. "Do I have dance class?"

"Yes," I remember, pulling her to my chest and cuddling. She pops her finger in her mouth and then tells me that she's hungry. The sun is barely in the sky and I try coaxing her back to sleep.

"But I'm hoongry. I'm so hoongry, Mommy. Can I have some cereal?"

"Okay." I throw the covers back. Two crawls up my body and demands to be carried to the kitchen. Rory and Liv are still asleep, so Two and I go downstairs. I listen at the basement door but I don't hear anything.

"Daddy down there?" Two asks.

"I'm not sure."

"How come he likes to be in the basement all the time?"

"He's having private time. What type of cereal would you like?" I say, changing the subject.

"Let me show you." She's climbing up my leg to get into my arms when I hear the basement door open and see Preston.

"Daddy!" Two shouts and runs.

Preston says nothing to me as he makes the coffee. I hear Rory on the steps and I walk to meet him at the bottom for a hug.

"Morning, son."

He holds me tight. "Liv is up. Can I have cereal?"

"It's on the table."

When Liv sees me she starts crying harder. My poor child probably thinks I've abandoned her again, and I scoop her from the crib and hold her to my chest. I could really use a dose of her healing energy, and I take her to the glider and rock her against my breast.

"Mommy!" Two shouts.

I head down the stairs.

"What do you need, Pudding?"

"A paper. I spilled it." She points to her milk.

Preston carries his coffee upstairs. I place Liv in the high chair and put on water for her oatmeal.

"What do you want to do today?"

"Can we go to the park?"

"We will see."

"I want to go to Chuck E. Cheese," says Rory.

Preston showers and leaves without saying a word. I'm done begging him for his forgiveness. I take all three kids with me to Two's ballet class in Montclair. The weather is summery and warm. I don't feel like being trapped in the house, so we head over to the Turtleback

Zoo. I know I'm supposed to go with Erica, but we'll just go again. It's so lovely having them back. I can't get enough of their voices, touch, and faces.

In the car on the drive back home, I keep having a two-sided conversation in my head with Preston over the split. I want the house and he will have to continue paying the bills and the children's tuition. The commercial should set me up as long as the hair thing isn't an issue. I'm Gran's offspring, so I do have a stash. I can cover regular expenses, groceries, and dance lessons, but he's still going to have to pay me alimony and child support. I hope a good divorce lawyer isn't expensive. And he's going to have to find an apartment in town because I want him to take the kids to school every day. These children deserve to have their father on a daily basis. He better not bring any bitches around them, either. I'm keeping my car and—

"Mommy, turn your brain on," Two says from the backseat.

"Huh?"

"When your eyes look like that, Mommy, your brain is off. You need to turn it on. I'm talking but you aren't listening. I see your face in the mirror."

"Sorry, baby. What is it?"

"I need a Band-Aid."

"Okay, dumplings. We are almost home. You guys want to hear some music?"

"Yes! Michael Jackson!" shouts Rory.

I hook up my phone to the system and play it.

As soon as we get home, Two is in my face, showing me an old scratch that has scabbed over, but still I oblige her with the Band-Aid.

"Rory, I'm going to go change Liv. You and Two may have a freeze pop."

"Yes." He smiles at me. "You're the best mom ever."

"No fighting."

Liv has exploded in her diaper, and not only does she need a changing, she also needs a full sponge-down and fresh clothes.

"Doesn't that feel better?" I kiss her neck. She squeals. When I come back downstairs my phone is vibrating with a text. It's Shayla.

I'm in your backyard.

That girl.

"Kids, let's go out back and play."

"Can I ride my bike?" asks Rory.

"Sure."

"Bubbles, Mommy? Please."

"Yes, Two."

I grab a few bottled waters, bubbles, sidewalk chalk, my cell phone, and sunglasses.

Shayla looks as if she has just stepped out of a high-end department store and was personally styled by the buyer. Her hair is straight and glossy and she's wearing orange pedal pushers with matching platforms. Everything on Shayla is done.

"Mommy, your friend is here," says Two.

"Hi, sweetie pies." Shayla bends to the kids.

"Hi, Auntie Shay-Shay."

Both kids mill over and wrap their arms around her. Rory loses interest the moment he spies his basketball and starts throwing it up toward the hoop.

I hand Two the bubbles and chalk. "Go play so Mommy can talk."

Shayla gives me a hug. I hug her back, hold her longer than I have since she's resurfaced in my life.

"What's wrong?"

"Everything. Hold the baby while I go get the bouncy seat."

I return with the baby contraption and two orange sodas I found in the fridge. Once Liv is settled and occupied, I sit across from Shayla.

"How did it go with Brave?"

"Everything went well." She slides my mortgage documents across the table. "You look like shit. What's happening with you?"

My belly flip-flops. "Shay, can I trust you?"

"Of course."

I look at her.

"I mean it, Faye. What the hell happened?"

In that moment I realize that there is no one else I can tell. Shayla is it. I look around the fenced-in yard to make sure my children are out of earshot, and then I scoot my chair closer to Shayla and recount everything. From Martin's phone calls to Preston pulling me offstage in front of the Dames. I tell her about him banishing me to Philly and how I went mad at Martin but it only took a second for that anger to thaw and for me to land in his bed.

"We did it so many times, I lost count."

Shayla listens as I tell her about Preston bringing the kids but refusing to talk to me. Crystal's crazy ass and Gran's will, and how I got back home because Rory was lost.

"I found him curled in the bottom of the linen closet, talking about he knew I'd come back to rescue him."

I sip my soda and then tell her the latest, how I told Preston about the baby but he didn't take it well.

"I'm tired of trying, Shay. I told him to draw up the papers, shit. That's where this is heading, anyway."

"Did you tell him about Martin?"

"Which part?"

"The most recent part, in Philly?"

"No."

"Good. Cause you don't ever tell a man something like that unless you want your family reading about you in the paper. Carry that to your grave."

"Okay."

Shayla whips her hair behind her shoulder as she leans in. "Listen, I know this all feels like you want to jump off the bridge with your children in your arms, but don't. You have it, Faye. You have what we dreamed about on Sydenham, right down to the picket fence."

"That fence is chain-linked, girl."

"You know what I mean. Faye, you've beaten the odds. You are giving your children something we never had. A good middle-class life with two parents. Don't throw this away over some past secrets that happened before you even met the brother."

"He doesn't want me, Shay," I say, feeling the strain in my throat. "What am I supposed to do?"

"Work this shit out." Her beautiful eyes bore into me. "Honey, it's cold out here. Trust me. I would trade my life for yours in a baby's heartbeat."

I let her words settle over me while I sip my soda. Rory goes up for a layup and somehow ends up on the ground.

"Sweetie, are you all right?" I move toward him and bend down to look at his leg. It's a scratch with no blood. He glances over at Shayla and tells me he is fine.

I smile at the effect she has on this family. When I sit back down, she grabs my hand.

"If not for any other reason, work it out for your children. Don't give up on this dream, Faye. You've come too far and I'm proud of you."

Her phone rings in her purse.

"That's Brave. I've got to go." She stands. "Oh, and I'm not one for apologizing"—she swings her hair—"but I'm sorry for blackmailing you to get Brave out. It wasn't right, but I knew you wouldn't say yes without the threat."

"Just don't let it happen again."

She taps the table twice with her knuckles, reminding me that her promises are golden.

"Be careful out there." I go in for a hug. She squeezes me good-bye so tightly, it feels like the last time I'll see her.

Shayla pulls out two sticks of bubble gum and hands one to each kid. "'Bye, cutie-pies."

She tips her chin at me, then sashays across the asphalt in my yard.

FORTY-FOUR

The Last Dance

Rory, Two, and Liv have long been tucked into their beds when I hear the front door push open. It's been hot and the wooden door rubs against the swollen wooden frame, causing a loud friction. Preston stops to flip through the mail, remove his shoes, tuck his keys into the second door, and walks in. I'm wearing terry cloth shorts and a fitted capped-sleeve top.

I look at him from where I'm seated on the living room sofa. He's wearing his golf polo and khakis. "How was your day?" I ask flatly.

"Nice, played eighteen holes."

His skin looks radiant from being in all that sun.

"Did you have dinner?"

He shakes his head. "I'll just order some Chinese."

"I made spaghetti. It's on the stove."

"This came for you."

It's a letter. It's addressed from the Dames. I stare at it. He stares at me.

"Aren't you going to open it?"

"Yeah." I run my finger along the inside of the envelope and pull at the seal. There is a single sheet inside. When I unfold it, it reads,

Dear Felicia,

Thank you for your interest in the Dames and Culture Club. I am pleased to inform you that the chapter has accepted your request for membership. We are excited and look forward to welcoming you to our family.

The letter continues with the steps I need to take to complete my membership. My face is frozen with shock. I made it in.

"What does it say?" Preston stands.

"I made it in. I'm a Dame." I can't stop the grin from brightening my face.

"Congratulations. It's what you've wanted."

"Thanks." I hold the letter and read it again. Preston moves into the kitchen. I poke out my lips and do a shoulder shimmy. *I am a mother-freakin' Dame.* I can't believe it. After everything that has happened to me in the past few weeks, I'm a Dame. I'm reading the letter for the third time, adding the listed dates to my electronic calendar when he returns with a bowl of food. He sits on the opposite sofa. I toss him the remote.

"You aren't watching this?" he asks, formal and polite.

I shake my head.

Next thing I know we are watching a special on Barbados on the Travel Channel. All of the two-sided conversations that I've had all day go flying out of my head. I feel shy to be the first to bring it up.

Preston finishes his spaghetti and goes for another bowl. "This is really good." He resumes his place on the couch.

"Thanks."

We watch television from our respective corners. When the Barbados show goes off, it's ten o'clock and he flips to our favorite show,

House Hunters, on HGTV. When the show gets down to decision time, Preston asks me which house I think they will pick.

"Number three."

"I knew you would pick three, but they're going to pick two."

They pick house number one.

"What? That's crazy," he says.

We have been occupying the same space for almost two hours. I have no idea what's going on with us, but I can't help but think of Shayla. *It's cold out here. I would trade my life for yours in a baby's heartbeat.*

But I'm not going to be anyone's doormat, either. No more apologizing.

Preston disappears up the stairs. I lower the television and play Pandora from my phone. Marvin Gaye comes up first, crooning, "Got to Give It Up." The song reminds me of the one good memory I have of my parents together. We lived in a little apartment around the corner from Gran. I woke up from a bad dream and when I scurried into the living room, they were in the kitchen, kissing and dancing. I think it was my father's birthday or their wedding anniversary. It's the only time I really remember them being happy. I question what happiness really means in a marriage. Could my parents have made it work, or did my mother throw in the towel too soon? Would things have turned out differently if she hadn't? Would he be alive? Would she be normal and whole?

When Preston returns, he has showered and is wearing loose pajama bottoms and a T-shirt that has two fists pictured with the word "Sandwich." He sits back down on the sofa. I glance over and he is chewing his bottom lip. He must be ready to discuss the divorce. I take a deep breath and brace myself.

"How did you feel afterward?"

"After what?"

"The baby died."

Relieved, I tuck my feet under me. "I didn't feel anything. I just shoved it down like it never happened."

"I'm sorry you had to go through that at such a young age. It must have been hard. Did you ever talk to anyone about it?"

"You know there was no therapy for what I was going through. I was expected to forget and move on."

"Right."

"Gran never even brought it up until I was just in Philly."

"What did she say?"

"Not much, but she gave me this." I reach into my purse that was tossed next to me on the sofa. I hold out the death announcement letter. Preston reads it and then looks up at me.

"Did she have a name?"

"I named her Angel, but I don't know what her family called her before she died."

He folds the letter carefully and hands it back to me.

"Are you okay?"

"I'm fine."

"Do you still love him?"

"Who?"

"The man from the church."

"God, no." I look at him dead on. "I love you."

Preston shuffles his feet.

"Thanks for dinner." He walks into the kitchen and then down into the basement.

The next evening our routine is the same. Preston comes in after the kids are in bed, eats what I left him on the stove, and asks more questions about my past.

"How was it that you were seeing this man and Gran didn't know?"

I answered him as truthfully as I could, not holding anything back. We watched *House Hunters* again, then he thanked me for the food and went to the basement.

When he left, I played Pandora on low, wondering when he was going to bring up the divorce or separation. I'm not moving again or giving up my children. I'll fight him with my mouth and teeth. He'll have to make the adjustments.

The next night he texted me before he came home.

I'm stopping for sushi. You want?

I text back. *Sure.*

The usual?

Yes.

When Preston walks in, I am in my favorite place, on the couch. I haven't bothered to shower tonight or add a little conditioner to my hair.

"You look pretty," he compliments me.

"Thanks."

"I'm going to set up the food in the kitchen."

I run up to check on the kids and then sit across from him at the table. I'm nervous. Like I'm sitting to eat with a stranger. Shayla's voice, Gran's voice, my mother's voice are swerving through my head. *Work it out.*

I squeeze a bit of wasabi on my spider roll and then drop a sliver of ginger on top. Preston has set up two ramekins with soy sauce and I dip my roll before putting it in my mouth. All the flavors combine and hit my taste buds at once. I feel euphoric while I chew and swallow.

"Good, isn't it?" Preston offers a hint of a smile. It makes me blush. "I found a new place in Union. Pretty addictive. This is my third run in a week."

"What are we doing?" I blurt.

"Getting to know each other."

"I already know you, Preston. Shouldn't we be making plans trying to figure—"

"Shh. Just be here for now. Tell me something else about you."

I slap my hand against my forehead. "I landed a commercial."

"The one in the city?"

"No, I went to Johnson & Johnson on my way to—Philly." I pause. "It's for their baby powder. I'm worried sick over my hair. It was long when I went."

"But you booked it. Your agent called and said it was yours?"

"Yes, the contracts came over but I haven't signed them."

"Then it's yours. Sign them and send them back. There's always hair extensions."

I shake my head. "No more hiding. This is what it is. Either accept me or let me go."

Our eyes meet, caress, and cling. I want so badly to kiss him. Tonight I'm the first to go.

"Good night. *Gracias* for the sushi."

"*De nada.*"

"Been working on your Spanish?"

"Watching too much *Dora* with the kids." He laughs and it reverberates through to my soul.

In our bed, sleep eludes me. I stare at the ceiling, counting the cracks, then counting sheep, then counting backward from ten to one over and over again, but nothing. My eyes stay wide open like a cartoon character. I picture them bloodshot. The covers are around my ankles and my mouth is dry. I look over at the clock: 3:33. I'm thirsty. I push myself from the bed, slip into my slippers, and pad softly downstairs for some water.

Preston is standing against the counter. The room is dark except for a sliver of light coming in from the side window. He is shirtless. My will feels weak as I pass him.

"Can't sleep." The voice coming from my throat has deepened, and my words sound husky, even to me.

"I haven't slept since you came home. It's like you've put a spell on the house."

Goose bumps sprout on my bare arms. I get a cup from the cup-board and reach past him to the sink. I turn on the water. He's so within reach I think I hear his heart pumping in his chest. We haven't been this close since I shoved him in the basement. We stand side by side, near but not touching. But I could feel him. Everything has changed, but we stood connected just the same.

I lean into him, pressing my hip into his thigh. Breathing his air.

"Foxy." He draws my name out like it's a tune. It sounds like the sweetest melody on his lips. The greatest love song.

Acknowledgments

I would like to thank God for blessing me with the gift of writing and the passion to pursue my dreams with tunnel vision. My angel in the sky, my love, Mommom. Thank you for weaving your stories into my heart and nourishing me with your humor and good will. Your memories sparked the magic and breathed life into this novel.

To a wonderful and supportive family, my parents, Nancy Murray, Tyrone Murray, and Francine Cross Murray for your amazing love and advice. My grandmother, Yvonne Clair, thanks for your effort to keep us together. To my siblings Tauja, Nadiyah, and Talib Murray for your constant companionship, it has always been us four. Twin nephews, Qualee and Quasaan you make my heart do flips. My in-laws, Paula Johnson for loving me like a daughter and Glenn Johnson Sr. for taking care of business. Pacita Perera for your wisdom, David Johnson, and Marise Johnson for always being available and lending me your children, Armani and Aarick. I have the best friends on the planet and I love you all.

To my mighty team: Cherise Fisher, I could not imagine my life without you. Wendy Sherman, Laurie Chittenden, Melanie Fried,

Dawn Michelle Hardy, Mary Brown, and the amazing staff at Thomas Dunne Books. Thank you for your hard work and dedication to this book and my career. I promise you the best is yet to come.

To the numerous book clubs who have supported me, fed me, and shared my novel. I need you now more than ever. A special thank you to Sharon Lucas, Lori M. Legette, Kelly Clemens, and Max Rodriquez. So many authors inspire and take me under their wing, but especially Benilde Little, Kimberla Lawson Roby, Trice Hickman, and Curtis Bunn.

To my dynamic and talented children Miles, Zora, and Lena Johnson, you three are my greatest creation. You make it all right in my world and I love you with fever. Remember, all things are always possible. To my best friend, partner in crime, and husband, Glenn, for believing with the faith of a mustard seed, catching me when I fall, and keeping me. Your love is my oxygen.